MW01600850

People can lose their lives in libraries.
They ought to be warned.

— Saul Bellow

Stacked for Murder

an elmwood mystery

Mark H. Bliss

Copyright 2025 by Mark H. Bliss

facebook.com/markhbliss15

mbliss3901.wixsite.com/elmwoodmysteries

amazon.com/author/elmwoodmysteries

All rights reserved. No part of this book may be reproduced or transmitted in any form or by any means without permission from the author. This is a work of fiction. All names, characters, businesses, places and events in this novel are either products of the author's imagination or used in a fictitious manner.

First Edition

Acknowledgements

I've always been fond of public libraries. Growing up in St. Louis County, my mother took my sister and me to the Kirkwood Public Library every Saturday to check out books. Library books have been a constant in my life ever since. So, it's not surprising that I wanted to center my latest Elmwood Mystery novel around a public library, this one patterned after the library in Cape Girardeau, Missouri, where I have resided most of my adult life. While this book is fiction, there has been an effort by some people to ban books at my local library, reflecting a nationwide trend. This issue serves as a backdrop to this murder mystery. As I've said before, people and places in Southeast Missouri inspire my novels. Sincere thanks to my wife Marcia and friend and fellow author Jim Wilder for their excellent edits. Lastly, I thank my loyal readers for their constant encouragement of my writing endeavors.

mbliss3901.wixsite.com/elmwoodmysteries

amazon.com/author/elmwoodmysteries

Chapter One

Alone in the Elmwood Public Library, Erica Stark eyed the rows of book-filled shelves stretching out before her like troops on the parade ground. The clock on the wall behind the circulation desk registered 9:20 p.m. The library in this Southeast Missouri river city closed its doors to the public at 9 p.m. Soon after, the rest of the staff departed. Silence enveloped the building.

Her hair dyed auburn to cover up the gray, the 59-year-old Erica wore blue dress pants, a blouse as white as her alabaster skin and open heeled shoes. A silver owl necklace adorned her neck. Although she wasn't married, she wore a large custom-made pear-shaped diamond on the ring finger of her left hand, a present to herself on her 50th birthday.

Slowly, she began walking through the library, making sure everything was tidied up. She visited the children's area first where she straightened the rows of colorful picture books with their cute illustrations of teddy bears and unicorns. Then, she moved on to the adult sections, working her way up and down the rows. She caressed the spines of the books. Erica loved the smell and feel of books with their ink-filled pages that excited her more than the touch of any man. To her, books were almost a religion. She embraced them with all her soul as if they could grant her immortality. Tonight, she lingered among the mystery books with their clever covers. Titles of some authors followed a pattern such as "Mortal Prey" and "Phantom Prey." For mystery enthusiasts, the titles themselves told you who wrote them. You didn't need a byline. Erica loved reading mysteries, trying to calculate the clues and find the murderer before the author revealed everything. The creative way writers committed murder in the pages of their novels never ceased to amaze her. If real criminals were this resourceful, we'd all be in trouble, she reasoned.

After working her way through the mystery section, she moved over to the nonfiction side. The library collection included books on everything from history to horticulture. She finished up with biographies, stopping at last at one of her favorite books on George Washington. A sudden sound interrupted her. Had she heard a footstep? Was someone else there? Maybe, she thought, someone had fallen asleep at one of the study desks at the back of the library and had just awakened. She turned around, but no one was there. She listened for several seconds but heard no sound other than her own heartbeat.

She shook her head, admonishing herself for being so jittery. She turned her attention back to the bookshelf. She reached for the biography. Suddenly, she felt a heavy blow to her head. Erica took a staggered step and fell to the floor, her head throbbing in pain. Blood oozed down the back of her neck. Strong hands choked her from behind. She struggled to free herself, kicking backwards at the assailant. She broke free, screaming as she rolled onto her back. Her assailant, wearing a black jacket and ski mask, pounced on her, plunging a knife into her torso. She felt the warm blood oozing across her chest, turning her blouse crimson as she lay dying, clutching her silver owl.

Chapter Two

Detective Adam Dade stared at the lifeless, pale body of Erica Stark as police department uniformed evidence techs scurried around investigating every inch of the crime scene. An open book covered the librarian's face. The back of her head was bloody and bruised.

Adam shoved his hands into disposable gloves, bent down and removed the book, exposing the victim's face – her mouth open as if she could still scream. Death shadowed her face; her eyes shown as dull as those on a manikin. He turned the book over. The title read, *Gender Queer*. He handed the book to an evidence tech who slipped it into a plastic bag. A biography of George Washington lay near the victim's feet. The detective advised another officer nearby to bag the biography. Adam wasn't sure if the book could provide any clues to the murder. Still, he didn't want to overlook anything.

Adam inspected the knife protruding from Erica Stark's chest. After several minutes, he rose and addressed the police chief who had been standing nearby.

"Anyone can see this knife is the murder weapon, but she wasn't bashed over the head with it," Adam said. "There's also marks on her neck. It appears her assailant choked her too."

"We'll need to do an autopsy, but any idea as to time of death?" Police Chief Blair Bonney asked.

"According to the library staff, the victim had stayed behind last night to close the library. So, she could have died any time after the library closed at 9 p.m. The victim's name is Erica Stark. She was the library director."

"I knew she looked familiar," said Chief Bonney. "I saw her working at the library's spring book fair last weekend. I stopped by, looking for a good bargain. Picked up some old Perry Mason books."

"I figured you see enough crime at work," Adam said, slightly amused.

3

"Fiction is more entertaining, and, unlike my day job, I don't have to solve it," the chief said.

"We could use Perry Mason on this case," sighed Adam. "We don't have any witnesses."

"What about security cameras?"

"The library has cameras. We're checking the footage," Adam said, "but it doesn't look promising."

"Why would anyone want to kill this woman? No evidence of robbery or sexual assault, I presume."

"No," replied Adam.

"Any idea why that book was placed on Ms. Stark?" asked Blair.

"No clue."

"Maybe the murderer hates gay people," the police chief speculated. "Was Ms. Stark gay?"

"Not that I know of, but I'll check into it. I need to talk to Julie Halston."

"Who?"

"The library's assistant director. She found the body when she arrived at the library around 8:45 this morning," Adam said, pointing to a woman with ash blonde, shoulder length hair, sobbing near the circulation desk.

"I'll leave you to it," said Blair. "I've been told the media's circling around outside. I guess I'll have to say something to those vultures," he grumbled.

"What are you going to tell them?"

"As little as possible."

Chapter Three

Connor Tate joined the scrum of reporters gathered in front of the public library on a cloudy, late-March morning. Sparked by police scanner alerts about the discovery of a dead body; print, television and radio reporters, videographers and photographers crowded outside. Uniformed officers blocked the front doors, barring the media from entering the building.

At age 56, Connor was the most senior reporter at the *River City Journal*, Elmwood's daily newspaper. Social media had circulated rumors that someone had died in the library. Police scanner traffic suggested it was a homicide. Impatient for official news from the police, Connor paced back and forth on the sidewalk in front of the library.

Built 10 years ago, the library stood on a grassy slope just south of the flood-walled downtown neighborhood, overlooking the Mississippi River. Once part of the grounds of a former Catholic seminary, the property was located just north of the river bridge, connecting Southeast Missouri with Southern Illinois.

With its glass and steel entry way and its even more modern interior design, the library contrasted sharply with the historic buildings in Elmwood's central downtown. Still, Connor felt the library's architecture suited the site, whose massive oak trees offered welcome shade in the summer. Amid the morning chaos, Connor heard the plaintiff cries of songbirds. He concluded the noise generated by the media had upset the birds.

Just then, a black F-150 truck pulled into the parking lot. Coroner Joe Sherill double parked his vehicle near the front entrance. He stepped down onto the pavement. The coroner wore black cowboy boots, dark blue jeans and a black and brown plaid, long-sleeve shirt that barely covered his beer belly. Gray hair peeked out from under the Stetson cowboy hat that topped his head. The coroner waved off reporters' questions and hurried into the library. Connor shook his head. Joe was sold on himself, but no one else was. The police viewed him as a joke. As a funeral director, Joe had seen plenty of dead bodies. But he had no training in forensic science. Adam often complained to Connor that Joe Sherill proved nothing but a liability at a crime scene.

Five minutes after the coroner entered the building, Chief Blair Bonney emerged. Unlike his scheduled news conferences, where he most often wore his dress uniform, Blair exited the library wearing a polo shirt and slacks. Connor observed the chief's graying hair and his bulging waistline. Sadness creased the chief's face like a twisted spiderweb.

Reporters shoved microphones at Blair while TV videographers aimed their cameras at him. Connor spotted Tyler Frazier, the *Journal*'s main photographer, standing at the edge of the scrum, snapping images of the chief with his Nikon, fitted with a zoom lens.

Blair cleared his throat and began. "The police department received a call shortly before 9 a.m. today, reporting that a body had been found in the Elmwood Public Library. When we arrived, we discovered the body of a woman. We are investigating the death as a homicide."

"Do you know the identity of the victim?" asked a local TV reporter.

"We do, but we will not release the name until we have notified the next of kin," the chief said.

"What about the cause of death?" asked a young, tattooed woman with a local radio station. "Was the woman shot?"

"She wasn't shot. She was stabbed once with a knife. That's all I will say at this time," Blair said. He turned and headed for his unmarked patrol car, ignoring further questions shouted by the media.

Blair's brief statement didn't surprise Connor. Behind his back, reporters called him "Bare Bones," a reference to the fact that the chief routinely insisted he would reveal nothing but "the facts." Of course, as Connor saw it, Blair viewed few facts worthy of disclosing to the press.

◆ ◆ ◆

Tears cascaded down Julie Halston's cheeks. "I can't believe she's dead," she sobbed. She wiped the tears away with the back of her right hand, smearing her mascara. Seated in her office, the

6

library's 35-year-old assistant director, attired in dress jeans and a long-sleeve black top with a flower motif, attempted to answer the police detective's questions. But she stumbled over her words.

"Take your time," advised Adam, seated across from Julie. "Tell me what happened when you got to work this morning? Was the front door locked?"

"No."

"Did that alarm you?"

"Not a bit. Erica always arrived before me or any of the staff. She always opened the library."

"So, you arrived around quarter to nine?"

"Yes."

"When did you notice the body?"

"After I stopped by my desk, I visited Erica's office. But she wasn't there. I...I figured she might be in the stacks. She liked to walk through the library first thing in the morning, making sure nothing was out of place, you know, in terms of books being left out on tables or atop other books on the shelves. I walked toward the other end of the library. That's when I...I found her; I saw Erica sprawled on the floor, bloodied. I screamed. Several other staff members had just arrived. They all came running over. One of the staff members called 911."

"Did Ms. Stark have any enemies?"

"In the past few years, she got a lot of hate mail."

"Who from?"

"Members of that Citizens for Decency group. They often disrupt our library board meetings. They want us to ban books dealing with homosexuality and ones they view as pornographic. Two months ago, someone threw manure at the library entrance."

"Do you think one of them could have murdered Erica?" Adam asked.

"I don't know. The leader of that group is Harold Presson. He's a minister. You'd think a guy like that wouldn't be so hateful. But I've never seen anyone so mean. Still, I can't envision he'd kill someone. What minister would commit murder? More likely, it's another member of that group, if you ask me."

"You said Ms. Stark received hate mail."

"Yes. I've gotten some too. Here," Julie said, pulling a typed letter from her desk drawer. She handed it to Adam. In 36-point type, the unsigned letter screamed: "Death Stalks Those Who Are Evil."

"They're worse ones. As library director, Erica received vile letters and emails calling her a pornographer and a child abuser. Some of the messages said they hoped she'd die," recalled Julie.

"I'll have the officers collect the hate mail. We need to look at it back at the station, analyze them for possible fingerprints. Maybe we can determine who sent those messages."

"Can we open the library back up?" Julie asked.

"Not yet. We need to finish processing the crime scene."

Julie nodded, showing that she expected that answer.

"Poor Erica," Julie said to herself as Adam exited the room.

Chapter Four

Adam, dressed in his favorite black suit and sporting an American flag tie, left the building before the body was removed as uniformed officers continued to process the scene. The media had scattered, except for a videographer from the local TV station. The detective assumed the cameraman was waiting to capture video of the victim being removed in a black body bag.

Adam climbed into his unmarked car and prepared to start the engine when he received a call from his friend Connor.

"I was wondering when you would contact me," the detective said, eyeing his gray-streaked hair in the rearview mirror.

"I just had a few questions," Connor said, calling from the *Journal* newsroom.

"I wouldn't expect anything less."

"I understand the victim was Erica Stark, the library director."

"Where did you hear that?" Adam asked.

"It's all-over social media. It appears a member of the library staff posted it."

"Damn social media," grumbled the detective.

"Can you confirm it?" Connor asked.

"There's no point in denying it. Yes, the victim was Erica Stark, but you didn't hear it from me."

"No, of course not. I just needed confirmation."

"We still need to notify the next of kin. She wasn't married. I believe she has a niece."

"Any suspects?"

"Not at this time."

"What about motive?"

"Still investigating," Adam said, being deliberately vague.

"The police chief said she was stabbed. Any idea when?"

"We'll have to wait for the autopsy results, but it appears she had been dead for several hours when the body was discovered. It may have happened last night. That's all I can tell you at this time."

"Thanks, pal," Connor said, ending the call. He turned toward fellow reporter Rachel Short, seated at an adjacent desk on the second floor of the more than century old brick building that looked out over the downtown with its streets sloping toward the river.

"We've got confirmation. The victim was Erica Stark, the library director," Connor said.

"My God, I just talked to her two weeks ago about book banning," Rachel said. "The story hasn't run yet."

The two reporters had been dating for several years. At age 41, she was 15 years younger than Connor. But what began as friendship, sparked by a love of jazz and journalism, had turned into romance. When they first met, Rachel wore her auburn hair long. Now, it was cut short and layered. She was fond of soft, V-cut blouses and skinny jeans that showed off her figure.

Connor lamented about his graying hair, but Rachel thought it made him look distinguished. Their relationship had improved his wardrobe. Instead of worn jeans, old sweatshirts and scuffed shoes, Connor embraced newer jeans, cotton dress shirts and Skechers. Still, he felt like a bum in the company of Rachel. Connor had failed at two marriages. Too late, he realized, he had been tied to his job. Still, some good came out of his marriages. He had two beautiful, smart, married daughters – one living in Texas and the other in Florida. Connor loved Rachel, but doubted he could commit to another marriage. Rachel hadn't pushed him. At least, not yet, thought Connor.

River City Journal editor Dave Lansmon stopped by Connor's desk, looking for an update on the homicide. Connor reported that he had confirmation that the library's director was the one who had been fatally stabbed.

"Good work. Get the story written. I want to get the article posted online as soon as possible. You can gab with your girlfriend later," the balding editor said. Lansmon wheeled around and marched back into his office.

Connor said nothing but turned his attention to the scribbles in his reporter's notebook. He quickly typed up a brief story, detailing the stabbing death of Erica Stark and mentioning that the victim's identity was first reported on social media. He quoted the chief's brief comments and described the army of police who descended on the library that morning. From the newspaper's electronic archive, Connor added some background on Erica, including the fact she had served as the library director for the past 18 years. He wrote a last line, pointing out this was a developing story.

Lansmon edited the short article and with a click of a button posted it on the newspaper's website, accompanied by Tyler's photo of the police chief holding an impromptu news conference.

Five minutes after the story popped up on the *Journal*'s website, the stout editor called Rachel and Connor into his office where piles of paperwork and newspapers cluttered his desk along with his computer screen and keyboard. A large, framed Shoe comic strip print of an ax-wielding, cigar-chomping blue bird and the message "Beware the Editor" adorned one wall. Rachel thought the print captured Lansmon's character. She was just glad Lansmon didn't have an ax.

Rachel and Connor joined their editor at a conference table. "We need to dig into this murder," began Lansmon, rolling up his shirt sleeves as if he had prepared to wash dishes. "We need to explore Erica Stark's life. It might help us discern why someone would kill her."

"I interviewed Ms. Stark for that book-banning story," Rachel pointed out. "I also talked to the assistant library director for the article. I could see if she'd talk to me. Maybe she could shed some light on Erica Stark and this tragedy."

"That's a good idea," Lansmon said. "See what you can find out. And where are you on that book-banning article?

"I've done all the interviews and written most of the story," Rachel said. "But what do I do with all of Ms. Stark's quotes now that she is dead?"

"Keep the quotes. Finish writing it. I want to run the article in the next edition. I'll add an editor's note explaining your interview of Erica Stark happened weeks ago."

"When I interviewed both women at the library they told me members of that book-banning group had verbally attacked them. Could that have been why she was murdered?" Rachel asked.

"Possibly, but let's not jump to conclusions. Personally, I think some of those people are nuts, but that doesn't mean one of them is a killer," Lansmon noted. "Still, we can't ignore the book-banning controversy. Your article can accompany the murder story."

Connor jumped in, describing the police investigation. "They're doing an autopsy," he said. "That should tell us when she died."

"What about next of kin?" Lansmon asked.

"My detective friend said he believes she had a niece," Connor said. "I'll see if I can track her down."

"And we need details on the murder weapon. Connor, you reported that Bare Bones said the victim was stabbed with a knife. What kind of knife? And have police recovered the weapon. We need some answers. Let's get on it," Lansmon ordered, signaling the meeting was over.

Chapter Five

Rachel met Julie Halston for a late lunch at Smooth Buns, a popular downtown bakery and eatery situated on the first floor of a former brick warehouse on River Street in the shadow of the Mississippi River floodwall.

Rachel had phoned Julie and convinced the librarian to talk to her. At first, Julie had said she wouldn't speak about it. But with police officers still on site, the library had remained closed to the public for the day. And Rachel explained she wanted her readers to know more about Erica Stark and what she was like as a person, not just a librarian. Grief stricken, Julie discovered she wanted to talk about her late boss and friend.

Julie had reapplied make-up, but it did little to cover her sadness. She stared at Rachel as if she had seen a ghost. Both women ordered the lunch special – soup and salad. Rachel sipped on sweet tea before pulling out her reporter's notebook and a small digital recorder.

"I just want to make sure I get everything right," Rachel explained, pointing to the battery powered device.

Julie nodded. Her right hand trembled as she ran her fingers through her hair. She took a big gulp of the lemonade she had ordered. She sighed. "You said you want to know about Erica, what kind of person she was."

"Yes. From what I could tell when I interviewed her a few weeks ago, Erica Stark seemed like a nice, friendly person."

"She was. She was my best friend," Julie said, tears forming at the edges of her eyes. Erica was much older than me, but we hit it off right away. I mean, we both loved books. Reading was our passion."

"I understand Ms. Stark was single. Did she have a boyfriend? Did she have children?"

"No. She wasn't dating anyone from what I can tell. She had dated some guys years ago, but those relationships never lasted. She had no children. The library was her life," Julie said.

"Did you have an intimate relationship with Erica?" Rachel asked.

"What? You think we were lovers?" Julie asked, her face reddening with anger. "I told you we were just friends, two single women who liked each other's company. We used to do things together on the weekend like visit wineries or go shopping or to concerts. We both loved jazz."

"How long have you worked at the library?"

"Ten years. I was hired as the assistant director. I came here from a smaller library in the Missouri Bootheel."

"Did Erica grow up here?"

"Yes. Her father died before I started working at the library. I believe he worked at the Procter and Gamble plant, making diapers. Her mother, Helen, was a schoolteacher. She retired before I came here."

"Her mother's dead?"

"Yes. She died several years ago from brain cancer. Erica took care of her. She saw to it that her mother received every possible medical treatment. She hauled her all over the country in search of a cure. But nothing worked. Helen spent her last years in one of those care facilities."

"That must have been expensive. Did Helen have money for such a place?"

"She had her teacher's pension, but it wasn't enough to pay for everything. All those treatments and cancer medicines were expensive."

"So, Erica helped with some of the costs?" Rachel asked.

"Yes, she was wonderful in that way."

"I assume Erica made a good salary as library director, but I imagine she still had to dip into savings to help her mom."

"Well, she told me she had some investments. She said it allowed her to help pay the medical bills."

"So, why would anyone want to harm Ms. Stark?"

"I don't know."

"What about the members of that book-banning group? Only weeks ago, I interviewed both you and Ms. Stark about the controversy. You both said you received hate mail and had been threatened by Citizens for Decency over the fact you wouldn't ban certain books that they felt were pornographic or dealt with topics such as child rape or homosexuality."

"Yes, we were threatened, but we weren't physically assaulted. They yelled and screamed a lot about our library, but I didn't believe any of them would actually murder someone," Julie said. "Besides, the group's led by a local minister. I don't see him murdering anyone even if he is a loudmouth."

"Maybe someone else in the group committed the murder," Rachel suggested.

"I don't want to believe it."

"But is it possible?"

"I guess so. Anything's possible. But I can tell you this, whoever killed Erica hated her with a passion."

"Why do you say that?"

"Because I saw her body," Julie said. "I found her on the floor in the biography section. She was bashed on the back of the head and then stabbed. The knife was still there, in her chest. Blood everywhere. She had marks on her neck too, like the killer tried to strangle her. Erica was the victim of pure rage. No doubt about it."

Chapter Six

Rachel paid for both meals, leaving cash on the table. Julie thanked her for lunch and hurried off, shock still registering with every step she took. Rachel watched her leave, knowing life would never be the same for Julie. *Erica Stark wasn't the only victim of the murder. Julie Halston was a victim too. She'd forever be haunted by the image of her dead friend.*

Back in the newsroom, Rachel rushed over to Connor, who had grabbed a snack from a vending machine and was waiting for a call from his friend Adam.

"Got some news," Rachel said, the words rushing out in a torrent. "Julie Halston, the assistant librarian, found the body. According to Julie, the killer struck Erica Stark on the back of the head. Julie said there were marks on Erica's neck, suggesting she was strangled. The killer stabbed Erica. The knife was still in her chest when Julie found her."

"Wow. I'll press Adam about it. I'll talk to the coroner too," Connor said.

"You think Joe Sherill can tell us anything about the murder?"

"I know the police believe he's clueless, but even someone with no forensic training can conclude it was a stabbing, particularly when the knife remained lodged in the body," Connor said.

"Well, good luck with that," Rachel said, returning to her desk. "I've got to finish my book-banning story."

Just then, Connor's cell phone buzzed. Connor answered. "Hey, Adam. Thanks for calling back."

"What are friends for?" Adam asked, laughing.

"I have some more questions about the murder," Connor said.

"More questions?"

"You know me."

"I really do. I just don't know if I am able to answer all your questions right now."

"You mean you may not be willing to do so," Connor replied.

"Fire away and we'll see what I can tell you."

"What can you say about the knife? We know the killer left the knife in the victim."

"How do you know that?"

"We talked to Julie Halston."

"Well then, you know as much as the police," Adam said.

"But what about the knife? Was it a butcher knife or a pocket-knife?"

"Neither. The killer wielded a KA-BAR."

"A what?"

"A fixed blade knife. Seven-inch blade. Very lethal. The U.S. Marines started using this weapon around 1942 during World War II. It's still popular with folks in and out of the military."

"Any chance the killer left his fingerprints on the knife?"

"I doubt it. But we're checking for prints."

"I understand Erica Stark was hit on the head and then stabbed. Also, it appears her assailant attempted to strangle her."

"I suppose that assistant library director told you that?"

"Actually, she told my co-worker, Rachel," Connor said.

"Yeah. Well, you don't need me to tell you that."

"But have you identified what the killer used to strike Erica Stark on the back of the head?"

"No. Some kind of blunt object, but we haven't located it. Maybe the killer took it with him."

"Or her?"

"Well, don't go all women's lib on me, Connor. You and I both know that it's far more likely that the killer is a man."

"So, why would the killer remove the blunt object but leave the knife?"

"I believe the killer left the knife as a message. He wants us to know he was enraged by this woman. It's personal to him," observed Adam.

"Does the library have security cameras?"

"Yeah."

"Then, the cameras may have recorded the crime," suggested Connor.

"We're checking the digital images now, but the location of the cameras inside the library may not help. It appears the murder occurred in a blind spot. That's off the record," Adam said.

"Can I say the library has security cameras and police are checking to see if those cameras recorded the crime?"

"Yes, that's okay. Just that one statement."

"Don't worry, I won't throw you under the bus," assured Connor.

"You better not."

"When will you have the autopsy results?"

"Maybe in a day or two. We had to ship the body to Farmington. I wish we had a forensic pathologist in Elmwood, but we don't."

"You don't want to rely on the coroner?" Connor asked, laughing.

"What a joke. Joe Sherill doesn't have a clue," Adam grumbled.

"Well, maybe in this case, he does. I mean, he can tell the librarian was knifed."

"Yes, but he doesn't know the first thing about investigating a crime scene," the detective said.

"You told me earlier that police have no suspects. But what about those book-banning folks. Could one of them have stabbed Ms. Stark?"

"Off the record, we're looking into that possibility, but we have no direct evidence suggesting that is the case. For all we know, the murder may have nothing to do with that issue."

"Have you contacted next of kin?"

"We have."

"A niece?"

"That's right. Angela Pierce. Ms. Stark was single. She had no children. Her parents are dead. Her sister and her sister's husband died in a car accident in Memphis last year. Their daughter, Angela, graduated from Elmwood College. She does clerical work for that high-priced criminal lawyer."

"Rush Johnson?"

"Yep. That's the one."

"I assume she didn't shed any light on why someone would kill Erica?"

"No, she didn't. As far as we can tell, Angela and Erica weren't close. Angela told me she hadn't spoken to her aunt in over a year."

"I wonder why."

"That's not my concern. The Elmwood Police Department is looking for a killer and Angela Pierce is just a dead end," Adam said. "If there's nothing else, I need to get back to work. We plan to put out a news release within the hour, although it will be pretty basic: victim's name and age, the fact she was hit on the head with a blunt object; stabbed with a fixed-blade knife, which has been recovered; and that we are asking for anyone who may have information related to this crime to come forward."

"Thanks, Adam. I owe you a beer."

"More than one, I would think."

"Yes, more than one," agreed Connor.

Chapter Seven

Blair Bonney kicked the wastebasket beside his desk after reading the Journal's stories the next day. "Damn reporters," he said aloud to himself. *Why couldn't they keep their noses out of our police investigation.*

The *Journal's* top-of-the-fold, front page story carried the bylines of both Connor and Rachel. The headline read: "Police seek clues in killing of librarian." The first paragraph said it all. *Elmwood Public Library Director Erica Stark, who had been criticized for not banning certain books, was struck on the head and stabbed to death in the library Thursday. Her killer has not been caught.*

The article went on to quote Julie Halston. *"She was my best friend. Erica was much older than me, but we hit it off right away. I mean, we both loved books. Reading was our passion."* Julie recounted the hate mail she and Erica had received over the book-banning issue. *"Erica was the victim of pure rage. No doubt about it."*

A description of the fixed blade knife made it into the story as did a statement from Adam that police were checking the digital recordings from the library's security cameras for possible clues to the killer's identity. It also mentioned police had no suspects.

A sidebar article by Rachel focused on the book-banning issue. An editor's note explained that the story contained information from an interview of Erica Stark weeks before she was killed. The article led off with this paragraph: *Libraries nationwide have become the front line in America's culture war over whether some books should be banned. Nowhere is that more evident than in Elmwood where the administrators of the public library have been yelled at and subjected to hate mail because they refuse to ban books that others view as pornographic or exposing children to LGBTQ lifestyles.*

The story featured comments from both Julie and Erica as well as quotes from members of Citizens for Decency, the local group leading the effort to ban books from the Elmwood library. It included comments from Pastor Harold Presson, who said, *"he was doing*

God's work" and wanted to *"save society from the devil's filth. "* A file photo of the group picketing the library last fall accompanied the article.

The police chief reread the articles. Paragraph by paragraph, he felt the bile rising in his stomach. The muscles throbbed in his neck as if he were lifting weights. He opened his office door and yelled for Adam. The department's lead detective came running.

"What's wrong?" Adam asked.

"Take a seat," said Blair, slamming the door. The chief returned to his cushy chair as Adam seated himself in a straight-back chair on the other side of the desk. "Have you seen the paper today?" Blair asked, barely containing his rage.

"Yes."

"Well, I know you're good friends with that Connor character, but what the hell is going on?"

"What do you mean?"

"The *Journal* has made this all about book banning. People will think we're blaming the killing on that minister or some other member of that Decency group," said Blair.

"We have not said that, and the articles didn't say we were focused on anyone in that group."

"But you and I both know we'll need to question that preacher. I just don't want Citizens for Decency to start attacking us, saying we support pornography. Politically, we need to be careful how we go about questioning members of that group."

"I agree."

"Good. Keep me posted. I want to know everything that preacher tells you. And, for God's sake, make it clear that we're not accusing him of anything. We just want information that might lead us to the killer."

"But Chief, what if Harold Presson is the killer?"

"Well, we'll cross that bridge when we come to it," Blair said. "Personally, I doubt the guy is our murderer. And I'm hoping the murder has nothing to do with book banning. Nothing good can come from us getting caught up in some damn culture war."

The Rev. Harold Presson sat stiffly in his leather desk chair in his spacious, book-lined corner office at his church. His brown eyes, seated under tangled eyebrows, stared at his visitor, Connor Tate, as if sizing up a venomous snake.

The 60-year-old minister had short, gray, curly hair and skin the color of a mocha latte. His angular face and long, thin nose made him look sophisticated to some and a snob to others. A former St. Louis police officer, he embraced a career in ministry at 39 years of age, enrolling in Eden Seminary. Three years later armed with a divinity degree, he took his first post as a Methodist pastor at a rural Missouri church where donations were sparse and the furnace barely worked in winter, turning the old wooden church into an icebox.

He had come to Elmwood as pastor for the Elmwood United Methodist Church. But he and most members of his congregation had split with the main-line denomination two years ago, believing that the United Methodist Church nationally had become too liberal when it came to LGBTQ matters. The 500-member congregation now operated as a non-denominational church.

The church, renamed GraceWorks, still occupied the rough-hewn stone building with its large stained-glass windows. Built in 1901, the house of worship's imposing architecture reminded Connor of an old English village church one would find in a Miss Marple mystery.

Connor, armed with pen and notebook, studied the pastor seated across the desk from him. Even at his age, Harold Presson's muscular frame stretched the fabric of his shirt sleeve. A regular at Elmwood's River City Fitness, he worked out four days a week as if his life depended on it.

"I'm not sure how I can help you," Pastor Presson said. "You said you wanted to talk about that librarian who was murdered. Such a horrible thing."

"Yes. I know you and your group, Citizens for Decency, had some disagreements with Ms. Stark."

"That's correct. But I don't see what that has to do with her death. We're a law-abiding, God-fearing group. Many members of our congregation participate in the group."

"You head it up," Connor said.

"True. I started the group about four years ago. It's a fluid group.

22

Members come and go, but we generally have about 100 people on our mailing list," the pastor said.

"We know that Ms. Stark and others on the library staff received hate mail. You and members of your group shouted at them at library board meetings."

"We had some heated disagreements," Presson conceded. "People get emotional. However, hate never solves anything."

"You accused Ms. Stark and the library staff in general of promoting pornography for not banning books that you and others don't like," Connor said.

"It's an abomination for our public library to contain such filthy literature. Our children should not be exposed to such books."

"Because they deal with LGBTQ issues?"

"Homosexuality is a mortal sin. The Bible tells us so," Presson insisted.

"The Bible also tells us to love thy neighbor."

"Sometimes, Mr. Tate, you have to shout, to take a stand against society's sins," the pastor replied. "But that doesn't mean my group had anything to do with the murder of Ms. Stark. We want to ban pornography, not kill people. Even Jesus Christ went into a rage when he threw the money changers out of the temple."

"Does it concern you that the police might view you or someone in your group as a suspect?"

"No. The Citizens for Decency have nothing to hide. We're patriots, not criminals. We should be applauded, not vilified. And, print this: We extend our sympathy to friends and family of Erica Stark and hope that the police soon will arrest the killer. Now, if you'll excuse me, I must attend to church business." Presson rose and marched out of his office before Connor could close his notebook.

Chapter Eight

Joe Sherill met Connor for lunch. Connor had phoned the coroner, hoping to secure a comment about the murder investigation. But Joe surprised Connor by suggesting they meet for lunch. Of course, the coroner made it clear he expected Connor to pay the bill. Connor doubted the *Journal* would reimburse him. Still, he was curious. Why would Joe agree to share his lunch hour with a reporter?

They dined on cheeseburgers and crinkle fries as they sat in a red and black vinyl booth in Hamburger Hut in Elmwood's Midtown neighborhood. The diner, a local landmark, featured a classic chrome lunch counter and a refurbished Wurlitzer jukebox that played old-time rock 'n' roll tunes for those willing to feed it with quarters.

The coroner wore jeans and cowboy boots. His white collared shirt stretched across his heavy-set frame like a circus tent. Gray hair peeked out from under his Stetson. Connor showed up in jeans, a blue plaid shirt and his favorite New Balance walking shoes.

Between bites, Connor questioned the coroner about the ongoing murder investigation. "Are we any closer to solving this killing?"

"I don't know. You'd have to ask the police," said Joe, wiping mustard from the corner of his mouth.

"But what about the evidence at the scene?"

"You mean the bloody shoe print?"

Connor tried to hide his surprise. "Tell me more," he said. But Joe heard the hesitation in Connor's voice.

"Oh, shit. You didn't know? I had assumed your police detective friend told you."

"Well, the news is out now. So, tell me. Did the police find a single print or were there multiple shoe prints?"

"Just one, Connor."

"Where was it found?"

"Near the body."

"How can there be just one footprint?"

"I don't know. Do I look like Sherlock Holmes? Maybe the killer wiped up the other prints. Maybe he tiptoed out of the library holding his shoes in his hand."

"What kind of shoe was it?"

"The tread appeared to be from a tennis shoe, but I doubt that will lead us to Ms. Stark's killer. At this point, we're still waiting for the autopsy results."

"You don't think police will find DNA evidence on the knife or body pointing to the killer?"

"Doubtful. This is the real world, not some TV show. In most cases, the killer is someone the victim knew. That's probably the case here. We all know that the preacher and his group disliked Ms. Stark."

"You mean Citizens for Decency?"

"Yeah, that's the one. Personally, I sympathize with their cause, but any investigator would be an idiot not to look at the group when it comes to this murder investigation. But, hey, I'm just the coroner."

"Thanks for talking to me," Connor said, putting down his pen and closing his notebook.

"Yeah. Well, hope it was worth it," said Joe, pointing to the bill the waitress had left on the table.

"I have no doubt," Connor said. "Besides, what is a murder investigation without a coroner?"

"You're right there," Joe said, standing up to leave. "I know what some people in the police department think. I know they joke about me behind my back because I'm not a forensic pathologist. But in most homicides, I can tell the cause of a death. It doesn't take a bunch of science experiments to tell if a person has been shot, stabbed, or strangled."

Chapter Nine

Connor drove his red SUV back to the newsroom, his wallet a little lighter for having paid for the meals at Hamburger Hut. At the office, he recounted to Rachel what the pastor and the coroner told him.

"Sounds like Pastor Presson isn't concerned that some people might blame him or his group for the killing of the librarian," Rachel said. "But from what you've told me, the coroner suspects the killer could be someone with Citizens for Decency."

"Yeah. Joe may have a point. It certainly seems a possibility."

"But can you see the preacher as a murderer?"

"Who knows? Anything is possible. One thing for sure, Pastor Presson is committed to the cause. He sees it as a fight between good and evil."

"In my mind, killing a librarian is evil," Rachel observed. Connor nodded in agreement. He moved back to his desk, sat down, took out his reporter's notebook and began typing his story. Forty minutes later, he finished the article. With the click of a mouse, he saved it. Editor Dave Lansmon reviewed the story and sent it over to the copy editors for final reads.

By 9 that night, the *River City Journal* posted Connor's story online under the headline: "Library murder focuses attention on book-banning group." The first paragraph read: *The killing of Elmwood's public library director Erica Stark has put a vocal book-banning group under an investigative microscope. Coroner Joe Sherill says any criminal investigator "would be an idiot not to look at the group."*

The second paragraph noted that Pastor Presson insisted that neither he nor his group were to blame for Ms. Stark's death. "We want to ban pornography, not kill people," he was quoted as saying.

Mayor Elroy James read the front-page story at his kitchen table the next morning as he ate a blueberry bagel. "Damn it. Why can't the coroner keep his mouth shut," he commented to his wife Martha as she ate a bowl of Cheerios.

"What, dear?"

"Oh, Joe Sherill suggested to the newspaper that someone affiliated with this Citizens for Decency book-banning group might be the killer," Elroy said, running a hand through his thinning, graying hair.

"Well, the group has been critical of the library director and staff."

"Yeah. But we don't need to stir up a hornet's nest. We don't need people accusing our local officials of supporting pornography."

"But won't the police have to question members of that Decency group?"

"Yes, but hopefully the police will do so quietly," Elroy said.

"It may be too late for that now," Martha observed.

Elroy threw down the paper and took another bite of his bagel. Sunshine and a soothing breeze had promised a good day, he had thought. But now this. Bad news. That preacher's group would get loud. He was sure of it.

Across town, Blair Bonney huddled in his office with Adam. The chief growled about Connor Tate's newspaper article. "Damn it," said the police chief. "Why did your reporter friend have to quote that idiot coroner. He's just made it harder for us to stay under the radar with this murder investigation."

"We'll have to question that preacher, Harold Presson," Adam said.

"I know. Do we have the autopsy results yet?"

"Yep. The forensic pathologist in Farmington, Dr. Matthew Burnett, said the librarian was stabbed in the chest. She didn't die instantly. She bled out. He figures she could have lived 10 to 15 minutes after she was stabbed."

"What about time of death?"

"He estimates Ms. Stark was killed sometime between 9 and 10 p.m. Based on the statements from the library staff, Ms. Stark closed up. So, the killing took place sometime after the library closed at 9 p.m."

"Any prints on the knife?"

"No. It appears the killer wore gloves," Adam said.

"What did the autopsy show about the victim's head wound?"

"Dr. Burnett said the librarian was struck with a blunt, wooden object. He found small splinters of wood in her scalp."

"We need to find that object. It could point us toward Ms. Stark's killer," the chief said.

"What about that preacher? You want me to talk to him now?" Adam asked.

"No. I'll talk to him. He's my pastor. I think he'll be more open with me."

"You think he killed her?"

"No, of course not. But maybe a member of his book-banning group stabbed her. We need to look at that possibility. And, it would be easier to do that if we can get Pastor Presson's cooperation."

"How are you going to do that?"

"On the golf course."

"What?"

"I play golf with him every other Tuesday when the weather cooperates," said Blair. "He says it helps him craft his sermons although I rather doubt it. Neither of us have inspiring rounds these days."

"Do you think you're too close to Pastor Presson to be objective? Maybe I should talk to him."

"Nonsense, Adam. I can handle it. If the pastor did the crime, he'll do the time. But, as I said, I don't believe he is the killer."

Chapter Ten

On Blair's orders, the police waited until Monday, four days after the murder, to release the autopsy results to reporters. The emailed news release stated that Ms. Stark bled to death after being stabbed in the chest and disclosed that the librarian had been attacked after 9 p.m. on the previous Thursday. According to the release, the autopsy showed she had been struck on the head with a flat, wooden object, which police had yet to recover. The police asked that any possible witness call the station.

After reading the release that showed up in his work email, Connor phoned Adam. "It took that long to get the autopsy results?" he questioned.

"No, it took that long for us to release the information," the detective said. "We had hoped to track down that wooden object, but no such luck. The killer probably dumped it."

"What about the bloody shoe print? Police made no mention of it in the news release."

"We don't want to disclose all our evidence," Adam explained. "We hope we can tie the shoe print to the killer."

"Why was there only one shoe print?"

"That is a mystery," Adam said. "It doesn't make sense."

"I assume you're going to question that pastor, Harold Presson?"

"Yes, of course. But there are others to question too."

"Others?"

"Other members of Citizens for Decency."

"So, the police investigation is focused on that book-banning group?"

"That is one avenue we are exploring, but it's not the only one. For all we know, Ms. Stark may have surprised a burglar."

"There was a burglary?"

"Nothing was taken that we can see. We're trying to retrace the victim's last movements. Maybe someone saw something."

"What about the security cameras?"

"The footage appears to have been erased, probably by the killer. There are no images of anyone leaving the library after the staff left for the evening. The system appeared to have been shut down at some point."

"How would the killer know where to access the security system?" Connor asked.

"We haven't figured that out. Off the record, it seems the murderer knew the library well, knew how to access the security system."

"Well, good luck with your investigation," Connor said. "Sounds like you need a break, some clue to point you in the right direction."

"You could say that, but that's off the record. I'm counting on you to do me right."

"Don't worry, Adam. I'm not about to take advantage of our friendship."

"See that you don't," the detective said, ending the conversation.

Connor wrote a short article, incorporating information from the news release and from his interview of Adam. By noon, the *Journal* had posted the article online under a headline that read: "Police to question pastor in murder case."

The article's first paragraph stated: *Elmwood police investigating the murder of a librarian plan to question a local pastor who had railed against the woman because she refused to ban certain books.*

According to the story, which would top the next day's front page, the library's security cameras held no clues. *Police said it appeared the killer disabled the security system before exiting the building.*

Police Chief Blair Bonney spent Tuesday afternoon playing a round of golf with Pastor Harold Presson at The Highlands Golf Club, located on the city's western edge. By the third hole, the conversation between the two men had turned exclusively to the murder. Blair asked the pastor about the actions of the Citizens for Decency.

"Do you think one of the members of your book-banning group could have killed the librarian?"

"Why are you asking me that? Are you trying to pin the murder on these fine citizens?"

"No, we're just looking for possible suspects. And, when it comes to motive, you have to admit that some of your members strongly disliked Ms. Stark. You, yourself, have complained about her."

"Hold on, Blair," the pastor said, raising his voice as he lifted an iron from his golf bag. "Am I a suspect? Do you really think I would commit such a sin?"

"I didn't say that."

"You implied that."

"No, I merely pointed out that you and others were not fans of Elmwood's head librarian."

"What of it? That doesn't make me a murderer."

"But you do know that she and other members of the library staff had received hate mail?"

"I had heard that."

"So, isn't it likely that at least some of that hate mail came from members of your Decency group?"

"I wouldn't know. I never sent any hate mail."

"But you did email Ms. Stark and other members of the library staff insisting that they should remove certain books and that to not do so would be a sin?"

"Well, yes. But that isn't hate mail, I never said I wanted her dead," the pastor said, wiping sweat from his brow as the temperature climbed on the freshly mowed fairway.

"Do you own a fixed-blade knife?"

"I have a pocketknife."

"No, I'm talking about a knife with a seven-inch blade."

"I don't have such a thing. If you don't believe me, check the parsonage, check my church office. I can't believe you, of all people, would view me as a suspect," the pastor said.

"Don't take it personally," said Blair. "I'm just doing my job. And, you should appreciate the fact that I'm asking these questions on the golf course and not at the police station."

"Yeah. Well, it feels like you're grilling me. I don't like it."

"But Harold, you do understand we have to ask these questions, and it would be best if you and your Decency members cooperate with us?"

"I guess so," the pastor grumbled.

"I need the names and phone numbers of all of the members of Citizens for Decency," Blair said.

"I'll email you the list," Harold muttered, throwing a club into his bag.

Chapter Eleven

Erica Stark's memorial service drew a huge crowd to the columned, Elmwood First Baptist Church. The church, three blocks from the river, could hold some 900 people. Connor and Rachel observed every pew was packed this Saturday, some two weeks after the murder.

Rachel was there to report on the service. Connor joined her out of curiosity. The veteran reporter found it interesting how people referred to someone after they died. Invariably, he thought, people said kind words about those who had passed. But did they really mean it?

Rachel spotted Tyler Frazier who had staked out a spot in the church balcony with his camera and zoom lens to capture images of the service for the newspaper. She marveled at the turnout. "I am surprised so many people showed up," Rachel whispered to Connor.

"I'm not. Erica was a member of this church, which has a large congregation."

"But she was vilified by Citizens for Decency," Rachel said.

"Right, but that group's actions no doubt irritated others. It made her a sympathetic figure to some."

As she had wished, Erica was cremated, and her ashes placed in an urn and buried in the family plot nearly a week earlier. Her will called for a memorial service. Her niece, Angela Pierce, made all the arrangements. Rachel spotted Angela, seated in the front row. She wore a collared, black dress. A string of pearls completed the outfit. Her combed-back dark hair fell to her shoulders. A tearful Julie Halston sat next to Angela. Several members of the library staff sat in the second row, their stiff faces showing the strain of coping with the death of a coworker.

Judge Michael Wachter sat next to Julie. The 55-year-old long-time circuit judge chaired the library's board of directors. He had worked closely with Erica and Julie for years. He led a successful effort to pass a property tax measure to fund construction of the new library a decade ago. In recent times, he and other board members had been vocal in support of the library and its opposition to book banning, even going so far as to write a letter to the editor.

Adam Dade slipped into the third-row pew next to Connor. "Are you here to pay your respects or are you on duty?" Connor asked.

"I wanted to see who showed up for the service."

"You think the murderer might be here?"

"Maybe. Killers have been known to attend their victims' funerals. It's worth a shot," Adam said.

"Harold Presson's over there," Rachel said, pointing to a pew on the other side of the aisle. "Have you talked to him?"

"No," Adam said.

"Why not?" Rachel asked.

"Blair talked to him."

"So, you aren't questioning him?"

"I didn't say that. Blair just wants us to use a little discretion in dealing with the pastor. It's a sensitive matter, but I'm sure I will be questioning him at some point. We'll be talking to every Citizens for Decency member, not just the Rev. Harold Presson."

The church's bell tolled, signaling the start of the service. Pastor Bob Matson like many Baptist clergy preferred civilian dress to clerical robes. Today was no exception. Dressed in a navy-blue suit and red tie, he stood behind a lectern, his Bible open to Psalm 23, "The Lord is my Shepherd." A poster-size, portrait photo of Erica stood on an easel next to the lectern.

"We are gathered here today to remember Erica Stark, a member of our congregation who had the heart of a servant. She loved her church, her community and all manner of history books including presidential biographies. As anyone who met her quickly learned, one of her favorite books was a biography of President George Washington. She loved the artistry of the written word. Her home was full of books. Conversations with her often resembled book reviews," the rotund, balding pastor said.

He went on to quote several passages from the Bible, including Psalm 23. The choir sang "Amazing Grace." The pastor then ended the short service with a final prayer.

"I'm surprised Erica's niece didn't say a few words," Rachel observed.

34

"From what I can tell, she wasn't close to her aunt. Angela told me they seldom spoke," Adam said as he rose to leave.

"So, she has no clue why her aunt was murdered?" Connor asked.

"I wouldn't say that," Adam replied. "She believes whoever killed her aunt was irate over the fact that Erica refused to remove certain books from the library."

"It all points back to Citizens for Decency," Rachel said. "Who else would want to kill a librarian these days?"

"I'd keep an open mind if I were you," Adam admonished. "For all we know, the murderer may have had an entirely different motive."

"But have you uncovered another reason?" Rachel questioned.

"Not at this time."

"Why would the Rev. Harold Presson show up for the memorial service?" Connor wondered.

"Maybe he wants people to believe he didn't hold any malice toward Erica Stark," Adam said.

"You think he's trying to convince people he isn't the killer?"

"Possibly, Connor. Or maybe he just hopes to polish the image of his book-banning group and convince people that the members of that group aren't a bunch of looney tunes."

Angela Pierce's movements distracted Rachel from the conversation. She watched as Angela headed toward Harold Presson. "I think Angela's going to confront Pastor Presson," Rachel said, interrupting the conversation between Adam and Connor. The two men looked toward where Rachel had pointed.

Angela stepped in front of the pastor before he could exit the pew. "You have some nerve showing up here," she growled.

"I came to pay my respects. Every human life is a gift of God," Harold said.

"You killed my aunt," she shouted, prompting those still in the church to turn back toward the confrontation.

"I did not," insisted Harold, his voice strained.

"Well, if you didn't, it was someone in your book-banning group," she yelled as Adam rushed over.

"Let's not get into an argument here," the police detective advised as Connor and Rachel gathered around.

"Well, the police better do something," said Angela, "or someone else on the library staff might get killed."

Harold started to reply but a look from Adam stopped him. "I'm leaving," the pastor said. "I don't want any trouble."

"It's too late for that," Angela replied as she moved aside to let Harold leave. As the pastor walked away, Adam addressed Angela.

"Ms. Pierce, please go home. Leave this to the police."

"For now," Angela grumbled as she headed for the exit.

Connor and Rachel returned to the newsroom. Connor busied himself with checking the latest sports scores while Rachel crafted a story on the memorial service. Twenty minutes later, Tyler arrived. The *Journal* photographer had stayed around after the service to grab shots of people exiting the church. He was outside when Angela confronted Pastor Presson inside the church. But he had snapped a photo of Angela when she exited the building.

Tyler scrolled through the photos on his camera, showing the digital image of Angela to Connor and Rachel. The photo captured the emotion. And, both Connor and Rachel thought, the emotion wasn't sadness. It was raw anger.

Rachel finished her story. She made no mention of the confrontation at the church, convinced Lansmon wouldn't allow her to write about the dispute. She notified Lansmon that the story was ready to edit. The longtime editor seldom worked on weekends but showed up this Saturday to review the memorial service article. He had instructed Rachel to focus on the service itself and not rehash the murder. Lansmon called up the story on his office computer and read through it line by line. Satisfied, he marked the article ready to post online. He clicked on the photo that Tyler had chosen to accompany the article. Lansmon shook his head. He strode to his office door and yelled, "Tyler."

The thick-haired photojournalist hurried into the office. "Where's the fire?" he asked, a little irritated by Lansmon's tone.

"We can't use that photo."

"Why not?"

"The woman looks angry. It was a memorial service. People came to show their respect for Erica Stark. There should be tears, not anger."

"But I figured you'd want to run a picture of the victim's niece since she was the only relative at the service."

"You figured wrong. Do you have another photo?"

"I have one I shot from the church balcony during the service."

"Send me that one."

"Sure," said Tyler, gritting his teeth. He preferred the other photo, but he knew it was a lost cause. What Lansmon wanted, Lansmon would get. Fifteen minutes later, the story and photo were posted online under the headline: "Memorial Service reflects on librarian's 'heart of a servant.'"

A half hour later, Rachel and Connor sat at a corner table in Smooth Buns, grabbing a late lunch. At 2 p.m., only two other customers were in the restaurant. The rich aroma of fresh bread greeted them in the riverfront eatery. Rachel and Connor ordered ham-and-cheese-melt sandwiches on thick, homemade rye bread and a side order of deviled egg potato salad.

"It's too bad we couldn't run the photo of Ms. Pierce," Connor said.

"I don't know. Running the photo wouldn't make much sense unless the story reported on the confrontation."

"True. And, I figure Lansmon didn't want to draw more attention to Pastor Presson at this time. He doesn't want Citizens for Decency to picket the newspaper, I assume."

"Angela seems convinced that Presson or someone involved with that group murdered her aunt," Rachel said.

"She may be right, but so far there's no evidence connecting anyone with that group to the killing."

"So, where do we go from here?"

"I'm not sure. I need to talk to Adam. Maybe the police have uncovered some new clues, something that would lead them to the killer."

"I will approach Julie again. Maybe she hasn't shared everything she knows," Rachel said. "After all, she found the body. She saw the crime scene before the police."

A red-haired, freckle-face waitress delivered their meals. Connor and Rachel said little as they ate lunch. Rachel sipped her glass of sweet tea. Connor drank a Coke. He told himself he needed the sugar high. He looked at the plump slices of pie in the glass case beneath the restaurant counter. He wanted a piece of pecan pie but ignored his craving as Smooth Buns owners Oliver Essner and his husband Truman Todt approached.

The two middle-aged men were fabulous cooks with similar culinary tastes, but they differed when it came to their clothes. Oliver wore comfortable, worn sweatshirts, jeans and scruffy tennis shoes. His husband, Truman, favored designer jeans, colorful long-sleeve shirts and expensive boots. Oliver was white; Truman, Black. Their friends, including Connor, called them, "Salt and Pepper."

"How are our two favorite reporters?" asked Oliver.

"The same as always," Connor replied.

"You mean as ornery as always," Truman remarked.

"I hope you mean that as a compliment," Rachel said, laughing.

"You know it," Truman said.

"I heard they had the memorial service today for that librarian," Oliver observed.

"Yes, we were there," Rachel said. "The First Baptist Church was crowded."

"I guess the book-banning people weren't there," Truman said.

"Well, Pastor Harold Presson showed up," Connor replied.

"The chief book banner himself. Wow, he sure had his nerve," Truman remarked.

"Yeah. After the service, Erica Stark's niece confronted the pastor," Rachel said. "She didn't appreciate him coming there."

"I can understand that," Oliver said. "That pastor had some nerve."

"You think that Presson fellow killed the librarian?" Truman asked.

"If you ask me," Connor said, "he's clearly a suspect. But so far, the police haven't linked him to the crime."

"So, maybe he didn't do it," Rachel chimed in.

"Maybe one of Presson's fellow book banners stabbed her," Oliver suggested.

"Or maybe it has nothing to do with banning books," Connor said.

"But if that's the case," Oliver said, "what possible motive would someone have to kill Ms. Stark? Who kills librarians? From what you all wrote, there's no evidence it was a robbery."

"No, the evidence suggests the attack was premeditated."

"You know, Ms. Stark often stopped by in the morning to pick up blueberry muffins and bagels for the library staff," Truman recalled.

"She was a nice woman. The whole thing is just so sad," Oliver said.

"And totally pointless," Truman said. "She didn't need to die."

"Tell that to the killer," Connor replied. "The killer had a motive. If the police figure that out, it might go a long way toward solving this case."

"Well, maybe you two can solve it," Oliver suggested.

"Don't be so sure," Rachel said. "We're not miracle workers."

"But you've got a solid track record," Oliver said. "You've solved several murders."

"If you keep this up, you might have to quit your jobs and become private investigators," Truman observed.

"I doubt we'd like that," Connor said. "The private eyes I've met spend most of their time spying on cheating spouses. It may pay the bills, but it's not something I'd want to do."

"Me neither," Rachel said. "I think we'll stick to being reporters."

"Well, I hope you both get to the bottom of it," Oliver said.

"Thanks," Connor said, placing cash on the table for his and Rachel's meals.

"Stay safe," Truman said. "You're our best customers."

"Oh, so it's all about the money," Rachel quipped.

"We have to make a living. Otherwise, we'll be living on the street," Truman replied with a laugh.

"We wouldn't want that," Rachel said as she and Connor headed for the door.

Chapter Twelve

Saturday evening—date night. Connor and Rachel swore to each other that they wouldn't mention the murder, not even for a second. Their brains felt mired in the murder of the librarian and they wanted an escape. It came in the form of shrimp lo mein at China Chan's restaurant followed by wine and dancing at Jello jazz club. Housed in an old brick building on River Street in the shadow of the Mississippi River floodwall, the club attracted a wide array of customers from college students to bank presidents. The dim lights overhead and the flickering battery powered candles at the tables set the mood.

Then, there was the music. Sultry sax. It settled in your bones. The kind of music you could slow dance too. Some of their favorites included *In a Sentimental Mood*, composed by Duke Ellington; *Just Friends* by Charlie Parker; and *Theme for Ernie* by John Coltrane.

It's where Rachel and Connor had first felt that spark of romance, dancing close, their bodies in rhythm.

Tonight, they relaxed, soothed by music from a local band, Soul Shades, which often played there. Rachel wore a black blouse, Capris, and flower-motif Birkenstock sandals. A turquoise necklace graced her neck. Connor wore dress jeans, a forest green Polo shirt and a pair of black athletic shoes. He smiled, inhaling the sensual scent of Rachel's perfume. They shared an entire $30 bottle of Chardonnay, savoring every drop of the smooth liquid. The older crowd started leaving by 11 p.m., replaced by college students, amped on hormones, for whom the night was young. Seated at a table near the back of the club, Connor and Rachel watched the college kids who mostly ordered bottles of beer and congregated close to the club's small stage. It felt good spying on them, eavesdropping on their conversations when the band took a break. Journalists were good at observing others' actions and conversations, Rachel concluded. Rachel and Connor viewed people watching as a recreational sport.

They nearly made it to midnight before heading to Connor's

downtown loft apartment on the second floor of an 80-year-old brick building, above a jewelry store. Large windows in Connor's place provided a sweeping view of the Mississippi River. Although Rachel kept her own place, a small, rented brick house near Elmwood College, she often stayed at Connor's apartment. Connor hugged her tight as they entered. He flipped on the lights and closed the door. She kissed him slowly before heading to the bedroom with Connor on her heels.

Chapter Thirteen

Rachel met Julie by the grave of Erica Stark. Rachel requested the meeting, which occurred mid-week. Julie had chosen the place. The librarian wanted privacy. The breezy cemetery with its massive oaks seemed the perfect meeting space on this early April morning, Julie thought.

A mound of dirt topped with shriveled bouquets of flowers marked the spot where Erica's ashes had been buried. A tombstone had yet to be erected. The Old Elmwood Cemetery, dating back to the city's founding in the early 1800s, sat on a hill overlooking the Mississippi River several blocks north of the downtown.

It's where the town's pioneers – French Canadian fur trappers, American settlers, Revolutionary War veterans, German immigrants, who opposed slavery, and slave holders were buried. So too were a number of Elmwood College presidents. The college's first president died in 1876 when the trench he was working in collapsed during an archeological excavation of an Indian mound as part of a Harvard field camp. A limestone obelisk marked his cemetery grave.

Over time, Elmwood opened two other public cemeteries. But the Old Elmwood Cemetery, with its wrought-iron fence and thick, hand carved wall of stone blocks, still drew genealogists to its grounds intent on gleaning the past from the words etched into its weathered tombstones.

"You realize Erica's probably the last person who will be buried here," Julie observed. "You can't be buried here now unless you had ancestors interred here. One of Erica's ancestors fought in the Revolutionary War in Virginia and then moved west, settling here in the early 1800s, shortly after the founding of Elmwood."

"It's a peaceful place," Rachel said. "Although, some people say it's haunted."

"That's just an old tale. It's no more haunted than the public library. Still, you didn't reach out to me to talk cemetery history."

"No," Rachel said. "I have some more questions about Erica's murder. I was wondering if it was unusual for her to close up the library. Didn't she have staff to do that?"

"Erica always locked up on Thursday. She insisted on it. I closed the other days, except Wednesday when various staff members would take turns closing."

"Did she say why she wanted to handle that chore on Thursdays?"

"No. It's just the way it was. I didn't ask. It wasn't a big deal to me or anyone else on the staff. Erica closed the library on Thursday nights."

"You saw the body. Do you remember anything else about the murder scene? The police seem baffled."

"I just remember the blood and the knife. It was horrible," Julie said.

"Anything else? I understand she was found in the biography section."

"Yes."

"Were any books dislodged?"

"An open book had been placed on her face," Julie said, closing her eyes as if to recall the scene more clearly.

"You didn't mention that when I interviewed you earlier."

"I wasn't thinking clearly when I spoke to you after the murder."

"What book was on her face?"

"Gender Queer."

"One of the books Citizens for Decency wanted removed from the library?"

"Yes."

"That suggests one of its members killed Erica," Rachel said.

"Seems so. Did you know that there were over 1,200 demands to censor or ban books and other materials in our nation's libraries last year? It's become an epidemic. And, it's happening right here in Elmwood. Some of these book banners are scary."

"I'm sure it's hard to be a librarian today, what with all the threats. Do you remember anything else? We understand the police found a bloody footprint."

"I don't recall seeing that. But I was in shock," Julie said. I just kept looking at the body. Oh, I do remember seeing blood on some

43

cash. The police bagged it for evidence, I think."

"What cash?"

"I saw two $100 bills. They were near her body."

"Was Erica in the habit of carrying around a lot of cash?"

"Not that I know of. When I was with her, Erica usually paid with a debit card," Julie said. "But I guess she must have had cash that night."

"It makes no sense," Rachel said. "Why would the killer leave the money behind?"

"Maybe the killer didn't notice the money," Julie said.

"Or maybe he meant to leave the cash."

"Why?"

"To send a message," Rachel suggested.

"But what message?"

"I haven't a clue."

"I hope the police catch her killer. If it's someone with that book-banning group, he might strike again. I'm not sure any of our library staff are safe. It scares me. I'm constantly looking over my shoulder, wondering if the killer might be stalking me."

"You should talk to the police," Rachel said.

"I have. They tell me not to worry. Easy for them to say. They haven't had death threats or been cussed out by some book-banning crazy," Julie said, fear gripping her voice.

"I'm sorry," Rachel said. "I wish I could help."

"Find Erica's murderer. That's the only thing that will help," Julie replied. She turned and walked toward her gray Ford Focus parked in the gravel lot beyond the cemetery gate. Rachel sighed. Questions rushed through her mind like a mountain stream. They all boiled down to a single word. *Why?*

Chapter Fourteen

Rachel returned to the newsroom to find Connor working on a piece about the city's aging water plant. The 93-year-old facility, despite some upgrades over the years, faced the real possibility of failing in the future without major improvements that would cost millions of dollars. Quoting city officials, Connor wrote that a tax increase would be needed to fund such a project.

"Connor, I need to talk to you. It's about that murder," Rachel said, stopping by his desk.

"I'm just finishing this city story."

"Very well. But it's important."

"Give me five minutes."

"Sure," Rachel said. Frowning, she retreated to her desk.

Connor finished the story and alerted the copy editors it was ready to edit. "Okay, what's the big news?" he asked Rachel.

"Erica Stark's killer left an open book on her face," Rachel said, recounting her conversation with Julie Halston.

"What book?"

"Gender Queer."

"Wow. That's news to me. The police never mentioned it."

"It suggests the killer may very well be one of the members of that book-banning group," Rachel insisted.

"It does indeed," Connor replied.

"There's something else. Two bloody $100 bills were found near the body."

"Adam didn't tell me about that either. Makes you wonder what else the police may be withholding."

"But why would the killer leave the cash? Why not take it?" Rachel asked.

"I don't know. That would seem to rule out robbery. Maybe the killer wanted to leave a message."

"That thought crossed my mind," Rachel said. "But what would be that message?"

"I haven't the foggiest."

"I wonder if police have a theory about the money."

"If they do, Adam hasn't mentioned it to me," Connor replied. "But I'm going to call and find out."

Connor picked up his cell phone and punched in Adam's number. The police detective answered with a question. "What?"

"Having a bad day?" Connor asked.

"You could say that. We're no closer to solving Erica Stark's murder."

"But the killer placed that Gender Queer book over Erica's face, and you found bloody $100 bills by the body."

"Who told you that?"

"Obviously, not you, Adam," Connor groused.

"We can't tell you everything. It's a police investigation."

"But are those things important clues?"

"We hope so."

"Have you questioned the members of the Citizens for Decency group?"

"We're working on it. There's some 75 people who claim to be members of that group. But most of them are only loosely involved, having showed up for only one or two meetings. There appear to be about 20 die-hard members who routinely have had run-ins with library staff. We're still trying to track some of them down. But so far, there's no solid suspect."

"What about Rev. Presson?"

"Chief Bonney talked to him. The pastor has cooperated, provided us with a list of the Citizens for Decency members and contact numbers."

"It doesn't sound like you really grilled him."

"Not yet. That's off the record. We aren't going to get heavy handed with him when there's no evidence the pastor killed the librarian."

"There's no evidence he didn't do it either," Connor argued.

"It seems unlikely," Adam said.

"Why?"

"He's a pastor. Don't quote me, but he and the police chief are friends. For God's sake, Blair attends the same church, Grace-Works."

"Let's hope it doesn't cloud his judgment," Connor said.

"If we find evidence linking Harold Presson to the murder, we'll arrest him. I promise you that. But so far that's not the case. We have no physical evidence tying him to the crime or anyone else with that book-banning group."

"Doesn't the placement of that book on the victim's face suggest the killer had ties to that group?"

"The book was one of those Citizens for Decency wanted removed from the library, but that fact alone won't solve the crime."

"What about the money? Why leave the money at the crime scene?"

"It's a mystery."

"Maybe the killer was sending a message," Connor suggested.

"What would that be?"

"You're the detective."

"Well, at this point, I haven't a clue. But I can tell you one thing."

"What's that?"

"Most killers aren't thinking about sending a message. They're just not that smart."

Chapter Fifteen

Connor and Rachel partnered on a story detailing the latest news on the murder. The first paragraph paraded the key facts. *The killer of Elmwood librarian Erica Stark left an open, controversial book on her face. Two bloody $100 bills also were found at the scene, police have confirmed amid the continuing investigation which has yet to produce an arrest.*

The second paragraph explained that the book, Gender Queer, had sparked outrage from Citizens for Decency, which accused the library of promoting pornography. The book, the article noted, was one of many that the group wanted banned from the tax-funded library. The story reported that Pastor Harold Presson was cooperating with police who were questioning active members of the citizens group. The article quoted Julie Halston's account of the crime scene, including the blood-stained cash. It noted that, according to the assistant librarian who was now the interim director, Erica Stark didn't carry much cash.

It also explained that Erica Stark insisted on closing the library every Thursday night rather than assign that duty to other staff members. The rest of the article rehashed information previously reported about the murder.

The two reporters reread their article and then marked it ready to edit. Lansmon read the piece and sent it on to the copy desk for a final review. Exiting his office, the balding editor approached Connor and Rachel. "Just wanted to let you know, the story's running inside. Interesting news, but there's not enough there to warrant putting it on the front page."

"But no one else has reported this information," Connor argued. "We've got an exclusive."

"Don't worry. People will read it. But we've already reported that Citizens for Decency had a beef with the library staff. We don't need to play it up. Besides, police haven't determined if anyone from that citizens group was involved in the crime."

"But what about the bloody $100 bills?" Rachel asked. "Doesn't it clearly show this wasn't a robbery?"

"I believe police already had made it clear they didn't view it as a robbery," Lansmon said. "For all we know, Ms. Stark may have offered the killer the money in exchange for her life."

"But," Connor began.

"No buts. Go home," Lansmon said.

Connor frowned. Rachel sighed as Lansmon marched off.

"Let's get out of here," Connor said. "I'm sure this murder story isn't going away."

"I wonder if the killer reads the paper," Rachel said.

"Now that's a thought."

"If so, he'll probably be grinning when he reads our story."

"Why?" Connor asked.

"Because now everyone will know about the placement of the book. The killer must have been sending a message. Why else stage the scene?"

"You believe he wants people to connect the crime to the book-banning controversy?"

"Yes, I do."

"It's the only thing that makes any sense."

"I agree," Connor said. "Enough about murder. Let's get some dinner."

"It would be a crime not to feed you," Rachel laughed.

"You know it," Connor replied as he and Rachel walked out the employee door into the coolness of an April evening, the sky aglow with the setting sun.

Chapter Sixteen

The news spread like wildfire. In the newspaper and online. Radio stations repeated the *Journal* story. TV reporters offered up soundbites from the police. Seated at his office desk, Blair Bonney raged at the news.

"Damn it. Why couldn't Julie Halston keep her mouth shut," he complained to Adam, seated across from him. "And why can't you rein in your friend Connor?"

"The story never would have come to light if that Halston woman hadn't spoken to the *Journal*," Adam noted.

"Well, it's out there now," the chief grumbled. "Where are we now on interviewing members of that citizens group?"

"I've questioned most of the active members. Just have a few more to contact."

"And?"

"Nothing much to report. Those questioned insisted they didn't do it."

"Do you believe them?"

"I do. They strike me as a bunch of loudmouths who hide behind their rhetoric," Adam said.

"Well, do me a favor, Adam."

"What's that?"

"Find me some damn evidence that will nail the bastard who murdered Ms. Stark. And find it now!"

Across town, *Journal* publisher Dan Steele had heartburn when he read the story. And that was before Harold Presson marched into his office and railed at him. "You've virtually lynched me and Citizens for Decency. How dare you," yelled the pastor. "You and I go back aways. I never thought you'd do a hit job on me. What trashy journalism."

"The story did say you were cooperating with police," Steele noted.

"Yeah. That makes me sound like I'm throwing my fellow Citizens for Decency members under the bus. Thanks a lot."

Steele said little else for the next ten minutes as he listened to the pastor berate the *Journal* and its reporters for "sensationalizing" the murder.

When Harold finished, he turned and strode out of the publisher's office. The pastor reached the front door of the newspaper building, yanked it open and stepped outside onto the sidewalk. He looked around to make sure no one could hear him before he cursed the newspaper to high heavens.

Five minutes later, Dan Steele barged into Lansmon's office, slamming the door behind him. Everyone in the newsroom could hear Steele shouting. A few minutes later, the yelling subsided. Connor and Rachel watched the event unfolding behind the window in Lansmon's office.

Steele scowled at Connor and Rachel as he departed the editor's office. No sooner had Steele left the newsroom than Lansmon called in the two reporters. Lansmon stood next to his desk. He didn't invite them to sit. Clearly, this would be a short discussion, Rachel reasoned.

"Dan's pissed," Lansmon said.

"About our story?" Connor asked.

"Yes, but it's more about the fact that Harold Presson cornered him, complaining that the newspaper had done a hit job on him and Citizens for Decency."

"We just reported the facts," Rachel said.

"Well, that doesn't matter. Dan has made it clear that Citizens for Decency and Presson are off limits for now. He doesn't want us to run anymore stories regarding them unless the police connect them to the murder."

"But," Connor began.

"No buts," Lansmon said. "It's Dan's paper. What he says, goes. And, I have to agree, we've pushed this book-banning angle as far as we can go without any solid evidence. Besides, I need you to work on some front-page stories that don't involve this damn murder."

Connor and Rachel nodded. There was no point in arguing.

They retreated to their desks as their co-workers looked on. Lansmon stood in the doorway to his office and eyed the other reporters. "Get back to work," he told them. "Show's over."

Chapter Seventeen

By late April, Adam had interviewed all but one of the active members of Citizens for Decency. On a Thursday, he questioned the last member on that list: Jeremy Law. The 42-year-operated Elmwood Treasures, a downtown gift shop in a brick building that in the early 1900s housed a bakery. Just blocks from the Victorian style clock that graced a downtown intersection, the shop sold everything from artsy note cards to scented candles. Adam conceded the place smelled good.

Law sported short, curly hair. He wore a pair of blue-framed reading glasses that complemented his blue collared shirt and slacks. He eyed Adam suspiciously from across the wooden counter on which his cash register stood.

"I've heard you've been talking to members of our Decency group. Sounds like you're trying to pin that murder on us," Jeremy said.

"Not at all," Adam replied. "We're just trying to find out who killed Erica Stark."

"Well, I'm glad that bitch is dead. She didn't care how many children she corrupted with those filthy books. Our town's better off without her."

"Did you send her hate mail?"

"Maybe."

"Now, we can do some forensic testing and match some of those messages to you. So, why not admit it?"

"Okay. Yes, I sent some of those messages. But I didn't kill her. I don't own some Rambo knife."

"But you seem to have hated Ms. Stark. So, you can see why we would suspect you killed her," Adam said.

"Maybe so. But I didn't murder her. You can't tie me to the crime."

"Did anyone else harbor the same hatred of Ms. Stark?"

"I imagine almost every member of Citizens for Decency. That librarian dismissed us as a bunch of jerks. We're not. We're just citizens who are concerned about the moral decay of our community," Jeremy insisted.

"If that's so, you should be concerned about the murder of a librarian."

"That's not my problem," Jeremy replied. "Just leave me alone, unless you're going to buy something."

"Don't worry. I'm leaving, but a word of caution. You're on our radar, Jeremy. And, if you killed Ms. Stark, sooner or later you'll foul up. We'll get you."

"Get off my case," Jeremy shouted. "I told you that I didn't kill anyone. You'd know that if you weren't so busy trying to frame me and the others in the Decency group."

"I'm not looking to frame anyone. We're just trying to solve this murder case."

"Well, do me a favor. Solve it somewhere else. I have customers to help," Jeremy said, turning toward a large-framed woman who had clamped her hands on a red, scented candle as if it were her last passion on Earth. "Can I help you?" Jeremy asked.

"Just browsing," the woman answered as Adam headed for the door. The detective sighed. Another dead-end. Thoughts jumbled around in his head. Try as he might, he couldn't see Jeremy Law as the killer. *What killer sells pretty notecards and candles?*

Chapter Eighteen

In early May, it wasn't flowers that took center stage. It was the monsoon season. Storms rolled through Southeast Missouri, seemingly one after another, bringing high winds, hail and tons of rain. The National Weather Service warned of flash floods and tornadoes. Fortunately, for Elmwood, the tornadoes went south. But the area received more than its share of wet weather, sparking flash flooding in low-lying areas.

Connor and Rachel spent the first week of May reporting on the storms that struck small, outlying towns, damaging mobile homes and flooding streets and houses. They spoke to the meteorologists at the National Weather Service so often they knew them all by name. Amid Mother Nature's wrath, a break occurred in the murder case. Adam phoned Connor with the news, which, he explained, was off the record.

Judge Michael Wachter, who chaired the library board, had informed police that he found a wooden paddle beneath a bookshelf. The judge had handed the paddle to police.

"Do you think the paddle was used to strike Erica Stark?" Connor asked after Adam finished telling him the news.

"Could be. Forensics should tell us if what appears to be dried blood matches the victim's blood," Adam said.

"What kind of paddle is it?"

"It's a fraternity paddle."

"How come it never showed up before now? I thought the police went through the whole place."

"We did, but we didn't look under every shelf. We had no reason to believe the killer left such a thing behind. Besides, the mysteries section, where it was found, is a good distance from the biographies section where Ms. Stark died."

"So, how did the judge find it?" Connor asked.

"He said he was looking to check out a James Patterson mystery after a library board meeting. He said he spotted the handle of the paddle sticking out from under the bottom shelf."

"I can't believe the killer would have left the paddle," Connor said. "And, why leave it there in the mysteries section? Was the killer trying to leave a message?"

"Don't know. Let's just hope this paddle will lead us to the killer."

"Damn. Why do you tell me all this off the record? Can't you talk on the record just a little?"

"Not yet. If we get a match on the blood, then we will disclose this publicly. Don't worry. We should have the forensic results soon," Adam said, ending the call.

Connor put down his cellphone, his face wrapped in disbelief. From her desk, Rachel cast a puzzled look at Connor. "What is it?" she asked.

"I just heard from Adam that a fraternity paddle was found in the library and that it appears to be blood stained. Police believe Erica Stark may have been struck with the paddle."

"I don't suppose any of this is on the record?"

"Not yet."

"This could be the big break in the case," Rachel said, her voice showing her excitement.

"I don't know. It doesn't make sense why the killer would leave that paddle."

"Who knows what goes through the mind of a murderer, especially one who kills a librarian," Rachel observed.

"Good point. Still, it seems more than a coincidence that this paddle suddenly just shows up after a library board meeting."

The Elmwood Police Department issued a news release the next day. It stated police had recovered a blood-stained fraternity pledge paddle that the killer used to assault Erica Stark before fatally stabbing her.

Police emailed the release to the news media fifteen minutes after Adam alerted Connor that police were going public with the information. Connor hurriedly typed the basic story before adding statements from the release. Twenty minutes after Connor finished the story, Lansmon posted it online under the headline: "Police tie fraternity paddle to Stark murder." The 10-inch article reported that Judge Michael Wachter, library board chairman, found the mahogany paddle under a bookshelf. It included a statement, attributed to Police Chief Blair Bonney, that blood found on the paddle matched that of the murder victim. Television stations aired the news on their noontime broadcasts, with reporters airing live reports standing outside the Elmwood Public Library. Seated in her office, Julie Halston read the *Journal* story and watched local TV news. She had seen the paddle. Judge Wachter alerted her to the supposed weapon after spotting it on the floor. Wachter had called the police to the scene. Julie had watched as Adam questioned the judge and crime techs bagged the paddle and processed the scene.

Julie pressed the remote, turning off the TV. The news didn't reassure her. Rather, the discovery of the paddle made her worry even more about her safety and that of her library staff. And, she wondered, why did the killer leave it behind. *Why not take it?*

Chapter Nineteen

Two days after discovery of the paddle, Connor sat in the spacious office of Judge Wachter on the top floor of the modern glass and steel Elmwood Justice Center. Wachter had phoned, asking the veteran reporter to stop by. The judge didn't explain why he wanted to chat.

Seated at a large, oak desk, Wachter eyed Connor from behind wire-rimmed glasses that made him look far older than his middle age. His charcoal-colored hair had turned increasingly gray. He wore a collared white shirt and a blue tie dotted with images of justice scales. His dark suit coat hung from an antique hat tree which stood against the wall near his desk.

The judge wiggled nervously in his leather, swivel chair. Connor showed up with pen and notebook. He didn't bother with the recorder. He sensed the judge wouldn't be rambling on. From covering trials, Connor knew Judge Wachter didn't mince words.

"Thanks for coming," Wachter said as Connor settled in a well-framed wooden chair. "I wanted to run something by you."

"Sure."

"This has to be off the record," the judge stressed.

"Ok," Connor said, reluctantly putting his pen down.

"It has to do with the fraternity paddle."

"The one you discovered at the library?"

"Yes."

"What about it?"

"Well, I don't know if the police told you but it's a Sigma Chi pledge paddle."

"Is that important?"

"It might be," Wachter said, pausing between each word. "See, Harold Presson is a Sigma Chi alum. He attended the chapter at Elmwood College. That was before he attended divinity school in St. Louis."

"How do you know this?"

"I have friends who are alums of that fraternity."

"Are you suggesting the pastor killed Erica Stark?"

"I must admit, the thought crossed my mind," the judge said. "He would have had a pledge paddle like the one I found in the library."

"Have you told the police?"

"No. I don't have any hard evidence that Pastor Presson murdered Ms. Stark. And, as a judge, I don't feel it's my place to hurl accusations."

"But don't you think the police should hear this?"

"Yes, but I was hoping it could come from you," said Wachter, his dark eyes focused laser-like on Connor.

"This isn't really about being a judge, is it? It's the fact that you chair the library board," Connor said. "You're worried that if you point the finger at Harold Presson, you'll face the wrath of Citizens for Decency."

"Well, yes. I don't want to make things worse for the library staff.. "So, will you do it and keep my name out of it."

Connor sat still for several minutes, unsure what to say. Then, he cleared his throat. "I'll do it, but on one condition."

"What's that?"

"If police arrest Pastor Presson and he's charged with murder, I won't keep your name and what you told me secret."

"I understand," the judge said.

Connor nodded and rose to leave. "One other thing, Judge."

"What?"

"Do you have any idea why the killer would leave the paddle and risk giving police a clue to his identity?"

"Not a clue. But as a judge, I've seen a lot of criminals in my courtroom. You know what they have in common?"

"No."

"They're not bright. If they were, they wouldn't commit crimes. In my experience, criminals are caught because of the evidence they leave at the scene. This likely is no different," Wachter said.

"I hadn't considered that. You're probably right," Connor said, heading for the door. Judge Wachter watched him leave before getting up. He walked across the room and opened a cabinet. Removing a bottle of Woodford Reserve, he poured himself a glass. He didn't sip it. He downed the bourbon. Then, he had another for good measure.

Chapter Twenty

They met on a Thursday over Po'Boys and cold draft beers at Alligator Alley. Adam showed up dressed in jeans and a Polo shirt in contrast to his usual formal attire. In between bites, Connor informed Adam of a source who said Pastor Presson was an alumnus of Sigma Chi and would have had a pledge paddle like the one tied to the Stark murder.

"That doesn't mean Harold Presson murdered Ms. Stark. I am sure there are other Sigma Chi members in Elmwood who would have similar paddles. Or maybe someone stole a pledge paddle," Adam said.

"Possibly. But don't you think it's worth investigating?"

"Of course," Adam replied. "I don't suppose you're going to tell me who your source is."

"I can't. I promised I wouldn't reveal my source unless Pastor Presson is arrested and charged with the murder."

"Of course, you did," Adam remarked. "Still, we'll check it."

"I hope it pans out," Connor said.

"Me too. We have recovered a set of fingerprints on the paddle. We just need to find a match."

"You haven't fingerprinted Presson?"

"Not yet. Blair doesn't want us going that route unless we have a reason to check his prints."

"But you do have a reason. I just gave it to you."

"I'm not jumping to conclusions," Adam said. "First, we need to find out if the pastor possesses a pledge paddle. If he does, it's unlikely that the paddle found in the library is his."

"I see your point," Connor said, frowning.

"Patience my friend. We can't go barging in like stormtroopers. We need to move carefully and deliberately. We need a solid case," Adam said. "By the way, are you buying dinner?"

"Yes, but only if you promise to keep me in the loop."

"Deal."

"Thanks, pal," Adam said, gulping down the last drops of his mug of Schlafly beer. Connor paid with cash, leaving a healthy tip for the blue-haired, freckle-faced waitress.

Adam Dade arrived at Harold Presson's church office the next morning, The pastor greeted him with a stiff handshake. Seated in the pastor's office, the detective eyed the photos on the wall. There were a lot of them. All showed Presson with various dignitaries, ranging from city council members to governors and congressmen. Today, Presson offered no camera-ready smile, Adam observed.

Presson sat in his comfortable office chair with his hands clutching the edge of his desk. "What can I do for you detective?"

"Well, it's the matter of the fraternity pledge paddle. We know it's a Sigma Chi paddle. It's embossed with the fraternity emblem."

"And you think it's mine?"

"I understand you were a member of Sigma Chi."

"That's true. I joined the fraternity when I attended Elmwood College. I wasn't planning on being a pastor then. Otherwise, I probably would have avoided Greek life," Presson said.

"Do you still have your paddle?"

"Of course. I keep it in my office."

"Why?"

"I guess it's because it reminds me of my youthful past. Some pastors act like they are so holy, but we all are sinners. Pastors are no exception," Presson said.

"So, can you show me your paddle?"

"Sure. It's over here," Presson said, rising from his chair. He stepped over to a corner cabinet. Opening the bottom door, he reached inside. Suddenly, he stopped. He turned toward the detective. "It's not here," he said.

"When did you last see it?"

"It was here last week. I'm sure of it."

"Did anyone break into your office?"

"Not that I am aware."

"But you believe someone stole your paddle?"

"I would assume so."

"You didn't lend it to anyone?"

"Of course, not. Besides, who would want the paddle? It's only important to me, to my past life."

"I'd like you to come down to the police station."

"Why?"

"We'd like to fingerprint you so we can hopefully rule you out as the owner of the paddle found in the library."

"I'm not the murderer," Presson said, raising his voice.

"Then, you have nothing to lose. We could seek a warrant to force you to be fingerprinted, but we'd rather not do so. We want to give you every opportunity to clear your name," Adam said.

"Fine. I'll do it. But then, I hope you will leave me alone and go find the real killer. Quit making me the scapegoat," the pastor grumbled.

Chapter Twenty–One

Adam sat in Blair's office. A day earlier, police fingerprinted Pastor Presson. His prints were found on the paddle. Still, Blair seemed reluctant to make an arrest.

"Why would Pastor Presson leave a paddle with his prints on it? If he were the killer, he wouldn't have left such a clue," the police chief said. "Besides, it was his paddle. Of course, his prints were on it."

"But there's no evidence the paddle was stolen from the church office," Adam noted.

"Any member of the church could have gotten into his office and taken it without his knowledge," Blair said. "We need more evidence."

'Like what?"

"What about the bloody shoe print? Can we tie that to Presson?"

"Not so far."

"Well, I've seen the pastor come to church in running shoes," Blair said. "We could search his office and the parsonage, see if he has a shoe that matches the bloody footprint."

"Not without a warrant."

"Well, get a warrant," Blair responded. "If Presson is innocent, let's clear his name. And, the sooner, the better."

The detective found Judge Wachter in his Justice Center chambers during a break in a trial of a two-time drug dealer accused of assaulting another low-life dealer. Wachter presided over such cases all too often. He noticed the faces of the jurors as the trial progressed. They'd convict the assailant. Wachter had no doubt.

Wachter listened as Adam outlined the reason for the requested warrant. When Adam finished, the judge nodded. "You've got your warrant," he said, signing the document. "But God help you if you're wrong. The whole congregation will be up in arms, not to mention those crazy Citizens for Decency folks."

"We're well aware of the situation," Adam said. "The chief hopes the search will clear any suspicion that the pastor murdered Ms. Stark."

"Let's just hope the search proves helpful in solving the murder," the judge said. Adam didn't reply. He left the office, holding the warrant as if it were a hot potato.

Two hours later, police led by Blair and Adam showed up at Presson's church office. Blair showed Presson the warrant. "You have no right to do this," the pastor shouted.

"I'm sorry, Harold. But we must do this," the chief said as Adam, two other detectives and four uniformed officers searched the office. Fifteen minutes into the search, one of the officers pulled a pair of Nike running shoes from beneath a pair of shorts and a Jesus T-shirt stacked on a lower-level shelf in the corner cabinet. A dark substance stained the treads of the shoe.

Adam examined the shoe. "Looks like blood," he said.

"That's not mine," insisted Harold.

"But you do have shoes like this?" Adam questioned. "And these are your clothes?"

"Yeah. I like to jog when I get the chance, which, these days, isn't very often."

"So, how do you explain this shoe?" Adam asked as the pastor took a closer look.

"I don't know. Someone must be trying to frame me for the murder."

"And you have no idea how this shoe could have ended up discolored like this?" Blair asked.

"No."

"Well, we've got to confiscate the shoes. We need to see if the one shoe matches the footprint found at the scene of Ms. Stark's murder," the chief explained. "The warrant allows us to search the parsonage too."

"Go ahead," Presson said, his face red with anger. "It's right next door. Check all my shoes. The next thing you'll tell me is that you want to check the shoes of every Decency member."

"We're not planning to do that. I don't think any judge would approve it," Blair replied.

"No. You'll just accuse me and my group of killing that librarian without any evidence. Meanwhile, you allow that library to expose Elmwood's children to pornography. You guys are a joke."

Blair didn't reply. He and Adam walked out of the church and led the uniformed officers over to the parsonage. They spent about an hour going through the one-story brick home but came away with no new evidence. Blair made sure the officers conducted the search as neatly as possible. He didn't want to be accused of Gestapo tactics. As it was, Blair and Adam both knew they had unleashed an emotional firestorm. Presson and Citizens for Decency soon would publicly blast the police. A shit storm was coming.

Chapter Twenty—Two

Forensic tests determined blood on the confiscated shoe matched that of the victim. A DNA test confirmed that Pastor Presson had worn the shoe. The arrest came on Monday. Blair had insisted that no arrest be made until then. He didn't want to interfere with Sunday's church service.

On Sunday, Harold Presson preached on the topic of false accusations. He talked about people who had served jail time in Missouri for crimes they did not commit. "As Christians, we should be compassionate of our fellow man. Not everyone accused of a crime is guilty. Not every police officer and prosecutor are innocent of wrongdoing. Evil can be found everywhere, even in the hearts of those in uniform," Presson told his congregation.

Blair skipped church. He feared the pastor's wrath from the pulpit. Fellow churchgoers called him after the service and recounted the pastor's condemnation. Blair called Presson and suggested he voluntarily turn himself in. Presson agreed, showing up the next morning at the police station dressed in a stylish blue suit complete with an American flag tie. After being processed, he posted bond and walked out of the station.

Blair watched him leave. He turned to Adam. "Now, you can alert the press," said the chief, satisfied they had avoided a media circus.

Adam phoned Connor with the news. "Sorry, I couldn't tell you sooner."

"Yeah, what a friend," Connor lamented.

"It was Chief Bonney's decision, not mine. He wanted to keep this under wraps until after the booking."

"So, I take it, you tied the paddle to Presson?"

"Yep, and the bloody shoeprint. It all adds up. We're putting out a news release within the hour," Adam said, ending the call.

Connor told Rachel the news and then hurried into Lansmon's office to alert him to the story.

"Write up what you have," barked the editor. "We're not waiting on the news release."

Connor returned to his desk and wrote an eight-inch story. The article began: *Pastor Harold Presson surrendered to police today on a charge that he murdered Elmwood librarian Erica Stark. Police alleged that a fraternity paddle and a bloody tennis shoe tied him to the crime.*

The second paragraph detailed that the GraceWorks pastor headed up Citizens for Decency, a group whose members had denounced Ms. Stark and other staff at the Elmwood Public Library for not removing books they deemed pornographic and promoting LGBTQ culture. Within the hour, Connor added in more details from the police department's news release.

Mayor Elroy James stormed into Chief Bonney's office the next morning. He'd read the *Journal* story and watched the TV news. None of this sat well with Elroy, who had feuded with the police chief for years. And, it was personal. Years earlier, Elroy's wife had been arrested for shoplifting. Blair had refused to drop the case. Elroy responded by orchestrating a cut in funding for the police department, forcing the chief to reduce staff. Then, there was the time that police arrested the mayor, wrongly accusing him of killing his nephew. The prosecutor eventually dropped the murder charge after the real killer was identified thanks to the investigative efforts of Connor and Rachel.

"What the hell are you doing, arresting that damn pastor?" Elroy asked, spitting out the words like bullets.

"We arrested Harold Presson because we uncovered evidence linking him to the murder."

"Seems circumstantial and rather suspect. Why would he leave his fraternity paddle at the scene of the crime and then hold onto a blood-stained running shoe? His Citizens for Decency gang may be a little crazy, but Harold Presson is no fool. If he killed that librarian, he wouldn't have left evidence behind."

"You're not thinking straight," Blair said. "Most cases are solved because criminals do stupid things, like leave tell-tale evidence at a crime scene. My officers know what they're doing. For God's sake, Harold Presson is my pastor. You think I wanted to arrest him? I didn't. But the evidence speaks for itself."

"You better be right because otherwise we'll be buried in a ton of crap from Pastor Presson and his crew. And, I'll hold you personally responsible for this mess."

"You do that. Now, get the hell out of here before I throw you out," Blair shouted.

Chapter Twenty–Three

Ducks swam lazily in the pond at Elmwood's city park, situated on a bluff overlooking the downtown. Connor sat on a park bench as one of the waterfowl eyed him, hoping for some bread crumbs or other morsel. Connor ignored the Mallard and the odor of duck poop as he waited for Adam on a breezy day in May as the temperature and humidity climbed. To the veteran journalist, it felt like summer had arrived. And, way too early.

Adam showed up in his usual suit, seemingly oblivious to the warm weather. Connor, on the other hand, wore a short-sleeve shirt and jeans. He wished he had worn shorts, but even the Journal's lax dress code didn't allow for such attire. Adam took a seat next to Connor. Then, he pulled out a bag of bread crumbs and threw it on the ground. The crumbs landed several feet away. A flock of ducks waddled over, competing for the food.

"What, are you seeking the ducks' affection?" Connor asked, laughing.

"No. I just feel ducky," Adam joked.

"You're the one who suggested meeting here."

"True. I thought it would be nice to get some fresh air. It gets a little stale in the police station."

"You said on the phone you wanted some information from me. What information?"

"Have you forgotten, Connor? You said you would reveal your source if we arrested and charged Pastor Presson."

"Oh, yes. It escaped my mind."

"Or you were hoping not to have to reveal it."

"No way. I keep my word. Judge Wachter told me about the paddle and its possible connection to Presson."

"You're kidding. The judge who approved the search warrant is your source?"

"Yes," Connor said.

"Seems the judge is more involved in this case than I realized."

"He didn't tell you because he chairs the library board, and the pastor is a vocal critic of the library. The judge said he felt it might make it look as if he was acting out of revenge."

"I see his point, but he should have spoken up. I'll need to interview him."

"Wachter knows the situation," Connor said. "I told the judge I wouldn't keep his name secret if you arrested Pastor Presson."

"Well, one thing is for sure."

"What's that?"

"Judge Wachter will have to recuse himself. He can't hear this case."

"Does the pastor have an attorney?"

"Yes."

"Let me guess—Rush Johnson."

"You're correct. The best defense lawyer in Elmwood," Adam said.

"And the most expensive."

"But money alone won't get him off. The evidence is substantial."

"Maybe so, but I wouldn't bet against Rush. He seldom takes a case he can't win."

"We'll see. But in this situation, there's motive, means and a lot of evidence," Adam said, rising from the bench. The police detective eyed the swimming ducks and smiled. Connor felt Adam would have loved to wade into the pond. But to the detective, it was a peaceful scene. Something he craved when most of his days were spent investigating bad people doing bad things.

Back in the newsroom, Connor moved ahead with a story on the city's crumbling streets and the efforts to repair them. Publisher Dan Steele had complained to Lansmon that the *Journal* had been too focused on the murder. Steele wanted more feel-good stories like the one Rachel was now writing. This one dealt with an upcoming, downtown music festival at the historic Flynn House, a Victorian-era home-turned-museum.

Connor wrapped up his story. As he waited for the copy editors to review it, his desk phone rang. Rush Johnson was on the line. Rush had a message. He and Harold Presson planned to hold a news conference at noon, an hour from now, to address the murder charge. Rush said the news conference would occur outside the Elmwood Public Library. Rush ended the call, saying he had other media to contact. Connor turned to Rachel and informed her about the impromptu press conference.

"Do you think Presson's Citizens for Decency members will show up?" Rachel asked.

"Of course. Rush would insist on it and so would Presson. They love a crowd, particularly one stacked in their favor," Connor said.

Chapter Twenty—Four

The news conference commenced promptly at noon. Rush Johnson showed up in a custom gray, Italian suit and matching silk tie. In his early 50s, the attorney's chiseled looks and tanned skin made him look younger. Harold Presson wore a blue suit and white collared shirt, but no tie. A gold cross hung on a gold chain around his neck. About 30 members of his Citizens for Decency group stood behind the two men. The group's members sported homemade signs proclaiming Presson's innocence and accusing the police of framing the pastor.

Rush and Harold stood on the sidewalk in front of the library entrance next to a bronze statue of two seated children reading books. Connor and Rachel joined the TV and radio reporters who crowded around the two men. Connor intended to write the story. Rachel tagged along because she wanted to hear what the two men had to say. Reporters thrust microphones at the attorney and pastor. Still others, including Connor, held digital recorders to capture every word. Rachel noticed that the local CBS station readied to cover it live. Rush didn't miss a trick. Nothing like a live report for the noon news, she thought.

Journal photographer Tyler Frazier climbed onto the bed of his late-model Ford pickup. Using a zoom lens, he shot images of the placard-waving Citizens for Decency members, along with close-ups of Rush and Presson.

Rush surveyed the media and launched into his remarks. "My client and I called this news conference to denounce the Gestapo-like tactics of the Elmwood Police Department and the decision of Prosecutor Richard Lamb to charge Pastor Harold Presson with a murder he did not commit. It's clear this is a witch hunt. Pastor Presson is being persecuted because of his involvement with Citizens for Decency," Rush said as members of the group shouted in unison, "Shame on the Frame." Tyler snapped several shots of the vocal crowd.

"It's clear my client was set up," insisted Rush. "The evidence suggests the fraternity paddle and shoe were stolen from my client's office shortly before the murder of Ms. Erica Stark. If Harold Presson had murdered Ms. Stark, why would he leave behind his fraternity paddle and a bloody shoe print and then leave that same blood-stained shoe in his office where police would find it? And if my client had left the fraternity paddle in the library, why wouldn't it have been found immediately after the murder? The police searched the entire library. They never spotted it. Then, more than a month after the murder, Judge Michael Wachter notifies police that he found the paddle under a bookshelf in the library. It seems strange that this judge, who chairs the library board and clearly is at odds with Pastor Presson, suddenly would find this so-called piece of evidence when numerous police officers never spotted it.

"And why would there be blood stains on a single shoe that match a single shoe print at the murder scene? Did the murderer hop on one foot? No. Any sane person would conclude that the killer stole one of Harold's tennis shoes , placed it down on the blood spatter, and then put it in some type of bag and carried it from the scene," Rush said. "The killer then returned the shoe to Pastor Presson's church office."

The attorney added that his client had waived the preliminary hearing. Given the judge's reported discovery of the fraternity paddle, Rush said he would ask for a change of judge. "My client deserves an unbiased magistrate, not one whose actions benefit the prosecution."

Rush stepped aside and Harold Presson took center stage. "This murder charge against me is a travesty. I am a man of God and would never take another person's life. I'm being persecuted to silence me and the decent citizens of my group who have advocated for the library to remove the pornography and filth that's corrupting our community's children. We will not let the Godless folks and perverts turn our library into a den of indecency," Presson said as his backers cheered.

"To my supporters I say, stick around. There's a food truck here. Tacos and burritos. I'm buying," Presson said. Connor and Rachel looked around. They eyed the green food truck, its exterior painted with images of tacos and chili peppers, parked at the rear of the parking lot.

"Wow," Rachel said. "You'd think they were having a festival."

"Everyone loves to eat free food," Connor said as they watched members of Citizens for Decency hustle over to the truck.

Julie Halston and her staff eyed the activity with suspicion. They had watched the news conference on TV. The screen now showed a live shot of the food truck. The Hispanic owner of the truck had not asked library officials if he could park his truck in the parking lot. But Julie decided against picking a fight with the eatery's owner. Elmwood had a growing Hispanic population. Many of the families regularly used the library. One thought consumed Julie. *No need to create more controversy.*

Chapter Twenty−Five

Back in the newsroom, Connor wrote a 15-inch article, quoting Rush and the pastor. Rachel reached out to the police and the prosecutor for comments without success. The *Journal* soon posted the story online under the headline: "Pastor claims innocence." Beneath it, a smaller headline read: "Attorney says client 'set up' for murder."

Connor looked at the clock on the newsroom wall that registered 1:30. Past time for lunch, he thought. "Let's get a bite to eat. I'm starving," he told Rachel.

"We could have had tacos," she replied with a laugh.

"Don't think so. Something tells me Harold wasn't going to buy our lunch. I didn't want tacos, not if I had to pay for them."

Rachel smiled as she and Connor headed for the exit. They dined at Smooth Buns. At this hour, few customers graced the place. They sat at a front table by a large window that allowed for a view of the mural-filled Mississippi River floodwall. They both ordered French onion soup and grilled cheese sandwiches.

"What did you think of the news conference?" Rachel asked after the blonde-haired waitress who sported a rose tattoo on her neck brought them their glasses of water.

"Despite the circus atmosphere, I think Rush has some points. It does make you wonder if someone framed Harold Presson. It's strange that Judge Wachter just happened to find that paddle. Seems a bit too contrived."

"Do you think Judge Wachter did it?"

"Framed Harold? I don't know. It's hard for me to see the judge as a killer. He doesn't strike me as the type. Besides, he chairs the library board. I don't see a motive."

"I agree. I can't see the judge as a murderer. And, it still seems likely the killer is someone who objected to banning books," Rachel surmised.

"Not necessarily," Connor said. "It might have nothing to do with the actions of Citizens for Decency."

"Why else murder Ms. Stark?"

"I don't know. I'm just saying it's all speculation at this point."

"Maybe so, but I have to believe the murder had something to do with the book-banning controversy. Why else kill the librarian? The police don't believe it was robbery. Two $100 bills were left at the scene. If the killer robbed Ms. Stark, why leave behind the cash?"

"Don't know. The police have said little about the money. Not sure why."

"Maybe they don't know what to make of the bills."

"I suspect you're right. If they could have tied it to the pastor, I believe they would have said so."

Halfway through their meal, Oliver and Truman stopped by their table to chat. The Smooth Buns owners wanted to know about the murder investigation.

"I heard about the news conference," Oliver said, wiping his hands on his grease-stained sweatshirt.

"Some of our customers were talking about it. They saw it on TV," Truman explained. His dapper attire screamed artsy to Connor, who could never imagine himself styled that way.

"You know what we know," Connor said.

"Do you believe the pastor's been framed?" questioned Oliver.

"Rush makes a good case, but the police seem sure they have the right person," Rachel said.

"Sounds like this book-banning controversy is at the heart of this case," Truman said.

"Maybe," Connor said.

"You don't sound convinced," Truman replied.

"I don't know. I know the book-banning controversy has sparked some hateful comments made to library staff. There's no love lost between the library staff and Citizens for Decency. And, one of the controversial books that's been at the heart of the debate was placed open on the victim's face. But the so-called evidence seems too well placed."

"You may be right," Oliver said. "But one thing is clear."

"What's that?"

"These Citizens for Decency folks want to eliminate from the library any book dealing with homosexuality. They don't see us as people," Oliver observed, putting his arm around Truman.

"Hate makes it easy to kill someone," Truman said.

"But if that pastor is innocent," Oliver said, "I don't want him convicted for a crime he didn't do even though everything about him sickens me."

"Let's hope the truth wins out," Connor said. "Meantime, I need to finish lunch."

"We'll let you get back to your meal," Truman said as he and Oliver headed back to the kitchen.

"You seemed a little short with them," Rachel remarked.

"Not at all. I didn't see the need to continue the conversation. At this point, we don't have concrete evidence that Harold Presson didn't kill Erica Stark."

"But that doesn't mean we can't talk about it," Rachel insisted. "You're always hangry."

"No, I'm not," Connor said, pouting.

"Yes, you are. So, let's finish eating so you'll be in a better mood when we go back to work this afternoon."

"Now, you're talking," Connor said, taking another bite of his sandwich.

Chapter Twenty–Six

Two days after the news conference, Connor and Rachel met Rush Johnson at Bourbon Balls, a trendy Broadway bar in downtown Elmwood that featured plenty of bourbon as well as beer on tap. The place also carried a limited menu, which included bourbon balls, those chocolate treats popular at the Kentucky Derby. Here, you could partake of the sweet treats year-round. Rush had invited the two reporters to the establishment, suggesting he had some information regarding his client, Harold, and the murder case.

Connor and Rachel entered the dimly lit bar at 8 p.m., ducking inside just as it started to rain. Customers, ranging from bankers to college students, crowded the bar, their boozy voices flooding the place. They found Rush seated at a table, still attired in a suit from a long day of court appearances on behalf of clients. Rush sipped a glass of Elijah Craig bourbon, savoring its sweet caramel and butterscotch notes that created the drink's smoothness. "Have a drink," Rush said, pushing the menu list of liquors toward Connor and Rachel after they sat down.

Five minutes later, they ordered two Schlafly beers from a dark, curly haired man who sported a cross earring on his right ear lobe. Rush added an order of bourbon balls. They chatted briefly about the wet weather, waiting on their drinks. After their beverages arrived, along with the bourbon balls, Rush said he had some information regarding the murder case that even the police didn't know.

"What's that?" Connor asked.

"First, let's get this straight. This is off the record. My client doesn't want this publicly known at this time although I expect it will come up if this case goes to trial."

"If it's off the record, why tell us at all?" Rachel questioned.

"Because I am hoping you can help me, help Pastor Presson."

"And why would we do that?" Connor asked.

"Off the record?"

"Yes," sighed Connor.

"Harold Presson says Erica Stark had blackmailed him, been doing so for years," Rush said.

"What?" Rachel asked. She and Connor stared in disbelief at Rush and what the attorney had just told them.

"You believe him?" Rachel asked.

"I do. He has a lot to lose if or when this blackmailing stuff becomes public," Rush said.

"What did Erica have on the pastor?" Connor asked.

"I'm not at liberty to say now. All I can tell you is that my client says he first paid $1,000 a month. Later, the monthly payments jumped to $1,500."

"Why would the pastor let himself be blackmailed? What did Ms. Stark have on him?" Rachel questioned.

"All I can tell you is that damn librarian was threatening to disclose information that would have been damaging to my client, both personally and professionally."

"I can't believe Erica Stark would be a blackmailer," Connor said.

"My client says he was instructed to leave cash in a biography of George Washington in the library."

"That would explain the $100 bills found near the victim," Rachel said.

"You said you wanted our help," Connor said.

"Yes. My client believes he wasn't the only person that Ms. Stark blackmailed."

"What makes him think that is the case?"

"Harold says when Ms. Stark first blackmailed him, she mentioned something to the effect that she 'knew a lot of things about a lot of people.'"

"So, you want us to find out if Ms. Stark had some dirt on other people?" Rachel asked.

"Yes. And, I want you to let me know of any information you uncover," Rush said.

"What do we get out of it?" Connor questioned.

"You'll get to break the story."

"With or without the stuff about Presson?"

"That depends," Rush said.

"On what?"

"On what you find out," the attorney replied.

"Bullshit," Connor said. "You're trying to protect your client."

"Of course, I am. That's what a lawyer does. I told you; I expect the blackmail will come out. I just want to put it in the best light for my client. If I can show that librarian blackmailed other people, I can give the jury a reason to doubt that my client killed her. And, maybe we can prove who killed Ms. Stark and why," Rush said, reaching for the bill. "I've got this. It's the least I can do for you guys."

"Hell, I would have had another drink if I'd known you were buying," Connor said.

"Yeah. Well, if you root out this blackmail scheme, I'll buy you both a steak dinner," Rush replied.

"We'll hold you to it," Rachel said as she and Connor rose to leave. Rush watched the reporters weave their way through the bar crowd. Then, he ordered another bourbon.

Chapter Twenty—Seven

The next morning, Rachel and Connor held a closed-door meeting with Lansmon. They told him about the alleged bribery scheme and the fact the information they had was off the record. They said they wanted to dig into that angle of the murder. Lansmon agreed, but suggested Harold Presson could be lying. "He's got every reason to make up a story that might get him acquitted," Lansmon said.

"You might be right, but we've got to look into it. If Ms. Stark blackmailed the pastor, she may have blackmailed others," Connor said.

"We've got to do a deeper dive into Erica Stark," Rachel said. "If she did blackmail others, how did she do it? Were the payoffs always made at the library?"

"And why did she do it? That's a question that needs to be answered," Lansmon observed. "And what do the cops know?"

"I don't think they know about this. From what we understand, Pastor Presson never mentioned the blackmail scheme to the police," Connor said.

"Not yet," Rachel said. "But Rush Johnson is sure to raise the issue if the murder case goes to trial."

"Well, let's see if we can uncover the truth. We need facts, not innuendo," Lansmon insisted. "Keep me posted. In the meantime, I expect you both to cover your beats. I can't afford to let you spend all your time playing detective."

"You mean you want us to churn out some front-page stories for tomorrow's edition," Rachel said.

"Yes, that's the idea," Lansmon said, grinning. "We can hardly go with a blank front page."

Connor and Rachel returned to their desks and spent the rest of the day reporting and writing stories on city government and the public schools. But the thought that the dead librarian may have blackmailed Pastor Presson and possibly others tumbled across their minds. After work, they took their thoughts to dinner at Elmwood's

Hamburger Hut. They settled into a booth. Both ordered cheeseburgers and fries. Rachel drank sweet tea. Connor had a Coke.

While they ate, they batted around ideas on how to delve into the blackmail allegations. "If only Harold Presson would go on the record," Rachel lamented.

"Yes, but Rush made it clear that won't happen right now. Still, that doesn't mean we can't look into it. We need to learn why he was blackmailed."

"I'll talk to Julie Halston. Maybe she knows something that will point us in the right direction," Rachel said.

"We need to know more about Erica Stark's finances. If she blackmailed people, there should be a financial trail. We should talk to her niece Angela. She might shed light on her aunt's bank records."

"Rush told us that Presson made blackmail payments at the library," Rachel said. "If so, maybe we can single out others who were blackmailed by reviewing security camera records. If we focus on individuals who routinely visited the biography section, maybe we'll get lucky."

"Maybe," Connor said. "But first we need to know if the police uncovered any information about the victim that could provide some clues. I'll talk to Adam."

"I wouldn't count on any help from the police. They seem convinced they have the murderer. They won't want to reopen what they see as an open-and-shut case."

"We'll see. Adam may be stubborn at times, but he's not stupid. If he knows there is a bribery allegation, he'll check it out. He's a good detective."

"I know you're friends, but Adam doesn't call the shots. Blair is in charge."

"Even Blair would be hard pressed to ignore this if we can show there's something to this bribery story," Connor said.

"That's a big if," Rachel replied. Connor nodded and ate his last fry.

Black clouds shot across the sky like cannon fire in June. Rain soon followed, drenching the Southeast Missouri town. Connor called Adam. The police detective had just returned from a family vacation. Seated at his desk, the reporter spent several minutes on the phone asking Adam about the vacation and chatting about the wet weather. Then, he got down to business. "I want to ask you something about the murder of Ms. Stark."

"What is it?"

"Did you ever look into the activities of the victim?"

"Why?"

"Was she involved in any suspicious activities? Did you look into her finances?"

"Hold on. What the hell is this about?"

"We have some information that suggests that Ms. Stark may have blackmailed people."

"Who told you this?"

"I'm not at liberty to say. I don't even know if the allegation is accurate. I'm just trying to get at the truth."

"Well, Connor, let me set you straight. There is no reason to think that the librarian was doing anything suspicious. You start spreading such allegations around and you're likely to be sued."

"So, you don't think there is any possibility that Erica Stark blackmailed people and one of them killed her?"

"I don't know what you're smoking, but you're out of your mind," Adam said.

"But what about the cash you found at the scene?"

"You're suggesting it was a pay off?"

"Maybe."

"Did Harold Presson allege the victim was a blackmailer?"

"I didn't say that."

"You don't have to. Who else would have made such an accusation?"

"What if the pastor didn't kill her? Shouldn't you at least explore the blackmail scenario? The murderer could be out there, right under your nose."

"You bring me a solid clue and I'll look into it. Otherwise, drop it, my friend," Adam said, ending the conversation.

Connor sighed as he put down the phone. He turned toward Rachel. "Adam dismissed the blackmail motive."

"I gathered that," she said. "I heard your end of the conversation."

"Well, I'm going to talk to Angela Pierce this afternoon."

"And I'm going to talk to Julie Halston," Rachel said. "If Erica Stark solicited bribes, maybe she picked up the money on Thursdays when she closed up. Julie said Ms. Stark insisted on closing only on Thursdays. Maybe that is the reason."

"You could be right," Connor said.

"Stick with me and you'll learn something," Rachel replied with a laugh.

"I'm not going anywhere."

Rachel smiled and picked up a notebook and her digital recorder. She headed out the back door. For a minute, Connor forgot about his upcoming interview. He had only one thought. *I love that woman.*

Chapter Twenty-Eight

Connor met Angela Pierce at the late Erica Stark's home, situated on a leafy avenue near Elmwood College. The two-story brick house, built in 1921, occupied a large lot. Angela was going through her aunt's possessions. She agreed to talk to Connor, but only because he insisted he had some important information about her aunt's murder.

Angela, dressed in denim shorts and a yellow T-shirt, ushered Connor into the home's formal living room. She sat on the immaculate leather couch. Connor took a seat in a nearby cushioned chair. He looked around. Modern paintings splashed the room with every color of the rainbow.

"You said you had some information about my aunt's murder," Angela said.

"Yes. It's possible your aunt was murdered because she was blackmailing people."

"What the hell are you talking about? My aunt, a blackmailer? What evidence do you have?"

"Well, nothing concrete. But I believe it may come up in Pastor Presson's trial."

"I get it. That sleaze-bag pastor intends to drag her name through the mud in an effort to convince a jury that he didn't kill her. He's pathetic."

"Must be hard for you to handle given that you work for Rush, who is defending Presson."

"Yeah. I'm not happy about it. But it's not my decision. Besides, everyone deserves their day in court, even that scum-bag pastor."

"I'm not sure he did it."

"What? Are you nuts?"

"Why would Harold Presson leave evidence that could incriminate him? He's not stupid. I was hoping you might have evidence that would show if the allegation against Ms. Stark has any basis in fact or if it is just bullshit."

"I know it's bullshit."

"I know your aunt took good care of her mother."

"For 10 years. Her mother received countless treatments, many of them experimental. Medicare didn't pay for all of that."

"I bet your aunt shelled out a lot of money for those treatments," Connor said.

"She did."

"And then there was the skilled-care facility. That cost money too," Connor said. "Erica Stark didn't settle for any old place. From what I understand, she put her mother in an expensive facility, not just your run-of-the mill nursing home."

"It was a classy place. It looked more like a country club. I visited there a few times. Medicare paid part of the bill, thank God, but not all," Angela said. "I've been going through my aunt's bank records. Her mother's nursing home cost $8,000 a month, which included medications. Lots of them. One of the meds cost $500 a month. Then, there were all the radiation treatments, on top of brain surgery. Some of the treatments were considered experimental. Insurance didn't cover any part of those treatments."

"That must have been a real financial burden for your aunt. Those expenses would have bankrupted many folks."

"Like I said, Medicare covered some of it. My aunt paid the rest. She was in good shape financially."

"As director of Elmwood's library?"

"Yes. She seemed to have plenty of money. She had nearly half a million dollars in investments. She had $75,000 in her bank account."

"Did you know she was so well off financially?"

"She told me several years ago that she had made some good investments. But I didn't know she had that kind of money in the bank."

"Maybe some of that came in the form of blackmail payments," Connor suggested.

"No way," Angela said. "My aunt wouldn't have done such a thing. I wouldn't be surprised if that damn pastor staged the crime scene to discredit Erica. It would explain the reports of cash found at the scene."

"You might be right," Connor said. He studied the richly decorated room. "These paintings. Are they originals?"

"Yeah. I looked some of them up on the internet. They're not to my taste. Some of them look like someone just dumped a bunch of paint on the canvas. But they're all expensive. This one here cost $3,000," she said, pointing to a large painting that appeared to depict ocean waves that featured heavy streaks of blue, red and yellow.

"She appeared to live a rich life," Connor observed.

"Yes. I never pictured her as being a big spender, but then we weren't real close. My aunt tended to keep to herself. I always felt that she valued her privacy. But she wasn't a blackmailer. I'm sure of that," Angela said, running a hand through her hair. "Now, if you don't mind, I need to get back to going through my aunt's stuff. You know the way out," she said.

"I do. Thanks for your time," Connor said as he headed for the door. Angela stood in the living room, watching him leave.

"Damn the press," she mumbled to herself. *Blackmail? Nonsense. Who ever heard of a librarian blackmailer?*

Rachel, accompanied by Sammie, her eight-year-old black and white border collie, met Julie on a concrete walking trail along the downtown Mississippi River shoreline, which extended from the city's main floodgate northward to the casino. Rachel asked Julie about her former boss, explaining that the newspaper had received confidential information suggesting Ms. Stark had blackmailed people.

"That's crazy," Julie said as she stooped to pet Sammie. "Who would say that?"

"I'm not at liberty to say, but the allegation might come up at Harold Presson's trial."

"That pastor won't stop attacking her. He's not content to kill her, now he wants to soil her character, make her out as the bad guy."

"But if she were blackmailing people, it could explain the cash found at the murder scene," Rachel insisted.

"That's garbage and you know it!"

"Tell me about Erica's Thursday night routine. You said she always closed that day."

"Yes. She insisted on it," Julie said as she and Rachel walked the trail.

"You saw the crime scene. The murder occurred in the biography section."

"Yes."

"Were any books from the biography section found near the victim?"

"Yes. A biography of George Washington. She loved everything about our nation's first leader. She kept another copy of that biography on her office desk."

"Did she say why she kept the book there?"

"Like I said, Erica loved histories about our first president. It seemed natural that she'd keep one of the biographies on her desk. She read and reread parts of it."

"Did you ever see anyone acting suspiciously in the biography section?"

"No, unless you count Rev. Presson. He'd come in once a month on a Thursday. I've seen him on the security recordings."

"Did he check out the Washington biography?"

"I didn't notice."

"What did the security camera recordings show?"

"Well, the immediate area where Erica was killed is in a blind spot when it comes to the security cameras. I've looked at the video. The killer wasn't visible. But then, the recording doesn't show anyone leaving after the murder. The police have reviewed the security footage too. They haven't found a single clue to the killer's identity."

"Police say some of the recording was erased, presumably by the killer," Rachel said. "That would explain why the murderer wasn't spotted entering or exiting the library. Did the police review security video going back a month or more?"

"I don't think so. They were focused on the hours surrounding the murder."

"I'd like to look at the security footage for Thursdays going back weeks before the murder."

"Why?"

"Maybe the murderer scouted out the place in advance of the killing."

"And how would you spot this person if it is not this Presson fellow?"

"I don't know. I guess I'd look for anyone who looks suspicious."

"I guess it wouldn't hurt to check the security recordings. Maybe it will provide proof that Harold Presson killed Erica."

"Or that someone else did," Rachel said as she, Sammie and Julie headed back down the riverfront trail as the afternoon sun painted the flowing current in shimmering shades of gold.

Chapter Twenty—Nine

Connor and Rachel watched as Julie opened the security folder on Erica's desktop. Rows of blue folders filled the screen, each one covering a two-week period. Two days after her conversation with Rachel, the now interim library director showed them the digital recordings.

"Can these only be accessed on this computer?" Connor asked.

"Yes," Julie said.

"Was Erica's computer on when you showed up for work and found her dead?" Rachel asked.

"Yes. But that wasn't a surprise. Erica seldom turned it off."

Rachel looked around the office, which somehow seemed impersonal to her. By contrast, literature posters adorned the walls of Julie's office across the hall. "You haven't moved in here," Rachel observed.

"To tell you the truth, I've avoided coming in her office since her death. I miss her so much. It doesn't seem right to be in here."

"But you're in charge now," Rachel said.

"At least for now. I'm just more comfortable in my office."

"How long do you keep the security recordings?" Connor asked, directing the conversation to the task at hand.

"We keep the records for three months, then they are automatically erased. But you can manually erase footage too from this computer. So, what do you want to look at?"

"How about Thursdays for the last three months," Rachel said.

"Why?"

"Erica was murdered on a Thursday," Connor said.

"I know what you're doing," Julie said, her voice tense. "You think Erica blackmailed people and the payments were made on Thursdays when she closed the library. I told you, Rachel, that Erica was no blackmailer. I don't want to help you tarnish her memory."

"Look, Erica may not have blackmailed anyone, but she was killed on a Thursday. The killer knew she closed on Thursdays,"

Connor said. "And the killer knew how to access the security system, override the system to erase the security footage. Police say the cameras were turned off, allowing the killer to walk out of the building undetected. How did the assassin know that? He or she had to have some inside knowledge. I assume the library has a burglar alarm."

"Yes, but Erica was killed before she finished closing up and activating the alarm.," Julie said. "Why all the questions?"

"We're just trying to find out who killed Ms. Stark," Connor said.

"The police already know who did it," Julie insisted.

"But what if the pastor was framed for the murder?" Rachel asked.

"You think going through these security recordings will prove if Harold Presson or someone else killed Erica?"

"Possibly," Connor said. "There are no guarantees."

"Well, you can click on each folder and fast forward to each Thursday," Julie explained. She started with the Thursday before the murder and scrolled quickly through the video, stopping only when library customers approached the biography section. "I assume you are only interested in anyone who might have lingered there," Julie said.

"That's right," Rachel said, looking at the black and white images.

"I'll leave you to it," Julie said, heading for the door. "I'll be right across the hall."

Rachel and Connor spent the next hour looking through the recordings. They skipped through much of the footage since they only looked at people who were spotted near the biography section. They observed several community leaders who made regular trips to those stacks.

"There," Rachel said, spotting Harold Presson on the security recording. She looked at the date on the video. The pastor had been at the library one week before the murder. And, the recording showed him heading toward the biography section and then leaving the library five minutes later. He did not check out a book.

Connor looked at the time recorded on Presson's visit: 8:45 p.m. Fifteen minutes before closing time. "Now, that seems suspicious, particularly since he spent only a few minutes in the library."

"We've just looked at one Thursday. We have 11 more to go through," Rachel lamented.

"Maybe he visited the library at the same time every week," Connor suggested. "We'll have to check to determine if we're correct." Rachel nodded. The two reporters spent the next hour checking the records. In all, the security footage showed Harold Presson visiting the library one Thursday each month at the same time.

Connor checked the dates he had written down. "That's it," Connor said, a sparkle in his eyes.

"What is it?"

"Harold Presson visited the library the week before Erica Stark was murdered. Based on his previous visits, he would not have come to the library again that month. If he was paying blackmail, he didn't do so more than once each month."

"That doesn't mean he didn't come back the next week and kill her."

"But why make another trip to the library? Why wouldn't he kill her on one of his regular visits? He could have stayed behind and then attacked her."

"If Erica blackmailed the pastor, what did she have on him?" Rachel asked.

"I don't know. But the security footage tells us something else. There were others who made quick trips to the library right before closing time."

"And approached the biography section and left without checking out a book," Rachel said.

"We need to talk to them," Connor said. Rachel didn't reply. Neither said what they were thinking. *Were these people, powerful community leaders, being blackmailed? And, if so, would they ever admit it?*

Chapter Thirty

The woman sobbed. "He didn't do it." Listening to her voice on his desk phone, Connor thought she sounded young. "I saw your stories in the newspaper. I don't want to get involved, but I couldn't let him be railroaded."

"Are you referring to Harold Presson?"

"Yes. I mean, the media's making him out to be some crazy person. But I know he didn't kill that librarian," she cried.

"How do you know that?"

"Because he was with me that night."

"All night?"

"Yes. His wife was out of town that day, visiting her sister in St. Louis. At least, that's what Harry told me."

"Harry?"

"Yeah, I don't like the name Harold. Too stuffy. I told him so the first time we met. So, I call him Harry. He doesn't mind. I think he kind of likes it," she rattled on.

"Are you willing to meet, answer all my questions?"

"For a story?"

"That's what I do, write news stories," Connor said.

"I don't want my name in the paper."

"Okay. I'll meet you wherever you like."

"Meet me at that jazz club."

"Jello?"

"Yes, say 6 p.m. Come alone."

"How will I know you?"

"I'll find you. I looked you up on Facebook." She ended the conversation without another word. Connor put down the phone and looked at Rachel, who typed away on a story on school safety.

"Rachel, I just talked to a woman who apparently is having an affair with Pastor Presson."

"What? The holier-than-thou pastor sinned?"

"Yeah, well this woman says Harold Presson didn't kill Erica

Stark because she was with him the night of the murder."

"She just gave him an alibi."

"Yes. She agreed to meet me tonight at Jello."

"Can I come along?"

"No. She insisted I come alone."

"Who is this woman?"

"She won't give me her name."

"Maybe Presson put her up to it. Maybe he is creating a fake alibi."

"I don't think so," Connor said. "She sounded sincere."

"Well, if this woman is credible, you have to run the story."

"Harold Presson doesn't want to go on the record about the blackmail, but I don't see how he can remain silent. We'll need to talk to Rush. He has to convince his client to go public with the blackmail accusation."

"But how will that play with his Citizens for Decency members? Do you think they'll turn on him?"

"I don't know. It's possible they'll rally around him just like voters did with Trump."

"Well, I doubt his infidelity will sit well with his wife," Rachel said. "Should we tell Lansmon?"

"Not yet. Let's wait until after tonight's meeting. Hopefully, Presson's girlfriend will provide information that will corroborate her statement."

"Call me after your interview."

"Why? Don't you trust me?"

"I just don't want you to get too close to your source," Rachel admitted with a smile.

"Don't worry. I don't date marriage wreckers. Besides, I have a girlfriend. A damn good one."

"Glad to hear it. Still, call me. I can't wait to hear what that woman has to say."

◆ ◆ ◆

Connor walked the short distance from his downtown loft apartment to the Jello jazz club on River Street. Heat and humidity gripped the late June night. Connor felt relief as soon as he stepped into the air-conditioned brick building. Members of a jazz band were setting up their equipment on the club's small stage. But for now, the club was silent except for the sound of quiet conversations among the few customers in the place. Connor knew the Jello's regular customers typically didn't show up until later in the evening. He looked around. He spotted a blonde sitting at a small round table in a corner of the room. She appeared to be in her 20s. Connor noticed she had a healthy tan. She wore her hair in a ponytail. She had on tight jeans and high heels. She wore a low-cut blouse that hugged her body like a glove. Lipstick painted her lips a dark wine color. In the dim lights of the club, the lipstick made her look almost sinister, Connor thought.

The woman waved to him to take a seat at her table. A waiter came by. Connor ordered a glass of Chardonnay. He offered to pay for her drink, but she refused. She ordered ice water. "When it comes to alcohol, I'm not a drinker," she explained.

After they received the glasses of wine and water, Connor pulled out a notebook and questioned the woman. She told him that she and the pastor had met on Tinder.

"How long ago did you hook up?"

"We first went out about four years ago," she said.

"Four years ago? He's been cheating on his wife all that time?"

"I didn't know he was married at that point. We went out about four times. Anyway, it didn't last. But he started coming around to where I work again two years ago. Things just clicked. Despite what some people think, he's a teddy bear. At least, with me."

"Where do you work?"

"I can't tell you that."

"Why not?"

"I need this job. It pays good money."

"Why would Pastor Presson visit your workplace?"

"I suppose because he wanted to see me."

"You look like you are in your 20s."

"Thanks for the compliment. I'm 32."

"Harold Presson is way older than you."

"He's 60."

"He's old enough to be your father."

"It may seem strange to you but Harry's a sweet guy. I haven't seen another guy like that in my lifetime. Even my dad was a jerk, a mean man when he was drunk. And he was drunk all the time."

"I see. And, just to be clear, Harold Presson was with you when the librarian, Erica Stark, was murdered?"

"Yes."

"At his place?"

"No. At a hotel."

"In Elmwood?"

"No, out of town."

"You need to give me some information that I can follow-up on to prove that you're telling the truth. What about receipts for gas, food and lodging?"

"I put all the expenses on my credit card. Harry didn't want his wife to know about the affair. He reimbursed me in cash. He even gave me extra money, so I came out ahead. I won't reveal the name of the hotel we stayed at the night of the murder. I don't want that information to run in the newspaper."

"Okay. I don't need to name the hotel, but I need some proof."

"Fine," she said, pulling out her cellphone and clicking on her gallery. She pulled up a photo and showed it to Connor. The selfie showed the pastor with his arm around the woman in a hotel bar. Connor recognized the place. He'd spent a weekend there with Rachel."

"Memphis. I know the place. The Peabody Hotel. Did you like the ducks in the fountain?"

"You promised not to disclose the place," she said, fear gripping her.

"I keep my word."

"You better."

"Why come forward now?"

"Harry told me he would keep our secret no matter what. But I don't want him to go to prison. You have to run the story."

"Even if it ruins his marriage?"

"What marriage? He and Priscilla may keep house together but, trust me, they lead separate lives. Harry keeps telling me he wants to get a divorce."

"Let me guess. He never follows through with it."

"Not yet, but he will. I've got to go to work. See you," she said, forcing a smile.

Connor watched her walk away, her head held high as if she were on parade. Connor paid his bill and walked back to his apartment. He found Rachel sitting on the couch.

"I let myself in," she announced.

"I see that," Connor said as he sat down next to her.

"So, tell me what she said."

"She said she's having an affair with Harold and that he was with her the night Ms. Stark was murdered."

"You believe her?"

"Actually, I do. She showed me a photo of herself and Harold being cozy at The Peabody Hotel in Memphis. I recognized the bar. You remember when I took you there for the weekend?"

"Of course, I do. We had a great time," Rachel said, grinning.

"We sure did."

"Then, maybe Harold Presson is telling the truth. Erica Stark might have blackmailed him. As a pastor and head of Citizens for Decency, he wouldn't have wanted it to come out that he cheated on his wife."

"Yep."

"But Rush says his client isn't ready to say Ms. Stark blackmailed him. So, how can we report this news?"

"We need to talk to Rush. He needs to convince his client to speak up," Connor said.

"What if he won't?"

"I've still got the story from his girlfriend."

"I'm concerned that this woman won't let you quote her by name," Rachel said. "And, without receipts, we can't check her story and neither can the police. From what you're telling me, the photo is the only proof that they went to The Peabody. But you don't know for sure that they even stayed there."

"I know. We need the pastor to confess his affair."

"Do you think he will come clean about his affair even if he won't talk about the blackmail?"

"I sure hope so."

"Otherwise, we only have the word of this mystery woman," Rachel observed. "Not sure Lansmon will run the story. By the way, how old is she?"

"She says she's 32 although she sure looks younger than that."

"Damn. Harold Presson is old enough to be her dad. What the hell does she see in him?"

"She says he's a sweetheart."

"Well, bless her heart," Rachel said, stringing out the words, imitating a southern drawl. Connor laughed. Leaning over, he kissed her on the lips. She wrapped her arms around him and pulled him close. "No more shop talk," she whispered.

Chapter Thirty-One

Connor and Rachel greeted Rush Johnson at his riverfront law office the next morning, insisting they had uncovered information about his client, Pastor Presson. Rush ushered them into his elegant, second floor office overlooking the mural-decorated floodwall and the Mississippi River it was designed to hold back.

Rush, attired in an expensive gray Italian suit and white shirt with gold cufflinks, seated himself behind his massive desk. Connor and Rachel sat across from him in wooden chairs that would have been right at home in *Architectural Digest*. They leaned forward on the edge of their seats.

"You two remind me of dogs chasing a fox," he said, laughing. "You've got your tails up."

"It's more like chasing the secret life of your client," Rachel said.

"So, what have you discovered?"

"An alibi for Harold Presson on the night of Erica Stark's murder," Connor said.

"Now, you're talking," Rush said. "What alibi?"

"I've talked to a woman who says she and the pastor were together at The Peabody Hotel in Memphis when Erica Stark was murdered."

Rush didn't look shocked. "Harold told me Ms. Stark blackmailed him over an affair."

"Well, we are looking to run the story. Now, I know we said we wouldn't disclose anything about the blackmail right now. But with the information we have about the affair, it would be better if your client speaks up now, admits to the affair. The way this woman tells it, Harold's marriage is on the rocks. She said he has talked about getting a divorce."

"Do you know the name of this woman?" Rush asked.

"No. Do you?"

"No. Harold insists on keeping her name secret, although it's likely we'll have to call her as a defense witness when this goes to trial."

"Can we get Pastor Presson to go on the record about being blackmailed?"

"I'll talk to him, but I'm not sure he'll go public about it at this time. I can't blame him. If he says he was being blackmailed over the affair, the prosecution will say that's all the more reason why he killed the librarian. That's why I hope you can find evidence Ms. Stark blackmailed others and that one of them killed her."

"We are looking into that possibility," Rachel said. "We have reviewed security footage at the library that shows that two other people, besides Pastor Presson, visited the library's biography stacks on Thursdays, right before closing time."

"And you believe they may have visited the library to drop off blackmail payments?"

"Perhaps."

"Any names?"

"Olivia Bolton and Michael Wachter."

"Holy, shit! If this is true, a jury would have every reason to find my client not guilty. As for Harold's infidelity, do me a favor. Hold off on the story for a day. I am sure Harold will want to break the news to his wife."

"Fine," Connor said. "Twenty-four hours, but then we'll go with the story."

"I could call your publisher and ask him to kill the story."

"But you won't," Connor replied, "because you want us to dig into this alleged blackmailing scheme."

"True." Rush smiled like the Cheshire cat.

"You want us to run the story about the affair," Rachel surmised. "You knew your client would have opposed such a move as long as possible."

"You said it."

"But will his supporters see him as a flawed man and abandon him?" Connor asked.

"I don't know. But my job is to mount the best legal defense possible for my client. And a rock-solid alibi, however sordid, could keep Pastor Presson out of prison. I call that a win," Rush said. "Besides, if you're old enough to remember, the church followers of

Jimmy Swaggart and Jim Bakker forgave them and continued to support the two preachers with prayers and cash. I'm sure a lot of Presson's parishioners—men and women—can relate to his indiscretions."

Chapter Thirty–Two

Twenty minutes after their meeting with Rush, Connor and Rachel delivered the news to their editor. Seated in Lansmon's office, they detailed the alleged affair. Connor recounted his interview with the woman who claimed she was dating Harold Presson.

Lansmon listened intently. When Connor finished, Lansmon frowned. "It's a good story, but you don't have Harold's side of it."

"We've reached out to his attorney and requested Harold Presson speak to us about the affair," Rachel noted. "Rush Johnson asked we give Presson 24 hours to tell his wife before we run the story."

"We need to know more about this lover of his," Lansmon said.

"She won't give her name," Connor said.

"But you said she indicated that Harold Presson visited her at work. What work?"

"She didn't say."

"Let's see if we can figure out where she earns her living. If we can nail that down, we might be able to identify her through social media," Lansmon said.

"But I promised we wouldn't identify her in the paper," Connor said.

"That's fine, but I want to know as much as we can about this woman before we publish this article, particularly if that pastor won't admit to the affair."

"We'll get on it," Rachel said as she and Connor headed for the door. They returned to their desks. Seated in her chair, she slid over to Connor's desk. "How can we track down this woman's employer?"

"I've been thinking. She said she didn't want to say where she worked because she needed the job. She also said the money's good. It doesn't sound like she's waiting tables," Connor said. "She works nights. She said she had to work last night."

"Anything else?"

"Now that you mention it, there was something about her appearance, high heels and all. Maybe it was the lipstick. Almost too theatrical."

"You think she's in show business?" Rachel asked.

"I don't know of any professional acting companies in Elmwood."

"Do you think she might be a dancer at a strip club across the river?"

"She said she met Harold Presson on Tinder, that online dating site. But she also said he started coming by her place of employment."

"So, maybe he was going to one of the clubs."

"There are several of them in Southern Illinois."

"And you know all about them, I suppose?"

"No more than any other old geezer," he laughed.

"Wouldn't it be risky for him to frequent such a place?"

"Maybe. But then again, who would think a pastor would go there? And the closest one is right across the river in East Elmwood, a village in Southern Illinois that quite frankly is falling apart. Wrecked by too many floods. Home to broken-down trailers, druggies and welfare moms."

"There are some decent folk there too."

"Yes, but they are the old-timers. There's very little business there other than Club Mardi Gras. There are other dives out in the boondocks where the dancers are mostly druggies. My friend Adam said his law enforcement buddies in Southern Illinois regularly police those places. They make plenty of drug busts. In contrast, Mardi Gras is fairly classy looking for what it is. I interviewed the club owner, Marissa Hue, several years ago when floodwaters inundated the town. I could contact her and ask. She doesn't put up with any nonsense. But it's doubtful that she would provide that type of information about her employees, even to me."

"We might need to pay a visit to this place," Rachel said.

"What do you mean, we?"

"I know you, Connor. You'll want to snoop around. That means an in-person visit. I'm not going to let my boyfriend go there without me."

"So, you can keep tabs on me?"

"It's not just that. I want to know what kind of woman we are dealing with. Women are a better judge of other women. It's a fact. Men are too busy looking at tits and ass."

"Wow. What a put down."

"I love you, Connor, but I wonder if this woman is telling you the whole story."

Late afternoon, the two reporters climbed into Connor's red Ford Escape and drove across the cable-stay Mississippi River bridge to East Elmwood. Perched along the state highway, Club Mardi Gras was a one-story, green and gold building. An elevated sign outside displayed the name in neon along with an image of a naked woman pole dancing.

They entered into a dimly lit bar that featured a small stage and strip pole. A few old men sat at the bar, drinking beer as they grumbled about failed jobs and miserable marriages. The so-called entertainment hadn't started yet. Connor spotted Marissa talking to one of the bartenders. He approached her. She glanced his way and smiled. "Connor, isn't it? How is my favorite reporter?"

"Just fine."

Marissa noticed Rachel, who had stopped next to Connor. "This is Rachel, another reporter at the *Journal*," Connor said.

"Nice to meet you. I remember seeing you guys together over in Elmwood, maybe at Smooth Buns or one of the other eateries."

"We both covered some of the flood events in East Elmwood," Connor said.

"Yes. And you questioned me about a college professor, who had ties to the East Elmwood area. As I recall, Connor, you stopped the guy from blowing up the concrete floodwall on the Missouri side. Of course, that didn't help East Elmwood. We had smaller, earthen levees that were no match for Ole Man River. Still, I don't wish anyone to be flooded out. Without the floodwall, the river would drown Elmwood, creating an economic catastrophe for Southeast Missouri's largest city."

"You have quite a memory, Marissa."

"I find it's useful in my business."

"Didn't you also own a pizza place and a small convenience store in East Elmwood?"

"Yes, I did." She sighed. "But the pandemic ruined those businesses. I closed them several years ago. Just another economic blow to an already struggling town."

"But you seem to be doing okay with Club Mardi Gras," Rachel observed.

"Well, I have loyal customers. You'd be surprised who comes here. After the bars close across the river, where do you think all those drunk college kids go? Over here, to my club. Not to mention, all the other late-night partygoers. But you didn't come here to listen to me talk about my club. What is it you want to know? Working on a story?"

"As a matter of fact, we are," Connor said. "I recently spoke to a woman, who may work for you?"

"What's her name?"

"She didn't tell me."

"Did she say she worked here?"

"No."

"Sounds like you're clutching at straws. What's this gal look like?"

"Blonde. Ponytail. Dark lipstick."

The Asian woman laughed. "Honey, that sounds like a lot of my girls, my dancers."

"She says she met her boyfriend, an older gentleman, on Tinder, but that they broke up and then later rekindled their romance. She says he visited her at work."

"And you thought she might work here?"

"Well, yes," Connor said.

"Who's the boyfriend?"

"A pastor," Rachel said.

"Are you talking about Harold?"

"Pastor Presson, yes," Rachel said.

"He's been here some, late at night. Nice guy, real polite. Not like some of our customers. I read that he's been charged with murdering that librarian. The Harold I know isn't a killer and, trust me, I'm a good judge of character. It seems to me the police have rushed to judgment because of this book-banning issue."

"Doesn't it bother you that the head of Citizens for Decency is spending time in a strip club?" Rachel asked.

"I'm not here to pass moral judgment on anyone. We all have faults. By the way, I prefer to call this a club. Some people might call it a gentlemen's club, but we've had women in here too, usually with their boyfriends. Just so you know, I run a tight ship here. My bouncers will throw you out if you cause trouble."

"So, this woman does work for you?" Rachel asked.

"Yeah. She goes by Diva Doll on stage."

"What's her real name?" Connor asked.

"Well, since she didn't tell you, I don't think I should reveal it. That's her business. You want to talk to her? Come back later tonight. She'll be dancing. You might want to bring some cash. She likes a good tip," said Marissa, laughing.

Connor and Rachel left the club. They climbed into the SUV. "I can't believe we found out where that woman works," Rachel said. "It was a shot in the dark. And, I can't believe a pastor like Harold Presson would frequent a strip joint."

"Why not? If Diva Doll is to be believed, Harold Presson is cheating on his wife."

"Yeah. You have a point."

Rachel and Connor returned to downtown Elmwood. They dined on Po'boys and seasoned fries at Alligator Alley. As they ate, they talked about the murder case.

"We need to talk to Rush again."

"I need to talk to Adam," Connor said. "I think we have enough evidence that police should reopen the murder case."

"I'm not sure the police will do so. They seem certain Harold Presson killed Ms. Stark. I doubt they will be convinced otherwise by the word of a stripper. I wonder if Harold is at home tonight confessing his affair to his wife?"

"If he is, it won't be a pretty sight," Connor said.

They finished their meals and Connor paid the bill. They landed at Connor's downtown apartment, concluding they had hours to kill before returning to Club Mardi Gras.

The "gentlemen's club" drew a crowd, but the place still wasn't full when Connor and Rachel returned around 9:30 p.m. A scantily clad woman paraded on stage, performing a suggestive dance with the stripper pole as mostly older men gawked with the anticipation of hungry hyenas. The younger crowd wouldn't arrive until much later, Connor concluded. To Rachel, the place smelled of sweat and beer. She spotted Diva Doll. The woman, wearing a loosely tied kimono that barely covered her tanned, toned body, conversed with Marissa at the end of the bar counter. Diva Doll appeared upset. Rachel nudged Connor and pointed toward the woman.

The two reporters approached. Marissa eyed them. "I hear you've stirred the pot," she said. "You've upset her," she said, looking at the stripper by her side. Tears streamed down the blonde's face.

"You talked to Harold's lawyer," the stripper said, wiping the tears. "You told him about me," she said, turning angry.

"The attorney said Harold had told him about the affair, but I don't think the pastor identified you," Connor said.

"Harold called you?" Rachel asked.

"About an hour ago. He said I had betrayed him. I told him I did it for him, that he needed to speak up about the alibi. It proves he's innocent of the murder."

"Did Harold talk to his wife?" Connor questioned.

"He said he and Priscilla argued. She threatened to kick him out. Harold said she called him a "lying sack of shit" and she could care less if he went to prison.

"She kicked him out of the house?" Rachel asked.

"Not yet. Harold said she locked herself in the bedroom. But he figures, he'll be moving out tomorrow."

"I guess he'll be living with you," Connor said.

"I don't know. He's mad at me, although he conceded that the alibi might keep him out of prison. Anyway, my apartment's small. He has more clothes than I do. I figure he'll rent his own place. You're destroying my life."

"We're just trying to uncover the truth about the librarian's murder," Connor insisted.

"You lied. You promised to keep my name out of the paper," she shouted.

"I didn't lie. Your name won't be mentioned."

"But you tracked me down, found out where I work."

"We just wanted to be sure you were telling the truth," Connor replied.

"I told you the truth. A lot of good it's done," she said, running a hand through her long hair. "Hell, I've got a show to do," she added, turning her back on the reporters. She took a deep breath and walked away.

"She should have kept her mouth shut," Marissa observed. "That pastor may beat the murder, but none of this will help her. People will view her as some gold-digger. It's a shame. She's a good person at heart and one of my best dancers."

Connor and Rachel didn't reply. They retreated toward the exit. Rachel saw the way some of the men looked at her. She felt like she was a piece of meat in a butcher shop. Pulsing music blared. She and Connor turned toward the stage. Diva Doll pranced onto the platform wearing a sailor's outfit. Five minutes into the routine, she began removing her clothes. She stripped to a glittery G-string and pasties as she twirled around the pole as if it were her lover. Diva Doll bent over the edge of the stage as customers tipped her in cash. Rachel tugged on Connor's sleeve. "Come on. I've seen enough. And, so have you. Let's get out of here."

"Yeah. I wonder what her real name is?"

"Does it matter?" Rachel asked.

"No. And, you know what's really sad?"

"What?"

"She may have given Harold Presson an alibi, but I doubt he's really in love with her. If he cheated on his wife, he'll cheat on her too."

"Maybe he already has," Rachel said.

"I know blackmail is a crime. But if Erica Stark blackmailed that sleazy pastor, a part of me says he deserved it."

"Yeah. Karma is a bitch."

Chapter Thirty–Three

The call from Rush came the next morning. The high-priced lawyer informed Connor that Harold Presson would not comment on the reported affair. "Maybe later. Not now," Rush said. Connor sighed. He had hoped the controversial pastor would have come clean about the affair. Connor thanked Rush for letting him know. The call ended; he turned to Rachel. "Presson won't comment about his fling with the stripper."

"I'm not surprised. Presson's probably still figuring out how to play it. Should he claim it's 'fake news' or play the 'I'm a sinner' role and appeal for forgiveness."

Connor agreed. He called his friend, Adam, and detailed the affair he and Rachel had discovered.

"So, he's a cheat and a murderer," Adam said when Connor finished. "It certainly won't make him a sympathetic figure to a jury."

"Don't you see? If Harold Presson cheated on his wife, he'd be a perfect mark for blackmail. Maybe he is telling the truth."

"Just because he cheated on his wife, assuming this woman is telling the truth, doesn't mean that Erica Stark or someone else blackmailed him. Has Harold told you that he was being blackmailed?"

"Not exactly."

"Right. I thought so. If Harold Presson has proof that he was blackmailed then he should tell the police. We'll investigate. But that hasn't happened. Leave it alone," Adam said, hanging up.

"Adam doesn't buy it," he told Rachel. "He isn't interested in looking into this blackmail allegation, thinks Harold is making it up."

"Let's talk to Lansmon," Rachel said, rising from her chair. She and Connor strode into the editor's office. They recounted their investigation. Lansmon stared at the ceiling as if trying to discern some hidden image. He returned his gaze to his two best reporters.

"I wish that woman had given you her name," Lansmon said.

"We tracked her. We know where she works. We know her stage name, but I already promised not to identify her in the story," Connor said.

"Look, I don't want to turn this into some *National Enquirer* story. Write it up, but don't mention this gal's stage name nor the specific strip club. Keep it simple. A woman claims that she is having an affair with a pastor who is charged with murder."

"Got it," Connor said. He and Rachel hurried back to their desks. Connor wrote the story. Rachel reviewed it and recommended some changes to the story, which Connor made. Lansmon read over the story paragraph by paragraph. Satisfied, he clicked a button on his computer, sending the story to the copy editors to check for typos. The *Journal* waited until evening to post the story online. It ran on the front page in the next day's print edition. The headline read: "Woman claims affair with pastor charged with murder."

The story began: *A woman, who dances in an Illinois strip club, claims she has been having a secret affair with a pastor charged with murder. The woman, who did not give her name, said she was with pastor Harold Presson at a Memphis, Tenn., hotel the night that Elmwood librarian Erica Stark was fatally stabbed.*

The article continued: *Presson refused to comment on the allegation. Police have not investigated the woman's story. The dancer said she and Harold Presson first met about four years ago through an on-line dating site and two years ago began a serious relationship. "Things just clicked. Despite what some people think, he's a teddy bear. At least, with me," the woman said.*

The news spread like a California wildfire. Television stations from as far away as St. Louis broadcast the story. That surprised Rachel, who expected the story to air only on local stations. But it didn't surprise Connor. "Sex and murder always make a good news story," he told her.

Elmwood Police Chief Blair Bonney complained loudly about the *Journal* story and the subsequent publicity when he met with Adam. The detective sat in the chief's office. "What garbage," said Blair, holding up the newspaper. "I assume that reporter called you?"

"Yes. Connor called. I dismissed the allegation. It has no bearing on the murder case," Adam said.

"Except, that now we have reporters calling about this affair and the woman's claim the pastor couldn't have killed Ms. Stark because she was with him the night of the murder. What is the paper trying to prove?"

"That Erica Stark was blackmailing people," Adam said.

"What? You're telling me that the newspaper is investigating a theory that Ms. Stark is a predator, instead of a victim?"

"Yes."

"Wouldn't that provide a motive for murder?"

"Yes. But Connor is looking into the possibility someone else murdered her."

"That doesn't make sense."

"It does if you believe that Erica Stark didn't just blackmail Harold Presson, that she blackmailed others."

"So, the theory is that another person was being blackmailed and that person killed Ms. Stark?"

"Correct."

"Well, your friend is out in left field on this one. We arrested the killer. There's no evidence placing anyone else at the scene. It's just a smokescreen, something imagined by Presson's lawyer to defend his client. Next time you talk to your reporter friend, tell him to deal in facts not fantasy. And, one other thing."

"What's that?"

"If any more reporters call, tell them I'm away from my desk. I don't want to talk to them."

Chapter Thirty—Four

The news conference caught Connor and Rachel by surprise. A day after the story broke about the pastor and the stripper, Rush Johnson met with reporters in front of the pastor's church. Harold and Priscilla Presson joined the defense lawyer. Rush, dressed immaculately as always, read a prepared statement.

"In light of the recent news regarding an alleged affair, my client, Harold Presson, wishes to speak to the fine citizens of this community," Rush said. He stepped aside and Harold, dressed in a blue striped suit and wearing a gold chain and cross, moved up to the mound of microphones topping a podium set at the base of the church steps. His wife Priscilla, wearing a black and white dress, stood next to him. Her pearl skin contrasted with her shoulder-length black hair. Rachel guessed she was in her late 50s, although she looked younger.

"I want to apologize to my wife, my friends, my church family and the Elmwood community for breaking my marriage vows. I have truly sinned by cheating on my beautiful, trusting wife," Harold said. "I also want to say I am sorry for misleading the woman with whom I was having an affair. I am deeply ashamed of having let down all the members of the Citizens for Decency group that I have the privilege to lead. I have always sought to provide moral leadership for this community and keep pornography out of our public library. But sin has stained me.

"While I have stumbled in my faith journey, I am thankful that my loving wife is standing by me. I ask that you respect our privacy as we work to rebuild our marriage. I also want to take this opportunity to tell you that I am innocent of the murder of librarian Erica Stark. I did not stab her despite the fact that she blackmailed me. She found out about my affair and threatened to go public unless I paid her $1,000 a month in $100 bills. Recently, she upped the required payment to $1,500 a month. I hid the payments from Priscilla and my closest friends. I have reason to believe that I wasn't the only person that Erica Stark blackmailed. I urge the Elmwood Police Department to reopen this case and find the real killer. Thank you."

Harold stepped back from the microphones. A TV reporter shouted a question to Priscilla. "Why do you stand by your husband?"

"I love him," she replied. "He let the devil lead him astray, but my husband is a good man. He deserves my love and forgiveness." She and Harold turned away from reporters, who were still throwing out questions. Holding hands, they retreated into the church, followed by Rush.

"I can't believe it," Rachel said. "I didn't expect Harold 's wife to stand by her cheating husband."

"Well, I think she played the role of a supportive spouse, but behind closed doors I'm sure she wants to kill him."

"After our previous conversation with Rush, I figured the allegations of blackmail wouldn't come out until the trial."

"Rush set this up. I should have seen it. He wanted us to break the story about the affair. It provided the perfect backdrop for Harold to allege blackmail."

"And maybe the public will see him in a more sympathetic light, with him acknowledging his moral failing."

"I know one person who won't."

"Who's that?"

"His girlfriend. You heard her. She thought Harold loved her. Now, she knows that was a lie."

"Maybe not. Harold might still love her. I wouldn't be surprised if Rush advised him to publicly commit to his marriage as a defense strategy."

Connor laughed. "You have a suspicious mind."

"And you don't?"

"Well, you have a point. Maybe that's why we're so good together." He reached out and gave her a brief hug. Then, they headed for Connor's SUV. They raced back to the *Journal*. They had a hell of a story to write.

Chapter Thirty–Five

The bomb-shell revelation led the noon news on the region's TV stations. The *Journal* posted a breaking-news report on its website even as Connor and Rachel worked on a lengthier, follow-up article.

The headline on the *Journal* story announced: "Murder suspect admits affair, accuses librarian of blackmail." The story began: *A pastor says he was being blackmailed by the Elmwood librarian he is accused of killing. Harold Presson said at a news conference today outside the GraceWorks Church he pastors that he had "truly sinned" by cheating on his wife. A dancer at an Illinois strip club said recently she had had an affair with Presson.*

The story, bylined by both Connor and Rachel, reported that Presson's wife and attorney joined him at the news conference. The article quoted Presson calling for the police department to reinvestigate the case and *"find the real killer."*

Late afternoon, Chief Blair Bonney convened a meeting in his office with Adam, Mayor Elroy James, city manager Don Ritter and prosecutor Richard Lamb. Blair vented his frustration, practically spitting out the words. "That damn lawyer is trying his case in the press."

"Do you think Harold Presson could be telling the truth?" Ritter asked.

"About the affair? Sure. I can believe he cheated on his wife. But that blackmail allegation is a bald-faced lie," Blair said. "He's dragging Ms. Stark's name through the mud, accusing her of being a criminal. Hogwash."

"I agree," Lamb said. "Rush Johnson trotted his client out for a news conference to seed doubt in the minds of potential jurors. I'm sure of it. But, Blair, your detectives need to investigate his allegation, find evidence that pokes holes in his claim."

Adam chimed in. "We'll need to dig deeper into the life of Erica Stark. Check her finances."

"Shit," Blair grumbled. "This is going to piss off a lot of people who liked that librarian. Let's do this as quietly as we can. Hold off telling the media until we have had a chance to do some detective work."

"What a mess," the mayor said. "We'll be pilloried by both sides – those who think we arrested the wrong man and those who believe we are unfairly attacking the librarian by even looking into the blackmail allegation."

"Yeah. It stinks," Blair said, throwing the newspaper into the trash can beside his desk.

"Well, Blair, you better get a handle on this quickly. It will be your ass if you screw it up," the mayor said. "I should have known something like this would happen."

"How dare you criticize me and my department. I run a great cop shop and my officers are some of the best in their field. Just keep out of my way."

"Let's hope you don't blow it. The public won't stand for it and neither will I."

"Don't flatter yourself, Elroy. You couldn't solve a crime if the clues were staring you right in the face. Go back to your damn office and leave the policing to the police."

"Stop, both of you," Ritter pleaded. "You two squabbling like children won't solve the problem. As city officials, we need to work together."

Lamb agreed. "Bring me some information that there's no truth to this blackmail."

"We'll get right on it," Blair said. "I've got my best detective on the case."

Those gathered in Blair's office mumbled agreement. They all rose to leave. "What happens if we discover Harold told the truth about the blackmail?" Ritter asked.

"It won't keep me from prosecuting the pastor," Lamb insisted. "If anything, it may speak to Harold's motive for killing the librarian."

Those at the meeting soon departed. All, except for Adam. The chief asked him to stay. "I want you to check Ms. Stark's bank records. And, talk to that damn reporter friend of yours. See if you can get anything out of him. I want to know everything that he knows about this case, and I want to know it now," the chief demanded.

Connor sat across the table from Adam at The Port, a popular restaurant and bar on River Street, just yards from the floodwall and the Mississippi River. The three-story brick building, dating back to the mid-1800s, once served as a dry-goods warehouse for the steamboats that stopped here. Later, it housed a steamboat company. Over the years, the building stored everything from furniture to beer. These days, its history is lost on most of the restaurant's patrons. What almost everyone notices, however, is the iconic Coca-Cola sign, originally painted on the side of the building in 1940 and later repainted.

Adam and Connor drank a few beers and shared an order of onion rings. Adam, who requested the meeting, said he would pay the bill. But the police detective said he wanted to know what Connor knew about the alleged blackmail.

"So, now police are taking the allegation seriously," Connor remarked.

"Chief Bonney wants the allegation investigated. That doesn't mean we believe Harold Presson is innocent of murder. But when there is an allegation of wrongdoing, we need to check it out. Of course, we have to consider that this allegation has been made by a man charged with murdering the individual who he claims was blackmailing him. If that's not a motive for murder, I don't know what is."

"Presson believes Ms. Stark blackmailed others too."

"I want to ask you about that," Adam said. "Have you uncovered anything to suggest that others were blackmailed?"

"Rachel and I reviewed the library security video going back three months."

"That must have taken a long time."

"Actually, we looked at only 12 dates. Ms. Stark was killed on a Thursday. We reviewed only footage from that day of the week for three months. We know from talking to library staff that she closed the library on Thursdays. So, we figured that she might be receiving blackmail payments on those days."

"And, did you discover anything from looking at the security footage?"

"Well, we found out that Harold Presson visited the library on one Thursday a month. He came in right before closing and headed toward the biography section. Of course, the security cameras don't have a view of that area. But I can tell you that Presson spent only a short time in the library and walked out of there without checking out a single book."

"You think he dropped the payments off at the library?"

"Yes, but here's the thing. Presson visited the library a week before Ms. Stark was murdered."

"And, you don't think he could have returned the next week and killed her?"

"Possibly, but I think it's likely someone else killed her and tried to frame Presson for the murder," Connor said.

"You've been reading too many mystery novels. It doesn't work like that in the real world of crime. The security footage doesn't exonerate Presson because we know some footage was erased and the system then turned off after the murder."

"But we spotted two other people who visited the library right before closing time on different Thursdays. It was the same thing. Each one entered the library, headed toward the biography section and minutes later walked back out. Don't you think that is suspicious?"

"Maybe. Did you identify these two individuals?"

"Yes."

"You know them?"

"They're community leaders."

"Who?"

"Olivia Bolton and Michael Wachter.

"You're talking about the president of Elmwood College and the judge," Adam said. "They seem unlikely candidates for blackmail. Are you suggesting that one of them killed Ms. Stark?"

"I don't know. Aren't you going to question them?"

"And accuse them of being blackmailed by a librarian? That's above my pay grade. We're not going to do that, not without solid evidence. Now, if you have such evidence, let me know. I'll be the first to question them. Meanwhile, I will check Ms. Stark's finances."

"Her niece says she had plenty of money when she died."

"That doesn't make her a blackmailer, but it's worth investigating," Adam said before eating the last onion ring. He stood up, put cash on the table to pay the bill. Connor followed Adam out of the restaurant. They walked across the street and through the flood-wall gate. Standing on the concrete tiered riverbank, they gazed at the Mississippi River flowing unceasingly southward toward New Orleans and the Gulf. To the west, the sun sank lower toward the horizon. Connor and Adam felt a gentle breeze. A couple sat a short distance away on one of the tiered steps.

"I never tire of looking at the river," Connor said. "It seems so peaceful."

"Yes. It takes your mind off all the evil in the world."

Adam and Connor stood still, silently admiring the majestic flow. Then, they turned and walked back through the floodgate.

Chapter Thirty—Six

Julie Halston entered the former office of Erica Stark on the second day of July. Outside, the temperature had climbed into the mid-90s amid high humidity. Miserable weather, she thought, as she appreciated the cool of the library's air conditioning. Although the murder of her boss had elevated her to interim library director, she still preferred to operate from her office across the hall. But today, she entered Ms. Stark's now largely unused office to search for paperwork associated with the library's fund-raising foundation. She combed through the desk. In the bottom drawer, she sorted through a pile of papers. She located what she needed and was about to close the drawer when she noticed a clipping from an education journal. She pulled it out. It was from *The Chronicle of Higher Education*. The article dealt with plagiarism among college educators. It detailed specific cases, including a Harvard professor's accusation that another college educator had stolen from his scholarly paper. Twenty years ago, the then provost at Drury University in Springfield, Missouri, authored a scholarly article on slavery in America. The Harvard professor claimed the educator had plagiarized much of the content from his paper. The provost denied the accusation, but within a year she had taken an administrative position at another school. Julie read the woman's name and gasped. The woman's name was Olivia Bolton. Ten years ago, she had been hired as president of Elmwood College.

Julie remembered what the *Journal* reporters told her after Erica was murdered. They wondered if her boss had blackmailed a number of individuals. Could she have blackmailed the Elmwood College president? Julie quickly abandoned the idea. How could she think her friend would have blackmailed anyone. Still, the thought nagged at her as she returned to her office. At lunchtime, it still bothered her. Finally, at 2 p.m., she phoned Rachel. "I need to talk to you."

A half hour later, Rachel met Julie in the librarian's office. A flustered Julie stumbled to start the conversation. She folded and unfolded her hands as she sat at her desk, eyeing Rachel, who was seated facing her.

"What's wrong?" Rachel asked.

"I found something in Erica's office. It's probably nothing. I shouldn't mention it."

"You called me here. You obviously want to talk about it."

"You can't quote me. This is totally off the record."

"Okay," Rachel said.

"I found an old clipping in Erica's office. It's from *The Chronicle of Higher Education*. It mentioned Olivia, but not in a good way." Julie explained the allegations of plagiarism and showed the article to Rachel.

"Wow," Rachel said after reading the article. "Maybe Erica blackmailed Olivia Bolton."

"I can't believe that," Julie said. "But it did make me wonder if someone might have blackmailed the college president. I don't plan to talk to the police, but I had to tell someone. I mean, could the college president be involved in some way. Harold Presson could have lied when he said he was blackmailed. Maybe he was the blackmailer and Erica found out about it, and he killed her."

"But what if Erica threatened to go to the police and reveal that the pastor had blackmailed the college president? Olivia Bolton wouldn't want the allegation of plagiarism to surface here. That would give her a motive for killing your boss," Rachel said.

"Oh, God. I hadn't considered that possibility," Julie said, a worried look on her face. She shook her head, refusing to believe it. "What woman would do that?"

"A college president who has a reputation to protect. Can I have the article?"

"Keep it. I don't want it."

"Thanks," Rachel said, rising to leave.

"I'm not sure I did the right thing."

"Don't worry. This may be nothing but old news. I'm just speculating here. Trust me, we're not writing about this plagiarism allegation unless we can tie it to this murder case."

"There's one other thing, I forgot to mention."

"What's that?"

"I don't know why I didn't think of it earlier."

"What?"

"It's about that biography on George Washington. I know we kept one on the library shelf. But as I previously told you, Erica kept another copy of that book on her office desk. But that book has disappeared. I don't remember seeing it after her murder. Do you think her killer took the biography?"

"I don't know why the killer would take it. Maybe as a souvenir."

"This whole thing is stressing me out. I just want it to go away," Julie cried.

Rachel felt helpless to comfort her. "You did the right thing," she said before leaving the office. Rachel could hear Julie sobbing halfway down the hall.

The call surprised Connor. He hadn't expected to hear from her. Her tone was harsh. Diva Doll was mad as hell. "That bastard. He told me he planned to leave his wife. Now, he's strutting about, telling everyone he's committed to his marriage," she shouted.

"Have you talked to him?"

"Not since he held that disgusting news conference."

"Does he come by the club?"

"No. He knows better than to do that. I'd have him thrown out on his ass, the bastard."

"Even so, does his alibi hold?"

"What do you mean?"

"You said he was with you in Memphis on the night of the murder."

"Yeah, I said that," she said, spitting out the words as if they were poison. "The thing is, that's not totally true."

"You and Harold weren't in Memphis?"

"No. We did go there. But Harold and I didn't leave for Memphis until nearly 11 p.m. I don't know where he was earlier than that."

"So, you weren't in Memphis at the time of the murder?"

"That's right. I told you we were there to give him an alibi. I loved him. I thought he loved me."

"Did Harold tell you to do that, give him an alibi?"

"I might have mentioned I was going to say something. He didn't tell me to say anything different."

"So, it's possible Harold killed the librarian," Connor concluded.

"I guess so."

"Did he seem out of breath when he picked you up? Were his clothes torn or bloody?"

"Of course not, you idiot. I wouldn't have gone with him if he looked like he had just killed someone. He looked great. I'd never seen him in such an upbeat mood. I assumed it was because we were going to spend the weekend in Memphis. I don't know anything about the murder. I just wanted you to know that I won't lie for that bastard. I don't care what happens to him," she said, ending the call.

Seated at his desk, Connor replayed the conversation in his mind. He spotted Rachel entering the employee entrance at the back of the newsroom. Connor waved her over. "Diva Doll just called me. She took back what she said about being together with Harold at the time of the murder. She wasn't with him until after the murder that night."

"Wow. That means he could have killed Ms. Stark."

"Yeah, but she says he was with her that weekend in Memphis. If Harold killed Erica, he would have had to go home, change clothes and then pick her up, all within a two-hour window if that woman's timeline is correct. She told me Harold picked her up shortly before 11 p.m."

"Maybe she's wrong about the time."

"Possibly."

"Well, I've just talked to Julie Halston at the library. Erica Stark may have blackmailed someone."

"Who?"

"Olivia Bolton."

"The college president?"

"Yep," Rachel said as she proceeded to detail her conversation with the library director. When she finished, Connor sat still for several seconds, contemplating what he had just heard.

"So, on the one hand, Harold could have killed Erica. But it also could be true that she was blackmailing people and one of those people might have been Olivia Bolton."

"How do we prove it?" Rachel asked.

"Good question. I don't have a clue."

Chapter Thirty—Seven

Connor and Rachel discussed the latest revelations with their editor. Lansmon had no difficulty deciding what to do. He instructed Connor to seek a response from Harold or his attorney. As for Rachel's conversation with the interim library director, Lansmon cautioned against jumping to conclusions.

"You don't have a story here," the balding editor explained. "The plagiarism allegations are old news. You have no evidence Ms. Stark used that information to blackmail the college president."

"But we could ask Olivia Bolton about the allegations and whether Erica Stark blackmailed her?"

"No, you can't just barge in and question her about this matter."

"Why not?"

"First of all, I doubt she would admit she was being blackmailed. If Ms. Stark was a blackmailer, why would Olivia Bolton say anything about it now? Ms. Stark is dead. Secondly, our publisher is good friends with the woman. I don't want Dan taking my head off or yours," Lansmon said.

"But," Rachel began.

"No buts. Leave it alone," he said, dismissing both reporters with a wave of his hand. The two reporters headed to their desks.

"Damn it," Rachel said. "I can't believe he just ignored this blackmail angle."

"Lansmon's right," Connor replied. "You don't have enough to turn it into a story."

"So, now you're taking his side. Traitor," she said, shaking her head.

"I'm not saying Erica Stark didn't blackmail the college president, but we need proof. We don't have any right now."

"So, how are we going to get it?"

"I'll talk to Adam, see if he'll look into it."

"I won't hold my breath. I know he's your friend, but so far he hasn't shown much interest in investigating any blackmail allegations regarding the librarian."

"He promised to look into Ms. Stark's background in light of the comments made by Harold Presson. That's something."

"I'll believe it when I see it," she said, sinking into her desk chair. Connor ignored the comment and sat down at his desk. He had a story to work on. No amount of pouting on Rachel's part would change anything, he thought.

Connor spent the next two hours crafting the story. He wrote up what the stripper had told him. He made repeated phone calls to Harold Presson and Rush Johnson, which went unanswered. He called his friend Adam and recounted what Diva Doll told him. Adam said he wasn't surprised. "I never believed that alibi to begin with. I told you, Harold Presson killed Erica Stark. All the evidence says so."

Rush finally returned the call. He dismissed Diva Doll's retraction. "She's just mad that Harold won't leave his wife for her," Rush said. "Nothing that woman says changes the fact that my client didn't murder Ms. Stark. Pastor Presson looks forward to proving his innocence in court."

"There's something else," Connor said. "My colleague Rachel has uncovered information that suggests Ms. Stark may have been a blackmailer. However, there's no hard evidence."

"What have you found?" asked Rush, sounding excited. Connor described the *Chronicle* article alleging plagiarism on the part of Elmwood College President Olivia Bolton.

"Do you have the piece?" asked Rush.

"Yes."

"I'd love to see it."

"I'll bring it by your office."

"Have you questioned Olivia Bolton?"

"No. And, our editor doesn't want us to do so without solid evidence. But I thought you might want to talk to her."

"I sure do."

"Any evidence of other blackmail victims?"

"Nothing concrete. We're still looking into that possibility," Connor said. "Do me a favor?"

"What's that?"

"Let me know what the college president tells you."

"If it's relevant to the case, you'll be the first to know."

"Thanks," Connor said even as he heard a loud click. Rush had hung up.

Connor turned his attention to the computer screen and added Rush's statement in support of his client. He finished the article and with a push of a button marked it ready to edit. Thirty minutes later, Lansmon emerged from his office and waddled over to Connor's desk. "Good work," he told him. Nearby, Rachel bit her lip, still feeling slighted by her boss.

The 10-inch story ran in the next day's edition at the bottom of the front page under the headline: "Former girlfriend undermines murder suspect's alibi." *The first paragraph read: The former girl-friend of murder suspect Harold Presson says she lied about the alibi she presented. The strip-club dancer says the Elmwood pastor was not with her during the time when librarian Erica Stark was killed.*

The story quoted defense attorney Rush Johnson, expressing support for his client. It didn't quote Adam, but said police all along dismissed the alibi and insisted the evidence pointed to Presson as the killer.

Elmwood's police chief smiled as he read the front-page story. "That alibi was garbage. Now, the public knows it," Blair told his top detective. "Adam, that reporter friend of yours did a good job for once. I hope our prosecutor is paying attention. Harold Presson has no alibi for the time of the murder. That fact, coupled with all the evidence our department has collected, should be more than enough to convict that damn pastor."

"I don't know," Adam said. "Harold's got one hell of a lawyer."

"Shit, why does everyone put Rush Johnson on some pedestal. He's won a few cases. I'll give him that. But I don't see how he can win this one, not when the evidence puts his client at the scene of the crime. And, one thing's for certain."

"What's that?"

"The pastor's wasting his money. If he were smart, he'd cut a deal and plead guilty," Blair said. "By the way, what about this blackmail business?"

"I've checked into Ms. Stark's finances. The last several years, she deposited between $1,000 and $2,000 cash into her bank account on some Fridays."

"Is that right?"

"Yeah."

"So where did that cash come from?"

"Don't know."

"Blackmail?"

"Possibly."

"So, Harold Presson could have been paying her."

"I don't know. Every week? I'm not sure the pastor could afford it," Adam said. "Maybe others were blackmailed too."

"Now you're sounding like that pastor. Let's not get ahead of ourselves. Keep digging. Someone must know something about this. If we can show Presson was blackmailed, we can prove the pastor had a strong motive to kill that librarian."

Chapter Thirty—Eight

It came to Rachel as she and Connor snuggled in her bedroom that night. She remembered something that Elmwood's favorite historian had once told her in passing. It had to do with Olivia Bolton. Rachel jumped up. "I'd forgotten about it."

"About what? You kind of ruined the moment."

"Sorry. It's just that I think I know how to delve into the plagiarism allegation."

"How's that?"

"It's something Henry Carter, director of Elmwood's regional history museum, said awhile back."

"What did he say?"

"He mentioned the college president, said she wasn't much of a scholar."

"When I asked him what he meant, he said that it's not just college kids who copy other people's academic work."

"Did he elaborate?"

"No. He changed the subject. I got the feeling he wished he hadn't said it."

"He thought she had plagiarized a scholarly paper?"

"I think so. I didn't know what he meant at the time. I've got to talk to him.

"Not right now," Connor said. "Come back to bed."

"Sure, love," she said, sliding her naked body under the covers. "Give me a kiss."

The next morning, Rachel rose early. She showered and dressed, eager to question Henry Carter. "Get out of bed. Time to go to work," she told Connor, who had made little effort to move from her bed.

"Wow. You are energetic today! I guess I have that effect on you."

"Don't flatter yourself," Rachel laughed. "It's Henry that has my attention."

"He's a little old for you," Connor joked as he climbed out of bed and hurriedly dressed. "Do you want me to join you?"

"No. I can question him all by myself," she said as Sammie, tail wagging, stood in the bedroom doorway waiting to be let outside.

"Suit yourself."

"I will," Rachel said, looking at herself in the mirror. She wore a white blouse, black jeans and her favorite checkered Vans. She added a silver butterfly necklace. She kissed Connor. She patted Sammie on the head and ushered him out.

"Don't forget to lock up," Rachel called back to Connor. "See you at work."

Henry Carter greeted Rachel on the wide front steps of the Elmwood Mansion, now the city's regional history museum. The plantation style, brick mansion, built in the 1850s by slaves for a descendant of one of the town's founding families, sat on a bluff overlooking the downtown and the Mississippi River. Converted into a history museum, it still retained its massive white columns, which hinted at its interior grandeur.

Stylish as ever, Henry wore a matching blue suit and bowtie. A history professor emeritus at Elmwood College, Henry, now in his late 70s, had retired into the job of museum curator more than a decade ago.

"Glad to see you again," said Henry as he ushered her down a hallway, past rooms filled with display cases exhibiting artifacts showcasing Elmwood's rich history. Carter led Rachel into a rear room that originally served as maid quarters. It now served as Henry's office. They sat at a small, round table, wedged into a corner of the room. Henry's antique, mahogany desk, covered with stacks of paperwork, stood nearby.

Henry and Rachel chatted for several minutes about the museum before she questioned him about the current college president's alleged plagiarism. "I need to ask you about Olivia Bolton?"

"What about her?"

"You told me once that in your opinion President Bolton wasn't much of a scholar. And that it wasn't just students who engaged in plagiarism."

"I remember."

"Well, we've discovered that the murdered librarian had kept a copy of an article from The *Chronicle of Higher Education* alleging that President Bolton, while provost at another university, had plagiarized much of the content of a scholarly article on slavery in America."

"Yes. I recall reading the article."

"Do you believe the allegations?"

"I do. But not because of that article. I know the Harvard professor who says she stole his work."

"You're talking about Dr. William Haywood?"

"Yes, Bill. He's a fantastic historian and my friend. Bill told me about the plagiarism. It occurred some two decades ago. When Olivia Bolton was named president of Elmwood College, I called him. He couldn't believe the college's board of governors would hire someone with her shoddy academic record to be president. But that's old news. I assume you think it's connected in some way to Erica Stark's murder."

"That's right. Connor Tate and I have been investigating Harold Presson's allegation that she blackmailed him and may have blackmailed others."

"You think that librarian blackmailed Olivia Bolton?" Henry asked.

"Don't you think it's possible?"

"I guess so. Dr. Bolton would be an easy target. As a college president, she would be at huge risk of losing her job if the allegation resurfaced. I could see her paying the blackmailer to keep quiet. But where's the evidence that the librarian blackmailed her? Those articles alone aren't convincing evidence."

"I agree," Rachel said. "The only real proof likely would have to come from President Bolton."

"You think she will admit to being blackmailed?"

"I don't know."

"I know you and your fellow reporter are persistent, but I doubt Olivia Bolton would confess, if what you say is true. It's not so much the blackmail itself as the allegation that she copied another educator's work and passed it off as her own. She wouldn't want that brought up again."

"You may be right. But ultimately she may be forced to talk."

"How so?"

"Rush Johnson, Harold's attorney, could subpoena her to testify at the murder trial."

"I hadn't thought of that," Henry said. "Oh, what a tangled web we weave when first we practice to deceive. It's a line from a play by Sir Walter Scott."

"And, here, I thought you were quoting Shakespeare. You're not only an historian, I see, but also well-versed in literature."

"You will find that history and literature often go hand in hand. "Tangled web just came to mind. It seemed appropriate," Henry said.

"It sure does," Rachel said, closing her notebook and putting away her pen. "I'll let myself out." Henry watched her leave. Then, he took out his cell phone and punched in Bill's number. His friend would want to hear this. *Imagine, Olivia Bolton having to take the stand.*

Chapter Thirty—Nine

In the newsroom, Rachel recounted her interview with historian Henry Carter. When she finished, Connor's face showed he relished the news. "Now, we can question Olivia Bolton," he said.

"You heard what Lansmon said? He forbade it."

"Because we didn't have solid evidence. Now, we have Henry Carter's statement. Surely, that's enough to broach the subject with the college president."

"Rush told us he would talk to her," Rachel pointed out.

"I'm sure he will, but that shouldn't stop us from interviewing her. We've got a reason to talk to her. Lansmon can't deny it. The worst that could happen is Olivia Bolton will throw us out of her office. But if she was blackmailed, I've got to believe she will disclose it at some point now that Erica Stark is dead. It just may take a little push."

"I think we should tell Rush about Henry's statement."

"We must talk to Olivia too. I'll let Rush know," Connor said, grabbing his cell phone. He called Rush and briefly described the interview with Henry Carter. Rush told him he had yet to question the college president. He thought it was a good idea for Connor to approach Olivia Bolton first. Then, the attorney could confront her and hopefully discover the truth. *Did Erica Stark blackmail her?*

Over the next week, Connor and Rachel made repeated calls to the president's office. They weren't returned. Finally, in mid-July, the president called. Connor and Rachel had said they needed to ask her about her possible connection to the librarian's murder. Olivia Bolton insisted she had no ties to the murder and any suggestion of it was ridiculous. But she agreed to meet the reporters, saying she wanted to put to bed any possible rumor that in some way she might be tied to the murder. And, she wanted to do it on her terms.

The interview occurred on a Friday morning in Olivia Bolton's spacious, second-story, wood-framed, tall-windowed office in Elmwood College's Academic Hall. Built in the early 1900s, a copper dome topped the massive, columned, limestone structure that dominated the south end of the hilly campus.

Unlike many women, the blue-eyed, 60-year-old college president didn't dye her hair. Her gray hair, cut short, framed an angular face. She wore little makeup. But there was a presence about her that made her stand out, Rachel thought.

Olivia Bolton greeted the two reporters with a thin smile that sought to hide her wariness about being questioned.

She waved for them to sit down in two chairs facing her desk. Olivia returned to her desk chair and positioned her hands face down on her desk as if she were trying to keep the furniture from moving. She stared hard at the two reporters. "So, what's this about?" she asked in a demanding voice.

"Well, as we mentioned on the phone, some questions have arisen that suggest you may have a possible connection to the librarian who was murdered," Connor said.

"You think I murdered her?"

"I didn't say that."

"Then what is it?"

"We believe Erica Stark may have blackmailed people and that you may have been a victim of that blackmail," Rachel said.

"You've got to be kidding! Why would that librarian blackmail me? I don't have a skeleton in my closet."

"You were accused of plagiarizing that slavery article," Connor said.

"That's old news," said the college president, laughing. "Besides, if you read the article, you'll know I denied that allegation. If this college's board of governors believed I had done that, why would they have hired me to be president?"

"Maybe they didn't do a good job vetting you," Rachel suggested.

"Well, they never asked me about it," said Olivia, her voice dismissive of the whole issue.

"But if Erica Stark blackmailed you, it would support Harold Presson's belief that the librarian didn't just blackmail him," Rachel said.

"So, this is about that preacher. Sounds to me like you're trying to defend that book-banning zealot. From what I've seen in the media, the evidence points to Harold as her killer. I certainly didn't stab that woman."

"We're not saying you did," Connor said. "But if that librarian blackmailed you, don't you want people to know her dark side, that she wasn't this lovely person that people talked about at her funeral?"

Olivia Bolton sat still for a minute, trying to decide how to respond. She twisted in her chair before straightening up. "I'll tell you something, but only on two conditions. First, you can't mention my name or associate me with Elmwood College. Second, you can't mention the plagiarism allegation."

"And if we agree to this?" Rachel questioned.

"I'll tell you something about that dead librarian."

Connor and Rachel eyed each other, wondering if they should agree to the conditions. Without a word, they both came to the same conclusion. "You've got our word," they said in unison. Connor added, "We'll keep your name out of it, for now."

"What does that mean?"

"If other information comes to light from the police or other sources regarding you and the dead woman, then we'll report what they say. And, of course, we'll contact you for any comment you might have," Connor said.

"But we don't have such information now," Rachel added, wanting to encourage Olivia to talk.

"Very well, I'll tell you this. That librarian called me some years ago and threatened to tell people about the alleged plagiarism unless I paid her $2,000 a month. Can you believe it?"

"Did you pay her?" Rachel asked.

"Of course, not. I wasn't going to give in to her little blackmail scheme. I told her to leave me alone, crawl back into her little hole. I made it clear I would go to the police, accuse her of blackmail. I told her I would bring so much bad publicity that the library board would have to fire her."

"So, what happened?" Connor asked.

"She backed off. I never paid her a dime. And I didn't kill her."

"So, do you think she blackmailed others?"

"I wouldn't be surprised," Olivia said.

"If that's the case, then Harold Presson wasn't the only one who had a motive to kill Ms. Stark," Connor said.

"You could say that," the Elmwood College president said.

Chapter Forty

Connor, on his cell phone, recounted the interview to Rush as he sat in the passenger seat of Rachel's Mini Cooper as she drove downtown to the newspaper office. Rush welcomed the news and the impending *River City Journal* story. He vowed to call the college president later in the week to tell her that he'd likely subpoena her as a defense witness. Rush also gave an on-the-record statement, which Connor wrote in his notebook.

Back at the office, Connor phoned his detective pal. He detailed his interview with Olivia Bolton, but without naming her. The news didn't thrill Adam.

"You call me with information from an anonymous source. What am I to make of that? How do you know this person is telling the truth?"

"I believe she is telling a half-truth," Connor replied.

"Based on what?"

"It's just a gut feeling."

"You want me to investigate a statement made by some woman whom you won't name. Not only that, but you're also telling me that without a shred of evidence you don't believe her full account. Which part don't you believe is true?"

"I believe Erica Stark blackmailed this woman and that this woman did pay up."

"Do you think this woman killed the librarian?"

"I didn't say that. I just assume you would want to dig into this matter."

"Give me a clue. What you've told me isn't enough. I need her name."

"I promised not to name her. But I will give you a clue. Google academic plagiarism on college campuses. Check out a *Chronicle of Higher Education* article from years ago involving a Missouri school."

"Fine," Adam said sullenly. "But you don't have any evidence that this woman killed the librarian. I don't think your wild theories will change the fact the evidence points to the preacher as the killer."

"Thanks, buddy, for at least agreeing to check it out."

"Yeah. But I still believe you're wasting my time."

"You'll thank me later."

"Don't count on it," Adam said.

The *Journal* editor listened as Connor and Rachel outlined the story. "Keep it short," Lansmon said after they finished. "It'd be better if this woman would let us identify her in the story. At least, Harold's lawyer commented on the matter."

"We will keep it short," Connor said, heading back to his desk. Within a half hour, he had finished typing the article, incorporating information from his and Rachel's notes. In addition to the new information, he briefly recapped the stabbing and subsequent arrest of Harold Presson. Connor closed the story and marked it ready to edit. Lansmon reviewed it. He made no changes before sending it to the copy editors for a final proofing. The story, bylined by both reporters, ran on page 3 in the Journal's print edition the next morning.

The police chief read it in his office. The first paragraph read: Elmwood librarian Erica Stark attempted to blackmail a local educator before she was murdered, according to the educator who requested anonymity. The educator claimed she refused to pay.

The second paragraph read: *Rush Johnson, attorney for Elmwood pastor Harold Presson, who has been charged with the librarian's murder, said the educator's story suggests others had motives to kill her. The celebrated lawyer called on police to investigate this latest claim. "Any competent investigation would show that my client didn't kill Erica Stark," Johnson said.*

Chief Blair Bonney didn't care for the story. He felt it left too much to conjecture. But the news didn't take him by surprise. Adam had alerted the chief to what Connor had told him. "I'm working to unearth that educator's name," the detective said as he sat in Blair's office.

"Do you think the educator killed that librarian?" the chief asked.

"I still believe the right person was charged with the crime," Adam said.

"So, do I. But let's find this educator," the police chief said.

Adam loosened his tie as he walked over to his desk, situated among a crowd of metal desks used by the police detectives. He removed his black suit jacket and hung it over the back of his chair. Once seated, he returned to the internet, hoping Connor's clues would lead him to the unnamed educator. He searched the *Chronicle's* website, but its electronic archives went back only so far. He needed to find a two-decade-old article. He phoned the *Chronicle's* office in Washington, D.C. Staff there transferred him to one person after another. Finally, Adam connected with a woman who searched through microfilm. She found several plagiarism stories but only one that mentioned a higher education official in Missouri. The detective asked for the name of that official. She told him: Olivia Bolton. She promised to email him the article. Adam thanked her.

The call ended; the detective tried to collect his thoughts. The news shocked him. Olivia Bolton, Elmwood College president, had been accused of plagiarism. And, from his conversation with Connor, Adam realized what that meant. *Olivia Bolton must have alleged Erica Stark tried to blackmail her. But was she telling the whole story? Was Connor right? Did Olivia Bolton fend off the blackmail or did she pay up? And, did the college president fatally stab the librarian?*

Chapter Forty-One

Olivia Bolton eyed the police detective sitting in her office. Adam Dade didn't look like a cop. Slightly balding with graying hair and a little overweight, he showed up in a rumpled suit. But it didn't take long for her to realize this detective was no fool. He had done his homework. Four days after being interviewed by the *Journal* reporters and two days after hearing from Rush Johnson, the Elmwood College president tried to mask her nervousness as she met with the police detective.

She quickly learned that Adam Dade had reviewed her bank account. Her mouth twitched before she spoke. "You looked through my bank records?"

"Yes. We were looking for any suspicious financial transactions."

"Well, you must have been disappointed, Detective Dade. I've got nothing to hide."

"No. It actually proved interesting. I found that every month you took out $2,000 in cash from your bank. Not only that, you took the money out on Thursdays, the same days that you visited the Elmwood Public Library just before closing time. What's curious is that security camera footage shows you never checked anything out."

"I don't believe visiting the library is a crime," said the college president, trying to take control of the conversation.

"No, visiting the library isn't a crime. But why did you take out so much cash?"

"That's none of your business. How I spend my money is my concern, not yours," she said stiffly.

"What I think is that Erica Stark blackmailed you and threatened to go public with allegations of plagiarism. That's why you took out so much cash every month."

"What are you talking about?"

"Don't take me as a fool," Adam said. "I read the *Chronicle* article that accuses you of copying another professor's work and

140

passing it off as your own."

"That was decades ago," Olivia Bolton pointed out.

"Yes, I know. But Erica Stark kept a copy of it in a desk drawer in her library office. Why would she do that?"

"How would I know what that woman did?"

"Because I believe you paid that blackmail money. You visited the library monthly to drop off the payment, leaving it in a book in the biography section."

"And why would I do that? I admit the *Chronicle* reported on those allegations of plagiarism, which I denied. But that's old news. Elmwood College's Board of Governors have faith in me. The board hired me. I don't recall anyone on the board raising that issue when I was interviewed for the job."

"Maybe board members didn't look that far back in vetting you. But if it came out now, the publicity could put you at risk of losing your job."

"This is all speculation."

"So, you say," Adam said, drawing out his words as he scribbled notes. "I've talk to the prosecutor. He could call you to the stand as a prosecution witness in the trial of Harold Presson."

"I admit, I have no use for that hate-spewing, book-banning preacher. But why would I be asked to testify about the murder?"

"Because you could talk about the fact that Erica Stark blackmailed you. Of course you would be under oath. You'd have to tell the truth or face a perjury charge," Adam noted.

"What the hell is going on? Erica Stark didn't threaten me, didn't blackmail me! You say the prosecutor wants me to testify. Well, Presson's attorney wants to call me as a defense witness, says he wants to show that others may have had a motive to kill her. But I don't know anything about the murder of the librarian or anything about some blackmail."

"Look, Ms. Bolton, you might as well tell the truth. Erica Stark blackmailed you," the detective said, eyeing her with a steely stare.

The college president fixed her gaze upon the detective. "I am telling the truth. Why are you badgering me?"

"I'm just being diligent with the investigation. Mr. Presson stated publicly that the librarian blackmailed him, but he insisted he is innocent of the murder. If that librarian was blackmailing people, anyone who was a victim of that crime could have had reason to kill her," Adam explained. "I have to ask, did you kill her?"

"Of course, not. Look at me? Do I look like a killer?"

"It's my experience killers come in all shapes, sizes and backgrounds."

"I didn't stab her. The prosecutor charged the preacher with murder, so why are you wasting my time?"

"As I said, I'm just covering all the bases. The murder victim had saved an article that mentioned the allegations made against you. Naturally, we needed to talk to you, see if you could shed any light on the matter. Thanks for your time," Adam said, rising and walking toward the door.

"Detective," the Elmwood College president said, "I'd prefer that you not come back here. I have nothing else to say."

Adam didn't reply. He walked out of her office. He didn't look back. So, he didn't see the fear in Olivia Bolton's eyes.

She sat at her desk for what seemed like forever to her. She looked at the clock on her wall. She'd been stuck at her desk for a half hour. She shook her head as if doing so would remove her crushing headache and her terrible fear that her secret would be exposed.

Her cell phone broke out in song, alerting her to a call. She answered it without even checking the screen to see who was calling. A male voice demanded, "You'll pay me $2,000 in cash monthly or your Board of Governors will learn about your academic cheating. Leave the cash under the computer terminal in the study area behind the biography section at the Elmwood Public Library."

"Who is this?"

"You heard me. Pay up or you'll be sorry," the man said in a raspy voice, ending the conversation.

Olivia Bolton looked at the phone number. She didn't recognize it. She thought of going to the police, but then the allegations of plagiarism would come out. No doubt, the police would learn that the librarian had blackmailed her. Now, she was being blackmailed again. Anger surged in her chest. Questions tumbled in her mind. *Who is this son-of-a-bitch? Was he a friend of the murdered woman? Do I keep quiet and pay up? Olivia bit her upper lip. One thing was certain, she thought. I'm screwed.*

Chapter Forty—Two

Adam stood on the wide steps outside Academic Hall, pulled out his cell phone and called Connor. He didn't bother with greetings but got right to the point. "I know your unnamed educator is Olivia Bolton. I just spoke to her. She said she wasn't blackmailed and didn't kill the librarian."

"Do you believe her?"

"It doesn't matter if I believe her or not. She denies being blackmailed and I have no evidence indicating otherwise."

"So, that's it? The Elmwood Police Department is done investigating this matter," Connor grumbled.

"At this point? Yes. Besides, whether or not she was blackmailed, I don't see the college president as a killer, much less someone who would have stabbed the librarian. If you're trying to prove Harold Presson didn't kill Erica Stark, you're failing miserably," Adam said.

"Thanks, pal, for the vote of confidence," Connor laughed.

"Bottom line: Harold Presson killed that librarian."

"I'm not ready to give up."

"Well, keep on digging. If you find something, let me know," Adam said.

"You can count on it."

The conversation ended, Connor turned toward Rachel, seated at her newsroom desk. "What is it?" Rachel asked.

"Adam questioned Olivia Bolton. She denied everything, said she wasn't blackmailed, didn't pay Erica Stark and didn't kill her."

"So, she lied, either to us or to Adam," Rachel said.

"Damn right."

"What do we do now?"

"Look for new evidence."

"That she killed the librarian?"

"Not necessarily. There's another possibility we haven't explored."

"What's that?"

"Judge Wachter."

"You think he is the murderer?" Rachel asked, a doubting look in her eyes.

"Possibly," Connor said. "At least it's worth checking out. It does seem convenient that he found the pledge paddle tying Harold to the murder. And, the security video showed the judge walking into the library near closing time on several Thursday evenings going back a number of months. In each case, Judge Wachter entered the library, headed toward the biography section and then, within minutes, exited without checking out a single book. His actions mirrored those of the pastor and the college president. If we believe that Erica Stark blackmailed both Harold and Olivia, then it suggests the librarian may have blackmailed the judge too."

"But the judge chairs the library board. So, isn't it possible he had a solid reason for his short visits to the library?"

"Maybe. But why visit so close to closing time? What possible business could be so pressing and take so little time?"

"I can't answer that. So, you want to investigate a sitting judge?" Rachel asked. "What possible dark secret could he have that would make him a blackmail victim?"

"That's what I want to find out," Connor replied.

"And how are you going to do that?"

"I don't know. But I'm not going to do this by myself. You're going to help me."

"Do I have a choice?" Rachel asked, a smile gracing her face, showing she already knew the answer.

"I just assumed you would want to participate in this investigative journalism."

"Damn. You know me too well."

"I figured you wouldn't want me to hog all the glory," Connor said.

"There's that too," she said.

Chapter Forty—Three

August rolled into Southeast Missouri like a sledgehammer, bringing with it oppressive heat and humidity that turned the outdoors into a sweaty sauna that sapped the strength of anyone who stepped outside, beyond the walled-in comfort of air conditioning.

But it wasn't just the weather that frustrated him. He and Rachel had found no evidence tying Judge Michael Wachter to the murder. Their inquiry had been hampered by their decision to do it in secret. They didn't inform Lansmon, worried their editor would have halted the investigation before it even began.

Connor and Rachel pursued their probe mostly evenings and on weekends. By now, they knew the judge's background so well they could have recited it in their sleep. Judge Michael Wachter was born in the Elmwood area. His father was a dairy farmer; his mother, a high school math teacher. A graduate of the University of Missouri Law School, he returned to Elmwood to practice law. He married his high school sweetheart, but the couple divorced five years later. Voters elected him as circuit judge 25 years ago when he was only 30 years old, making him the youngest person to be elected to the bench in the history of Elmwood. By all accounts, he was viewed as an able judge by lawyers who practiced in his court.

Connor and Rachel interviewed members of the local library board. They all praised his work as board chairman. And, Michael Wachter had repeatedly lauded the efforts of the now murdered library director. He had publicly defended Erica Stark and the library from the verbal assaults made by Harold Presson's Citizens for Decency. He routinely opposed the group's efforts to ban books they viewed as pornographic.

One evening as the reporters cooled off in Connor's loft apartment, Rachel slammed down her notebook on the kitchen table. "Damn it. This is a waste of time."

"I'm frustrated too, but we've got to continue to find out more," Connor countered. "We just haven't found the right clue."

"And what would that clue be? Everyone we've chatted with has sung the judge's praises."

"No one is that perfect," Connor insisted. "There has to be at least one skeleton in his closet."

"You've read too many mystery novels," Rachel said, laughing.

"What if there is something in his background that we've missed?"

"You mean blackmail material?"

"Right."

"Maybe Julie knows something. She worked with Erica. If Erica did blackmail the judge, maybe she let something slip in passing in a conversation."

"It's worth asking."

Rachel sat in Julie's book-cluttered library office the next morning, hoping the interim library director held a clue to the murder. Deep down, she questioned why she was even here. She had stories to write back at the office. She found it hard to believe the judge could have murdered Erica. Julie's mouth stiffened before Rachel said a word. Rachel noticed it. Clearly, Julie Halston wasn't happy to see her. "Why do you want to know about Judge Wachter?" Julie asked.

"I am just wondering about the judge's background. Could someone have blackmailed him?"

"You mean Erica?"

"I didn't say that."

"But that's what you meant," Julie lashed out. "I've told you Erica Stark didn't blackmail anyone. Harold Presson lied so people would feel sorry for him. He wants people to believe he was the victim. Well, I know that preacher killed her because she wouldn't agree to the demands of his group to remove certain books from the library."

"How do you know? Do you have evidence of that?"

"Well, no, but it's the only scenario that makes sense."

"Maybe."

"Why do you want to sully Erica's character? I was around her a lot. She was both my boss and a friend."

"But is there anything in the judge's background that might result in his being blackmailed?"

"None. He is a gentleman. He doesn't have a black mark against him."

"I understand he's single. Does he have a girlfriend?"

"Not that I know of, but he does like women. I remember Erica once told me that Michael was the most eligible bachelor and he liked to keep it that way. But as far as I know, that's not a crime. And, I certainly see why women are attracted to him."

"What do you mean?"

"He keeps himself in shape and he knows how to treat a lady. Most guys aren't like that."

"It sounds like you know about this firsthand."

"I've dated some guys over the years who have been less than stellar. But thankfully I didn't marry any of them."

"So, you've never married?"

"No. Not that it's any of your business."

"Anything else you can tell me about Judge Wachter?"

"Well, he's done a great job leading the library board despite the hell-and-brimstone attitudes of that book-banning group, whose members say the vilest things," Julie said. "It takes a strong person to deal with those people and Michael is such an individual. He makes my job easier."

"Does he have any hobbies? What does he do for fun?"

"I never really asked him."

"He must have some hobbies."

"I believe he's mentioned playing golf."

"Anything else?"

"Not that I remember," she said, casting stern eyes upon Rachel as if she were boring a hole in her brain.

Chapter Forty–Four

Sultry, soft sounds of jazz played inside Jello as Rachel and Connor shared a bottle of Prosecco and a plate of roasted garlic hummus and pita chips. Friday night and the lights were low. A perfect date night, one the couple badly needed. Their investigation had all but fizzled out, leaving them frustrated and mentally exhausted. Julie Halston had revealed Judge Wachter liked the ladies. He had been married for a short time, but that was years ago. From what Julie had said, the judge was a committed bachelor now who liked a good time. But that didn't seem like blackmail material, Connor and Rachel thought.

At Jello, they put work aside. A 20-something Black woman stood on the small stage, backed by a trio of musicians on horns and piano. Dressed in a low-cut red dress that hugged every curve of her body, she sang Billie Holiday's soulful "All of Me."

Connor gazed approvingly at the singer. Rachel eyed her boyfriend. "Don't strain your eyes, Connor."

"Don't worry, I'm listening to the song."

"Yeah, but I'm certain you've noticed her too."

"The singer?"

"Yes, the singer."

"Well, I admit she's good looking, but I'm not dating her. She's a little young for me."

"Glad to hear it," Rachel said.

"Don't think I don't notice you," Connor said, turning his gaze on her. Dressed in a sleeveless blue top, topaz earrings and black skinny jeans, she returned his gaze. Her eyes smiled at him in her inviting way. He loved that look. It amazed him. How does she do that? They drank a couple glasses of wine before hitting the crowded dance floor. They loved slow dances, their bodies pressed together, moving as one to sax-filled rhythms, their shoes scuffing the old wooden floor. As they danced, Rachel spotted Julie Halston seated at a round table in a corner of the club. Julie didn't see her. The library director wore a periwinkle blouse and a matching skirt. Her eyes focused on the well-dressed man seated next to her. His right hand lay atop hers as she whispered something in his ear. Rachel didn't know the man, but he and Julie appeared very cozy.

"Julie's here," Rachel told Connor.

"Julie Halston?"

"Yes."

"Good for her."

"She's with some guy."

"Who is he?"

"I don't know," Rachel said. Connor peered around Rachel. He spotted the couple. The balding man, attired in a tan suit and open collared white shirt, drank a beer as Julie sipped a glass of red wine.

"That's Bob Benson," Connor said.

"How do you know him?"

"Bob Benson's a public defender. I've covered a number of his cases. I feel for him and other public defenders. The state government doesn't provide enough funding. The result is that there are too few public defenders in Missouri and the ones we have are saddled with too many clients. Of course, these defendants are poor. They can't afford to hire a lawyer. Their only choice is to be represented by a public defender. In most cases, the defendants plead guilty. For a public defender, success is getting clients to accept plea deals, which typically means lighter sentences."

"Sounds like a tough job," Rachel said.

"Yeah, and the money's not as good as what you can get in private practice."

"Well, money isn't everything. Look at us. We're working for a small newspaper and we're certainly not doing it for the pay."

"Good point," Connor said, throwing a smile her way. "He seems a little overdressed," he noted of Benson.

"Not everyone wears jeans. Maybe he wanted to impress her," Rachel said. "We should go over there."

"Why?"

"To be polite."

"I doubt she wants to talk to us now. Erica Stark was a close friend. Julie sees us as smearing her friend's name."

"What? You're afraid to approach her?"

"Of course, not. But this isn't the time or place."

"I want her to realize we're just searching for the truth."

"She thinks she knows the truth. She's certain Harold killed her friend."

"Well, I'm still going to say hi."

"Suit yourself," Connor sighed.

"Come on," Rachel said, grabbing his arm. Grumbling under his breath, he followed her as she walked toward the table where Julie and Bob were seated. Julie spotted the reporters and tried to turn away. But it was too late. Connor and Rachel stopped at the table.

"Hi," Rachel said. Connor nodded at the couple.

"What do you want?" Julie asked in a steely voice, betraying her unhappiness at having to deal with the two reporters once again.

"I didn't know you liked jazz," Rachel said.

"Julie does," said Bob, inserting himself into the conversation. "I prefer rock n' roll."

"These are the two nosy reporters I told you about," Julie told Bob.

"I can't say I've heard good things about you," Bob said. "But then most lawyers don't like reporters."

"Well, we can't please everyone," Connor replied. "But then I'm sure it's the same in your line of work, defending those accused of murder, rape, assault and other crimes."

"Everyone deserves to be represented in court, even those accused of horrible crimes."

"You have a reputation for getting your clients to plead guilty rather than go to trial."

"It's the smart move for most of my clients, who, let's face it, are guilty. I generally advise them to accept a plea deal where they admit to a lesser crime and receive a shorter prison sentence or even get probation."

"That makes sense," Connor agreed.

"Are you looking for Judge Wachter?" Julie asked, breaking into the conversation. "If you are, I'm sure he doesn't want to talk to you. Rachel, I phoned him after you questioned me. I told him that you two were digging into his background, saying he might have been blackmailed by Erica. You know what he did? He laughed, said you two must be high as a kite. He told me no one blackmailed him, and he has nothing bad in his past. Why can't you leave him alone?"

"You two are barking up the wrong tree," Bob said.

"Do you think the preacher did it?" Rachel questioned.

"No way. He talks tough, but I can't see him stabbing that librarian."

"You don't believe Presson when he says Erica Stark blackmailed him?"

"How would I know?" the lawyer replied.

"Maybe another blackmail victim killed her," Rachel suggested.

"I think you're too focused on the blackmail scenario. There could be a much simpler reason for murder," Bob said.

"What's that?"

"To get rid of a cheating husband by framing him for murder."

"Wow. That's out of left field," Connor remarked.

"Not really. In my line of work, I represent a lot of less than stellar people."

"You mean criminal types."

"I prefer to call them my clients. But whatever you want to call them, they hear stuff."

"Like what you just told us?" Rachel said.

"Yeah."

"You're suggesting Harold's wife killed the librarian in order to frame her husband because he was having an affair?" Connor asked.

"I'm not suggesting anything. And, I didn't say she did it. I said it's been suggested she could have plotted to frame Harold."

"And paid someone to do the deed?" Rachel questioned.

"That's one scenario," the public defender replied.

"But you have no evidence that's the case," Connor said.

"No, I have no evidence. I'm just telling you what my clients have told me. And, I hear a lot of stuff from them, not all of it true. I practice in front of Judge Wachter all the time. One thing I know, he's not a killer."

"And he'd never kill Erica Stark," Julie insisted. "I mean, they liked each other."

"Were they sweet on each other?" Rachel asked.

"I won't say that, but they enjoyed each other's company."

"Well, we've taken up enough of your time," Connor said.

151

"You can say that again," Julie said.

"Yeah, well have a good night," Rachel said.

"It will be better as soon as you leave."

Connor grabbed Rachel's hand and led her back to their table. He paid the bill, leaving a sizable tip for their waitress. Connor and Rachel exited the club and into the thick night air that felt like a warm, wet, wool blanket.

"Well, that was sure interesting," Rachel said.

"You mean the part about Priscilla Presson?"

"Yeah. Bob Benson implied she could have schemed to frame her cheating husband for the murder."

"He said he had heard rumors from some of his clients, but I wonder how reliable that is. Most of his clients are anything but honest. And, if Bob Benson had any serious evidence that Priscilla Presson was involved, I have to think he would have sought a plea agreement for one or more of his clients in exchange for that information."

"Maybe he did."

"I don't think so. I'm sure he would have bragged about such a plea deal if it had happened."

"Maybe it's more than rumors."

"If so," Connor said, "then Priscilla killed the librarian or hired someone to do it. And, I find it hard to believe Priscilla killed Erica. She doesn't seem like the stabbing kind."

"When a person is mad enough, he or she can do almost anything," Rachel insisted.

"Maybe so, but Mrs. Presson seems to me like a person who'd hire someone to do the killing. She wouldn't do it herself. Too messy."

"And, if that's the case, then the murder was just a means to frame her husband. That would be one ruthless woman."

"Yep. We need to know more about her."

"We need to find out of if there is any evidence that could link her to the murder. But that may be a difficult challenge. Police have found no shred of evidence to support such an accusation," Rachel said.

"Yes, none that we know of. But that's doesn't mean Priscilla Presson didn't frame her husband. Think about it. What a perfect crime. Who would believe a preacher's wife would do such a thing?"

"You've got a point. Of course, who would believe a preacher and a stripper would fall in and out of love?"

"Right," Connor said as the couple strolled along, hand in hand, past the closed antique shops and jewelry stores and the crowded eateries and riverfront taverns, bathed in the soft glow of streetlamps. As they headed back to Connor's loft apartment, they tried to shelve talk about the murder. Afterall, they had embraced date night. A chance to put aside work. But try as they might, they couldn't ignore what Bob Benson had told them. It's all they could think about as they fell asleep, nestled together in Connor's bed.

Chapter Forty–Five

The man's bad luck left him downing glasses of bourbon at the Isle Casino bar, served by a big-breasted gal whose eye makeup, he thought, made her look like a raccoon. Middle-aged and a little on the heavy side, the man told himself he needed to get in shape. But the thought went nowhere. He couldn't escape his addiction. He played them all: slots, card games, roulette and craps. He lost at them all, especially blackjack. Once he hit big on progressive slots, winning $5,000. But he never scored like that again. Over the years, he'd lost tens of thousands of dollars. He'd gambled away his marriage. Spent hours in casinos at judicial conferences across the country and on occasion maxed out his credit cards. Now, he'd gone through nearly $1,000, playing high-stakes poker on a Friday night. And, that didn't include the money he'd spent at the casino on food and drink.

The casino sat just north of Elmwood's downtown on a rise overlooking the floodwall and the Mississippi River beyond it. The gleaming, modern façade with its blue neon lights beckoned college kids out for a good time, as well as hardcore gamblers and visitors hoping for a little luck. The rows of colorful slot machines, with the constant tumblers, bells and whistles created a cascade of sound. The deft hands of dealers shuffling decks of cards mesmerized him. The clicking of a spinning roulette wheel could be heard as gamblers watched the bounce of the ball. Excited screams signaled the ecstasy of those who had just won a card game or hit the winning combination on the slots. But none of that came his way. He adjusted his glasses and finished his drink. He closed out his tab, tipped the bartender and slowly headed for the exit. Worse still, he thought, he was going home alone. Earlier, he had made a pass at a 20-something, tanned woman with a tattoo of a cat on her right arm. She had rejected his advances before he could even get out a second sentence. The man reached his black Mercedes, climbed in and started the engine. He took his foot off the brake and slowly steered out of

154

the parking lot. He was careful. He knew he'd had too many drinks. It wouldn't do to get stopped. He didn't think he could talk the cops out of arresting him for drunk driving.

A woman closely watched him leave. From a distance, the woman had observed him gamble for hours. She'd done it before. Several times within the past month. Almost always, she saw him lose, saw his frustration. She'd spent some time at the slot machines, mostly watching him. Still, she found herself distracted, watching others play the slots with their colorful spinning reels of cherries and the desired row of lucky sevens. Brightly lit, the machines beckoned with bold colors and names like Dragon Link, Mega Joker and Fruit Blaster. Some gambled away their money on several machines at once, staking their claim with the tenacity of a tiger.

The slot machines gave her cover. She positioned herself so she could see him playing poker, losing and then losing some more. He was stubborn. She gave him that. He also was in debt. She wondered. *What would he do to feed his addiction? What had he already done?*

Private investigator John Wilder Brumley operated out of a former downtown tavern. Another investigator, Lou Lockhart, operated from that place before he was murdered. Within months after the murder, Brumley bought the place. He had it renovated with new white paint on the walls, modern light fixtures and furniture. Brumley kept the bar counter and stocked the shelf behind it with bottles of vodka and bourbon. He kept a refrigerator stocked with Bud Light. He'd partitioned off the front part of the first floor to use as an office. He used the upstairs for storage. A former small-town cop in the Missouri Bootheel, the 42-year-old Brumley moved to Elmwood a decade ago; found it far more profitable to be a private investigator, chasing down cheating spouses and from time to time finding witnesses for defense lawyers seeking to keep their clients out of prison. Brumley thought most of the defendants were guilty of the charges they faced from assaults to home burglaries, but he was paid to find alibi witnesses. And he was good at it. If some guilty scumbag high on meth got off, well, that wasn't his problem. Brumley operated out of a midtown location above a medical marijuana shop before relocating downtown five years ago. He missed the smell even though it was a better location.

Only days after talking to the public defender, Connor interviewed Brumley at the suggestion of his friend Adam. The police detective had advised Connor that Brumley earned a living chasing down unfaithful husbands and wives. Who better, thought Connor, to ask about whether Priscilla Presson knew about her husband's affair long before the preacher admitted to it.

Brumley, wearing an Eagles band T-shirt, sat behind a scarred, cherry paneled desk that seemed to Connor as almost as massive as the investigator. Built short and stout, with leathery tan skin, Brumley reminded Connor of a human cigar. His short black hair peaked in the front. He had a slight beer belly, which broke over his worn jeans. Black Tecovas cowboy boots covered his feet. His muscled upper arms and thick-knuckled fingers revealed a man who knew his way around a bar fight, a useful trait for a private eye. Connor smelled the leathery, woody aroma of cigar smoke even though Brumley wasn't smoking. The ceiling fan whined as it whirled. It reminded Connor of a scene from an old black-and-white Bogart movie.

Brumley ran his fat right hand across the desktop. "I love this piece," he said. "You know what's special about this desk?"

"It's old," Connor laughed.

"More than that. It's historic. I bought it from a guy in Arkansas. He claimed Judge Parker used this desk in his courtroom."

"Judge Parker?"

"Judge Isaac Charles Parker. They called him the 'hanging judge.' He served as a federal judge in Fort Smith, Ark., for 21 years in the late 1800s, after the Civil War. Did you know that his jurisdiction included all of the Indian Territory? That was the Wild West back then. All sorts of murderous, thievin' outlaws. That judge was the law. He sentenced 160 people to death. Seventy-nine of them were executed."

"And you're sitting at a desk used by Parker in his courtroom?"

"Well, that's what the guy said. I don't know if it's true. Could be crap. But there are historic accounts that Judge Parker had such a desk. And, I like to tell the story. Of course, you're not here for a history lesson. You said on the phone you wanted to ask me some-

156

thing about a cheating spouse and that it might relate to the murder of that librarian."

"Yes. I talked to a lawyer who says the word on the street is that Priscilla Presson may have plotted to kill her husband."

"And you think I know something about it?"

"Well, if she did want to kill her husband, then it likely was because he cheated on her. She would have sought evidence of his infidelity before even thinking of murdering him. I assume she would have hired an investigator, someone like you. I've been told that tailing cheating spouses is your bread and butter."

"You think Priscilla Presson hired me to find evidence if her husband cheated on her?"

"It seems plausible."

"What if I told you, it's none of your business?"

"I would keep asking."

"You journalists are like sharks when you smell blood in the water," Brumley grumbled.

"Look, I just want to know if Priscilla hired you to follow her husband, find evidence of his adultery."

"Okay. Yeah. Off the record, she did. And, yes, I discovered Harold Presson had an affair with that stripper. And she wasn't the only gal he had on the side. He often engaged prostitutes in the Bootheel. I tailed his ass all over the place, practically every shady motel from here to Memphis. Of course, he did spring for a room at The Peabody Hotel for that one stripper. But she had his balls in a sling."

"So, Priscilla Presson knew about her husband's activities before Erica Stark was murdered?"

"You bet," Brumley said. "I gave her my report at least a month before the librarian was murdered."

"How did she take it?"

"Like a woman who already knew her husband was a cheating bastard. She didn't break down. She just thanked me and wrote a check for my services."

"Do you believe she could have killed Ms. Stark?"

"Not by herself. She would have paid someone to do the job and then framed her husband for murder," Brumley suggested. "But that's just speculation. Don't quote me. But it would be one hell of a way to get rid of your cheating spouse."

Chapter Forty–Six

The gritty voice spilled out in anger. "Pay up by tomorrow or everyone on your college's Board of Governors will know you're an academic fraud," the caller told Olivia Bolton, spitting out each word. Verbal missiles. The Elmwood College president felt the muscles stiffen in her neck and shoulders. Fear gripped her mind. *Who is this damn blackmailer?*

"Plagiarism. I bet the college board would love to know what you did. Stealing another person's academic work," the caller said.

"You don't scare me," said Olivia, trying to hide the strain in her voice, the heart-stopping fear.

"You don't fool me," the voice said. "The board will kick out your ass."

Olivia cut off the call, slammed her right hand on her desk. She turned and stared out one of the large windows in her spacious Academic Hall office. Below, shorts-clad students with backpacks walked along the concrete sidewalks, making their way across the hilly landscape to morning classes.

Olivia Bolton bit her lip. She felt like a wounded, trapped animal. The caller had become increasingly angry with each call he made. For several weeks, she had made excuses. No longer. Now in mid-August, the caller had given her a final deadline. She paced and shook her head, hoping to free herself, to find a way out of this dilemma. *Twenty minutes later, she had a plan. She wouldn't be a victim. She'd go public, admit her mistake.* The Elmwood College president thought of the unknown caller, the ugly, attacking voice. She vowed she'd silence it. She imagined strangling the caller, pictured his dying breath. And for the first time in a long while, Olivia smiled.

Brumley gazed around the spacious, richly decorated office of Rush Johnson. From the second-story office, Brumley took in the view of the floodwall and the Mississippi River beyond, its waters flowing toward New Orleans. A large, acrylic painting of Elmwood's river bridge occupied one wall of the posh office. Rush had invited him to his headquarters. The stylish lawyer had a job offer. Brumley showed up dressed in a brown suit and bolo tie, accented with cowboy boots and a Stetson. He smoked a cigar before walking several blocks from his sparse downtown office to Rush's. The aroma clung to his clothes.

Rush, dressed in an Italian suit and leather dress shoes, took a seat at his ornate desk. Brumley thought to himself that Rush's attire probably cost more than the private eye cleared in a month. The investigator routinely did jobs for area defense lawyers, not all of them reputable. But he wasn't in the same league with Rush. The high-priced attorney rarely hired him to conduct investigations, preferring to hire investigators from St. Louis. So, naturally, Rush's invitation to meet intrigued him.

Rush eyed the private eye seated across from him. "Thanks for coming. I have a job, which is right up your alley."

"What's that?"

"I need you to investigate Priscilla Presson, find out if she plotted to frame her husband for the murder of Erica Stark."

"What? I guess you don't know that Ms. Presson hired me to obtain evidence that Harold Presson cheated on her. I obtained the evidence. I detailed it all in a report to her long before that librarian was murdered."

"Yes, I know. That's precisely why I want to hire you. You have rapport with Ms. Presson. That makes you the ideal person to spy on her," Rush said.

"How did you know that I worked for her?"

"I have my sources."

"Yeah. Those damn newspaper reporters."

"I didn't say that."

"You don't have to. I'm not stupid. I just talked to those *Journal* reporters off the record. Clearly, they didn't keep their word."

"If you must know, I learned about your investigation from my client. After Harold was charged with murder, his wife told him that she had suspected his infidelity, that she had hired you to find evidence of his cheating and that you had provided such evidence."

159

"I see," Brumley said. "So, you think Priscilla Presson killed Erica Stark and then framed her husband?"

"It's a possibility, I believe. And I need you to check it out."

"I don't know," Brumley mumbled.

"Are you still working for her?"

"No. She paid me for my investigative work. But I also did something else."

"What's that?"

"I taught her how to shoot."

"She has a gun?"

"Yeah. She came to me after I gave her my report on what a lying, cheating guy her husband was. Priscilla bought a Colt Model 1911."

"A semi-automatic pistol?"

"Yep. Seven rounds, .45 caliber. Nice piece."

"Did she tell you why she needed a gun?"

"Priscilla told me she feared her husband might harm her because she had confronted him about his cheating."

"Did you believe her?"

"I didn't give it much thought. I mean, I don't really think her husband would kill her. He's already charged with one murder. Still, she might fear him like she said."

"Or maybe she's thinking of shooting him if a jury finds him not guilty of murdering the librarian," Rush suggested.

"Possibly."

"So, are you up to spying on her?"

"That depends?"

"On what?"

"How much you'll pay me."

"How about $5,000?"

"Plus expenses?"

"Verified expenses."

"Deal," Brumley said. "Just one question. What if I can't find any evidence she was involved in Erica's murder and/or framing her husband for the crime?"

"Then, you've made a lot of money for nothing. Of course, I expect you to find me some evidence that indicates my client didn't kill Erica Stark. You said you taught Priscilla how to shoot. I assume you took her to an indoor gun range?"

"Yeah."

"Any witnesses?"

"Yes."

"Good. Plus, I'll need a statement from the shop where she bought the gun. It would be great to know if she confided in anyone besides you that she feared her husband might harm her."

"You don't believe her story?"

"I believe Priscilla Presson is the type of person who would hold a grudge and might very well have contemplated killing her husband."

"But she didn't kill him."

"No."

"Wouldn't that have been better, from her point of view, than stabbing the librarian?"

"Not if you wanted to eliminate the blackmailer too. You've got to see it from Priscilla's viewpoint. Erica Stark knew about the infidelity. She blackmailed Harold but also kept quiet about his cheating ways. That would be unforgivable to Priscilla."

"You could be right. I've dealt with all kinds of shady people. If Priscilla Presson killed the librarian and framed her husband, I'll find the evidence," Brumley said.

"Good. Don't let me down," Rush said, showing him the door. Once alone in his office, Rush took air freshener out of a desk drawer and sprayed it all over. "Damn cheap cigar," he said aloud.

Chapter Forty—Seven

Water dripped off her red, hooded raincoat as Olivia Bolton entered Smooth Buns. The rain had drenched the city for hours. Now, in mid-afternoon, the storm showed no signs of letting up. The Elmwood College president spotted Rachel, seated at a corner table near the rear of the dining area. None of the other tables were occupied. Olivia sighed with relief. She had scheduled to meet Rachel at 3 p.m., for that very reason. She wanted some privacy. Although when she thought more about it, she realized nothing would be private for long. Not after she confided in Rachel. Not after what she was about to reveal.

Rachel sipped sweet tea through a straw. Olivia took off her raincoat, shook off the rain drops and placed it over an empty chair. She sat down opposite Rachel. A red-haired waitress stopped by. Olivia eyed Rachel's drink and ordered the same. "Thanks for meeting me," Olivia said after the waitress left.

"I wasn't going to say no, not after you told me it was something important and that you couldn't wait to tell me."

"Still, I'm glad you came. I'm more at ease talking to you than that other reporter."

"Who, Connor?"

"Yes. I wanted to talk to a woman. I feel you might better understand why I did what I did."

"What did you do?" Rachel asked.

"You know. Off the record, I had told you I plagiarized an article some years ago, before I became the president of Elmwood College. I also told you Erica Stark tried to blackmail me, but that I refused to pay. Well, the last part isn't true. I did pay. Month after month, I left cash in a biography in the library. I wanted you to know, and I'm telling you this on the record."

"Why are you willing to go public now?"

"Because someone else is trying to blackmail me."

"Who?"

"I have no idea. It's a man for sure. It sounds like he's trying to disguise his voice. But he sounds oddly familiar. I keep thinking I may have met this guy at some point. But no one comes to mind. As college president, you can imagine that I meet a lot of people at fundraisers and other events."

"When did this start?"

"After Erica was murdered."

"He phoned me and threatened to go public with the accusation if I didn't pay up."

"And did you pay?"

"No. That's why I'm talking to you. If I don't pay up by tomorrow night, he's going to reveal everything."

"I figure the only way I can fight this blackmail is to go public myself. Confess everything. Then, there won't be any reason for him to blackmail me. I just want him to leave me alone. Will you write this story? It needs to make the next edition."

"Of course, I will. But I do have a question."

"What's that?"

"How did this man know about your secret?"

"I don't know for sure. But he must have known that Erica Stark blackmailed me."

"Why do you say that?"

"Because the caller said for me to leave $2,000 in cash each month under the computer terminal in the study area behind the biography section in the public library. Why would he pick the library as the drop-off site unless he knew about the librarian's blackmail scheme."

"You might be right. It may indicate he feels right at home there. Maybe he has something to do with the library or he's a regular customer. Or maybe he and Erica were in it together. Erica made the demands, but this man may have conspired with her. Now that Erica's dead, this guy wants to keep blackmailing you and possibly others."

"I never considered that."

"It's just speculation. But if we could figure out what connects this man to the Elmwood Public Library, we might be able to discover his identity."

"Well, I must go. I need to make some phone calls, talk to my board."

"You think you'll get fired?"

"I don't know. I hope they'll forgive me for my actions. But I must admit there is a good possibility I will lose my job. Still, I won't live in fear. I've done that too long. Whatever happens, I'll live with the consequences."

Olivia reached for her purse. Rachel stopped her. "I'll get this."

"Thanks. Got to go." Olivia put on her raincoat and hurried out the door into the storm.

Chapter Forty—Eight

Rachel's story detailing the blackmail of Olivia Bolton would be front-page news. But Lansmon wanted more than a single-source story. He instructed Connor to secure a comment from the police and attorney Rush Johnson.

"Talk to Chief Bonney. I don't want some sanitized written statement from the police. Get the chief on the record," the *Journal* editor said. "I want to know what the police will do with this new evidence. As for the defense attorney, we need to get his reaction on the record. How will it impact his defense of the preacher?" Lansmon told Rachel to ask the chairman of the college's Board of Governors whether the board would consider terminating Olivia Bolton's contract because of the plagiarism. With the editor's instructions in place, the reporters tackled the breaking news.

Rachel began crafting the story as Connor sought comments to add to the piece. He chose not to call the main number to the police station for fear the public information officer would run interference, keeping him from talking directly to the police chief. Connor had Blair's personal cell number. He used it sparingly, afraid that if he called too frequently, the chief would ignore the calls.

Seated in his office, Blair answered the call. "What do you want?"

Connor told the chief about Olivia's disclosure. The reporter asked, "What will you do now that Olivia Bolton has gone public with the allegation that Erica Stark blackmailed her and someone else is attempting to do the same thing?"

"Well, it's already been alleged that the librarian was a blackmailer. That doesn't change anything when it comes to the murder charge against Harold Presson. You're not suggesting that college president killed the librarian?"

"No. I didn't say that," Connor said. "She insists she didn't kill her."

"It doesn't matter. The evidence points to the preacher as the killer. Nothing Ms. Bolton says or doesn't say will change that reality."

"What about the fact that Olivia says someone else is now trying to blackmail her?"

"If she reports it to us, we'll look into it. But from what you just told me, there seems to be little to go on. I'm focused on sending a murderer to prison, not some plagiarism incident involving a scholarly article that few Elmwood residents know about or much less read."

"Doesn't it bother you that there could be another blackmailer out there?"

"We take any report of criminality seriously. But we don't spend our valuable time and manpower investigating something because of what you and your colleagues write. Some sensational article isn't evidence," Blair grumbled, ending the conversation.

An hour later, Rachel finished the story, having added information obtained by Connor. Lansmon reviewed the article, which included comments from the police chief as well as Rush Johnson and the chairman of the Elmwood College Board of Governors. Lansmon rearranged a few paragraphs and tightened the writing. Then, he marked it ready for a final proof by the copy editors. By mid-afternoon, the *Journal* had posted the Rachel-and-Connor bylined story online.

The story began: *Elmwood College President Olivia Bolton says librarian Erica Stark repeatedly blackmailed her for plagiarizing a scholarly article and that after the librarian's death she's been the target of a blackmail attempt by an unknown person. Bolton insisted she did not kill Stark. She said she refused to pay the latest blackmailer, whom she described as having a "raspy" masculine voice.*

The story quoted the police chief, insisting the revelations provided no new evidence as it related to the murder and expressing little concern about the latest blackmail allegation. Rush Johnson served up a quote. He said the latest information showed that Harold Presson wasn't the only person blackmailed by the murder victim. The lawyer suggested police should question Bolton and take steps to find out if Stark blackmailed others. Christian Clack, chairman of the college's Board of Governors, told the *Journal* that board members would review the admitted plagiarism. But he said that while it's a *"serious academic issue,"* no one on the board had called for her resignation. Clack added that the board was "shocked" that the college president had been the victim of blackmail and voiced concern that Olivia again was targeted. Clack urged police to *"get to the bottom"* of this latest extortion effort.

Seated in his city hall office the next morning, Mayor Elroy James read and reread the front-page story. Each time, he grew angrier. Finally, he threw the entire newspaper into the trash can beside his desk. "Damn, reporters," he mumbled. *Why can't they leave it alone?* But his real anger was reserved for the police chief. *Why the hell hadn't the police discovered the blackmailing of Olivia Bolton and its connection to the murder victim?*

Thirty minutes later, the mayor barged into Blair's office. "What kind of police department are you running?" Elroy asked, the veins on his neck bulging. Blair eyed the red-faced mayor with contempt.

"You've got some nerve coming into my station with your childish temper-tantrum."

"Did you read that front-page story?"

"The one about Olivia Bolton?"

"Yeah."

"Of course, I read it. It's a nothing story."

"What do you mean, nothing?" Elroy screamed. "The *Journal* is reporting that Erica Stark blackmailed the college president and now that the librarian has been murdered, another scumbag has surfaced demanding payment."

"Hold on," Blair shouted. "What Olivia Bolton told the newspaper doesn't change anything regarding the murder. The evidence shows that Harold Presson killed that librarian."

"But Bolton is now saying someone else has attempted to blackmail her and that person, apparently some guy, has ties to the library. According to the story, the blackmailer wanted a monthly payment to be left in the library in the vicinity of the same section where Erica Stark was stabbed to death. You don't see the connection?"

"I see a newspaper trying to sensationalize a case and offer up a narrative that the preacher is being framed. That someone else, possibly this college president, had motive to kill the librarian," Blair said.

"You're missing the point. According to the *Journal*, we have another extortionist out there, and what are you doing? I'll tell you. You and your department are sitting on your asses doing nothing, not a damn thing!"

"How dare you make such an accusation," Blair loudly replied. "Olivia Bolton never told our officers she was blackmailed by Erica Stark or that she was now being blackmailed again. Had she done so, we would have looked into it."

"Well, if your officers had done a little investigating, you surely would have uncovered that Stark had extorted the college president. And, you would have learned that there's another blackmailer out there. Judging from the article, it sounds like you aren't too concerned about this latest extortion."

"Don't lecture me. Of course, we'll look into it. But now that Olivia Bolton has gone public and admitted to the plagiarism, I imagine this blackmailer will crawl back in his hole. He's got no hold on her anymore."

"So, you're going to sit on your lazy butt and do absolutely nothing," the mayor yelled.

"Listen, you idiot. I told you we'd investigate. Now get the hell out of here before I throw out your sorry ass."

"Don't threaten me, Blair. I'm the mayor. I run this town."

"Ha. That's laughable. Even your fellow council members can't stand you."

"One of these days," Elroy began.

"What?" the chief interrupted.

"I'm going to get you fired. Elmwood needs a real police chief, not some incompetent prick."

"Well, try it. Oh, but you can't. There's a little thing called the city charter. The city manager makes hiring and firing decisions regarding city staff, not the mayor," Blair said.

Elroy shook his fist at the chief. The mayor stomped out of the office, cursing as he went. Blair walked to his office door and slammed it shut. He returned to his desk, sat down. He had been certain the mayor would have popped a blood vessel, maybe suffered a stroke. It hadn't happened. But one thing was for certain. *It was only a matter of time. He was a ticking time bomb.*

Chapter Forty–Nine

Connor sat at a rear table at Smooth Buns listening to Adam. The police detective harped on the issue that bugged him. Connor hadn't tipped him off regarding the Olivia Bolton story.

"The least you could have done was call me. I had to hear it from the police chief, whom you called for a comment. You called him, but not me. What the heck were you thinking?"

"I'm sorry. I should have contacted you," Connor said. He paused and sipped his tea. "My editor instructed me to call the police chief directly. I was focused on getting hold of the chief."

"That's no excuse. You'd think you could have called your best friend and, frankly, your only friend at the police department."

"I know I'm not on the Christmas list at the cop shop. I'm sorry. I should have let you know the situation."

"Darn right you should have," Adam said, sipping on a glass of lemonade as he and Connor waited for the sandwiches ordered for lunch.

"Are you checking out Olivia's story?"

"Yeah. I talked to her by phone this morning. She told me the same thing I read in the newspaper."

"No new details?"

"No."

"What about this new blackmailer? Do you think you'll find him?"

"It depends. If he doesn't contact Ms. Bolton again or try to blackmail someone else, we may never find him. He could just fade away."

"You couldn't trace the call?"

"No. He must have used a burner phone. No way to trace it."

"Don't you believe he could be connected to the original blackmail?"

"In what way?"

"Well, the caller instructed Ms. Bolton to leave a payment be-

169

neath a computer terminal at a study desk in the library. Why pick that location if the blackmailer had no connection to Erica Stark and the library?"

"Maybe it's as simple as the fact that the murder occurred in the library. Plus, Harold Presson told the media where he dropped off the money demanded by Stark. It's natural that a copycat blackmailer would use the same drop-off site."

"You don't believe this latest blackmailer could have been involved in the original scheme?" Connor asked.

"I don't see it. I think you're looking at a copycat blackmailer."

"But how would he know Ms. Bolton incorporated another scholar's writing into her academic article?"

"You were the one who mentioned the issue surfaced in the *Chronicle of Higher Education* publication long before Ms. Bolton ever became president of Elmwood College. Anyone could have googled the woman's career and discovered that fact."

"True. Do you believe Presson and Bolton were Stark's only blackmail victims?"

"I don't know. There could be others. But if true, why wouldn't they come forward?" asked the detective as a college-age waitress brought over their food – a Philly steak sandwich for Connor and a pulled pork sandwich for Adam. The two friends ate in silence for several minutes.

Adam finally spoke. He suggested his friend not read too much into Bolton's story. "You must remember, Connor, most criminals are dumb. They're lazy too. So, the most obvious solution typically is the correct one when it comes to crime. Don't make it complicated. It almost never is."

Connor smiled. But deep down, he felt uneasy. *Something seemed out of place. But what? Could Olivia Bolton have gotten away with murder?*

Chapter Fifty

John Brumley stared out the front window of his battered, black Chevy Silverado. The truck had nearly 200,000 miles on the odometer, but he had no plans to replace it. Not yet. As a private investigator, he spent a lot of time in the truck, trailing cheating spouses and others he was asked to check out. To Brumley, it felt like a second home. Even the coffee stains on the seats appealed to him.

On this day in early September, he sat in the truck cab with the window down. Brumley puffed on a cigar, a ring of smoke floating away into the sun-setting sky. He had parked the Chevy in the Elmwood casino's massive parking lot. It wasn't the first time. He'd spent the last few weeks tailing Priscilla Presson, discovering where she went and whom she saw. He staked out her spacious brick home many times. Enough to know that even though Priscilla and her cheating husband Harold still shared the house, they led separate lives. Brumley predicted to himself that Priscilla would soon divorce her husband. He couldn't blame her. He'd learned that Priscilla often visited the neon-lit Isle Casino. At first, he followed her inside, assured she had a gambling habit. But he soon discovered that gambling wasn't her thing. She appeared to be spying on another man, someone well known, someone he recognized.

The times Brumley had tailed her inside the casino, he'd seen enough. Besides, he worried Priscilla might realize she was being watched if he spent too much time maneuvering among the slot machines. Staying in the truck seemed a better option. He wiped sweat from the fatty folds of his neck as he waited for Priscilla to leave the casino. He longed for cooler fall weather. But that was weeks away, he knew. Heat and humidity pressed in on the Mississippi River city this first week of September. He finished smoking and rolled up the window. Brumley turned the air conditioning fan to full blast and boosted the volume as he listened to his favorite Classic Rock station.

By the time Priscilla left the casino, night had crept in. But the parking lot was well lit. Brumley had no trouble seeing her as she walked to her silver Toyota Highlander. She climbed in, started the engine and put it in gear. She drove slowly through the lot. Brumley followed at a distance.

The detective woke up with a pounding headache, which he blamed on too much bourbon. He hadn't planned to finish the bottle when he went back to the office. Now awake, he realized he'd spent the night there. He ran a hand through his disheveled hair. From a desk drawer, he pulled out a green bottle of Polo and slapped some of the cologne on his chubby cheeks. He left his office and walked two blocks to the Fuel Stop coffee bar where he ordered a cup of hot, black coffee. Armed with the drink, he returned to his office. An hour later, fueled by the coffee, he felt better. His headache was gone. But he soon felt nagged by a concern, one he needed to address.

Thirty minutes later, he pulled his truck into a weed-filled, pot-holed, asphalt lot south of Elmwood's Mississippi River bridge. The lot adjoined the now defunct dry docks on the Mississippi River shore. He spotted Robbie Glenn. The long-haired, hawk-nosed man sat in a blue Lincoln Navigator. Brumley had called him and asked to meet. Robbie had agreed.

Brumley exited his truck and approached Robbie, who motioned for the private investigator to climb in. "I hope this is worth my time," Robbie said as Brumley settled into the passenger seat. The car smelled of marijuana and cheap beer.

"You know it's worth it."

"Because I'm your informant," Robbie said, grinning through crumbling teeth, revealing his meth addiction.

"You're a drug dealer," Brumley said. "And I need some information."

"What's it worth?" Robbie asked. He'd been in and out of prison over the years on drug distribution and possession charges. Robbie claimed he'd beat his addiction to meth. Brumley didn't buy it. He'd seen enough drug addicts.

Brumley pulled a $100 bill from his wallet. Robbie shook his head. "Come on man, I'm taking a risk just meeting with your sorry ass." Brumley pulled out another $100 bill.

"Take it or leave it," Brumley said.

"I'll take it," said Robbie, grabbing the cash. "What information do you want?"

"I need to know if Priscilla Presson sought someone to kill her husband?"

"You talkin' about that holier-than-thou preacher?"

"Yep. I've heard a rumor that Priscilla Presson wanted to kill him because he cheated on her."

"I heard that too. People say a lot of shit."

"Is it true?"

"Hell no."

"You sure?"

"I'd know if that bitch had wanted to put a hit on that bastard. Course, from what I hear, that preacher will be doing time. So, why kill him?"

"Yeah. Well, you never know," Brumley said.

"Would I lie?"

Brumley laughed. "I won't answer that."

Chapter Fifty-One

Fall felt far away in mid-September with the area blanketed in heat and humidity. Connor and Rachel ate turkey and Swiss paninis at Smooth Buns. Seated at a table wedged into a corner, they watched lunchtime customers crowd into the downtown bakery and eatery. Rachel noted with satisfaction that she and Connor had arrived ahead of most of the noontime crowd.

Connor spotted Harold Presson paying for a to-go order at the counter. "This is the first time I've seen him in weeks."

"He's been keeping a low profile. Wouldn't you, if you were charged with murder?" Rachel asked.

"He didn't shy away from publicity in the past."

"Well, these days, his attorney seems to be doing most of the talking in Harold's behalf."

Harold Presson finished his transaction and turned to leave with his bagged sandwich and chips order. The preacher spotted the reporters and headed for their table. Worry lines creased his face. To Rachel, he looked worn, buffeted by the legal woes that now defined his life.

"I just wanted to say, 'Thanks,'" Harold said.

"What for?" Connor asked, surprised by the remark.

"Rush tells me you both have done a lot, investigating the murder, trying to find the killer. That's more than the cops and that lazy prosecutor have done. They just want to pin it on me. They're not interested in the truth," grumbled the preacher, his voice strained.

"Well, we just want justice done," Connor said.

"As I've told you, I didn't kill that librarian. Someone else did. My money is on that college president. But, of course, most people won't believe it. They find it hard to think a woman would stab someone. However, to my mind, a woman could do the deed. Particularly, if she is confident she can get away with it."

"You might be right," Rachel replied.

Nodding to the reporters, Harold turned and walked out of the restaurant. He never looked back.

"Did you hear Harold?" Rachel asked.

"That he suspects Olivia Bolton?"

"No. How he sounded?"

"What?"

"Harold Presson's voice. It sounded raspy."

"Oh, God. You think he's the one trying to blackmail Olivia now?"

"Maybe."

"But then, are you suggesting the cops are right, that he's a murderer?"

"No. I think someone could have framed him, possibly Olivia," Rachel said. "But I also believe Harold could have decided he'd blackmail the college president, particularly if he assumed she framed him for the murder."

"This all seems too mixed up to me."

"It's no less plausible than any other theory right now," Rachel insisted.

Just then, Smooth Buns owners Truman and Oliver interrupted the conversation. "You two look deep in thought. I saw you talking to the preacher," Oliver said as he and his husband Truman eyed the reporters.

"You think he did it?" Truman asked. The restaurant owner, Rachel thought, looked as sharp as ever, outfitted in custom jeans, designer shirt and alligator-skin boots.

"I still have my doubts," Connor said. "Harold suspects Olivia Bolton."

"The college president? I don't see that being the case," Oliver said. His grease-stained T-shirt, fraying jeans and dirty tennis shoes contrasted with his partner's stylish image.

"But we do have to tattle a little," Truman said.

"What about?" Rachel asked.

"Well, Olivia and Harold Presson's wife had lunch together here yesterday."

"I didn't know they knew each other that well," Connor remarked.

"No. That's the thing," Truman said. "We've never seen them in here together before."

"Separately, they've eaten here. Just not together," Oliver added.

"We couldn't hear them. But they seemed to be having an intense discussion," Truman said.

"And, one other thing. They each paid for their meal and then left separately," Oliver said.

"Olivia left first," Truman recalled.

"Why would they be meeting?" Connor asked.

"Maybe they were discussing the whole murder thing and the blackmail," Oliver suggested.

"What if they were partners in crime?" Rachel questioned.

"Are you serious?" Truman asked.

"Think about it. Priscilla Presson wants to frame her cheating husband for murder. Olivia Bolton wants to kill her blackmailer, Erica Stark. So, they conspire together."

"That's one hell of a theory," Oliver said, shaking his head.

"It might not be so farfetched," Connor said. "It makes sense that Priscilla would desire to get revenge on her husband. She could have convinced Olivia to murder the librarian."

"But how would she know that Erica blackmailed Olivia?" Truman questioned.

"I don't know," Connor said. "She had to know that her husband was being extorted. So, maybe she suspected Erica Stark blackmailed others. We know she hired a private investigator to get the dirt on her husband. Maybe she paid him to look for other possible blackmail victims. Once she had information on Olivia, she approached her and the two plotted the crime."

"You should write a mystery novel," Truman said. "It's one hell of a plot."

"Or maybe it's just fantasy," Rachel sighed.

"We need to talk to Priscilla," Connor said.

"What about the private investigator?" Rachel asked.

"I've talked to him, but we need to question him again. What is it he's not telling us?"

"All you've got is questions," Truman observed.

"You're right," Connor said.

"However, there's one thing you're not questioning," Oliver said.

"What's that?" Rachel asked.

"The food here. You don't seem to have any questions about the meals."

"No, we don't. There's nothing to question on this menu," Rachel said, grinning. "It's all good."

Chapter Fifty—Two

John Brumley sat in Rush Johnson's majestic office. He'd previously emailed his report to the lawyer, outlining his investigation of Priscilla Presson. The private investigator knew Rush had read the report because the attorney had mentioned the findings when he scheduled the meeting. The investigator didn't bother trying to impress Rush. Brumley showed up in a Jackson Browne T-shirt, worn jeans, scuffed Tecovas boots and his favorite Stetson.

Rush eyed the investigator the way he would a trial witness whose testimony he wanted to carefully examine. Brumley knew that look. He'd been on the witness stand himself a time or two. He didn't like being grilled by anyone, especially a lawyer. But he put up with it. Afterall, it meant he'd get paid.

"So, you didn't find any evidence that tied Priscilla Presson to the murder of Erica Stark?" Rush asked.

"No. There were plenty of rumors, but none of them checked out."

"You wrote in your report that you had a confidential source."

"Yes."

"You trust him?"

"I wouldn't go that far. But I would say I know when he's lying. He told me Priscilla Presson didn't hire anyone to kill that librarian and frame the preacher. I believe him."

"That's too bad. I was hoping to somehow tie her to the murder."

"Would Harold let you cast suspicion on Priscilla?"

"There's no love lost between the two of them. All that holding hands stuff is just for show. You could say things in that household are pretty frosty. Harold's sleeping in one of the guest rooms."

"I'm not surprised. She strikes me as someone you don't want to cross."

"Your investigation did surprise me in one way."

"What's that?"

178

"Priscilla Presson spent a lot of time at the casino."

"Yeah, spying on Judge Wachter."

"I wonder why?"

"From what I discovered, the judge is a habitual gambler. And, he's lost a lot of money."

"Do you think Erica Stark knew that and blackmailed him?"

"Don't know. It certainly would have been odd because the judge chairs the library board. He dealt regularly with Erica. Would he have stayed on the board knowing that she blackmailed him?"

"Good question. But if she did blackmail him, it would provide a powerful incentive for murder. Not to mention, what better way to cover up your crime than by framing Harold Presson who had publicly feuded with Erica Stark."

"I can't argue with your theory," Brumley said. "You want me to tail the judge?"

"Not now. I don't want to piss him off, at least not yet. I have other clients I have to defend in his court," Rush said, handing a check to the investigator.

Brumley looked approvingly at the check. "Nice doing business with you," he said, casting a brief smile at the lawyer.

Rush rose from his chair and ushered the private eye toward the door. "Do me a favor?"

"What's that. Don't breathe a word of your investigation to anyone."

"Of course, not. Why would I?"

"Because, Mr. Brumley, I know you like to talk."

"Not if it might lose me future business," the investigator replied.

"Glad to hear it," Rush said as Brumley exited the office.

Once outside, Brumley looked at the check again: $5,000 plus another $1,000 in expenses. Time to celebrate. He took out a cigar and lit it. Then, he walked back to his downtown office, a huge grin stretching his fat face.

◆ ◆ ◆

Two hours later, Rush dined at The Port restaurant with Connor and Rachel. Connor had phoned the attorney with new information. Rush had responded that he also had new information. They agreed lunch should be on the menu too.

Everyone from realtors to downtown shop owners frequented the old brick building, with its worn walls and first-floor antique windows that looked out at the floodwall just yards away. This day, the place was packed. Rush, Connor and Rachel squeezed into a corner, taking the last available table.

While they dined on barbecued shrimp flatbread, they reviewed the murder case. Rush disclosed what Brumley had learned: Priscilla Presson spied on Judge Michael Wachter. Connor and Rachel revealed what they had heard from Oliver and Truman: Olivia Bolton and Priscilla Presson had conferred at Smooth Buns.

None of them could be sure what it all meant, but they had suspicions. "I believe Priscilla suspects Wachter may have killed Erica and framed Harold," Rush said. "That scenario has merit, given that the judge found the incriminating paddle. He could have placed it there."

"But how would Harold's wife have known about the judge?" Connor asked.

"I don't know," Rush replied. "And, now you tell me that Priscilla and Olivia met."

"Priscilla and Olivia could have conspired to kill the librarian and frame Harold for the murder," Rachel suggested.

"But then why would Priscilla spend time tracking the judge?" Rush asked.

"Don't know," Rachel said.

"I think we need to dig into the judge's life. Could Erica have blackmailed him?" Connor questioned.

"But what would she have on the judge?" Rachel wondered.

"Brumley told me that Wachter has gambled away a lot of money," Rush said.

"I can't see where that fact would be enough to blackmail the judge," Connor said.

"The judge is a public figure. Such news could be a major embarrassment," Rush said.

"What if it was something else?" Connor asked.

"I don't know, but maybe Priscilla found out and told Olivia," Rush said. "It makes sense that Olivia, who admits the librarian blackmailed her, would desire to know who else was a target."

"Or Olivia and Priscilla are looking to frame the judge if it becomes clear to law enforcement and the prosecutor that Harold Presson didn't commit murder," Rachel said.

"We plan on talking to Priscilla," Connor said. "We need to find out what she knows."

"And you believe she'll tell you?"

"Not sure about that, but I know we have to ask her," Connor said.

"You need to talk to your police detective friend," the attorney replied. "Maybe you can convince the police to reopen their murder investigation."

"I can't work miracles," Connor said. "But I'll see what he says. Just don't hold your breath. The police seem sold on your client as the murderer."

"I know, but it just doesn't add up," Rush said. "What does add up is this lunch," he added, looking at the bill.

"We can pay for our meals," Rachel said.

"No. I've got this. It's all part of the expenses associated with this case."

"And your client will pay the bill," Connor said.

"No doubt," Rush said.

"I hope he's getting his money's worth," Rachel remarked.

"I'm certain he is. He'll know so when I get him off," Rush said, leaving cash on the table.

Chapter Fifty—Three

The interview occurred in late September. Priscilla was reluctant to talk at first. It took some convincing. Brumley proved key to getting her to open up. And the private investigator didn't do it out of the goodness of his heart. He was bribed. Rush Johnson gifted a box of premium Padron cigars to him.

On this afternoon, Priscilla sat behind the desk in Brumley's downtown office. The private investigator stood off to the side, smoking a Padron. Connor and Rachel sat across from Priscilla, who showed up attired in a frilly white blouse and black pants. Sunglasses topped her straight black hair.

"So, I understand you're investigating Michael," she began. "That's why you want to talk to me, right?"

"Yes," Rachel said. "Judge Wachter seems to be tied up in this murder case. Afterall, he found the fraternity paddle that led police to suspect your husband killed Erica Stark."

"And we know that you recently spied on the judge. You were seen following him at the casino," Connor said. "The question is why?"

"You do know that he has a gambling problem?"

"So, we've heard," Rachel said.

"Well, I believe that wagering problem left him open to being blackmailed."

"You think the librarian would have blackmailed the head of her library board?" Connor questioned.

"I'm sure it sounds unlikely to you, but I know something about that woman. She was a piece of work."

"We know Harold and his group didn't like her," Rachel observed.

"I don't give a damn about all that."

"So, what do you know?"

"This is off the record?"

"If it has to be," Rachel said.

"It has to be."

"Okay. Tell us," Connor said.

"Harold cheated on me. You know that. But I didn't just sit around, waiting for him to come home. I found companionship elsewhere. I found it with Michael."

A surprised look crossed Rachel's face. "You dated the judge?"

"I wouldn't call it dating exactly. I mean we didn't go out in public, except to the casino. And, then I would hang out in the bar while he gambled. Nobody really saw us together. Mostly, I went to his place. Stayed late. Had sex. Went home."

"Harold didn't know about this?" Connor asked.

"No. He was too busy shagging that stripper."

"How did you hook up with the judge?" Rachel asked.

"He approached me at the casino bar, the one upstairs with a view of the river. I was drinking Chardonnay alone. He bought me a second glass and then another. I was feeling lonely. He drove me back to his place and we made love. Then, he took me back to the casino so I could get my car. Two days later, we met up again and soon we were together two or three times a week."

"Did he know who you were?" Rachel asked.

"You mean that I was married to the preacher who led the book-banning effort? Yeah. I told him."

"That didn't bother him?"

"No. He rather liked the fact that he was screwing Harold's wife."

"So, are you still seeing the judge?" Rachel questioned.

"No. I broke it off when Harold was arrested for murder. I was afraid the press would find out about my affair. I didn't want to be the subject of rampant gossip. And, to be honest, I didn't want people to feel sorry for Harold."

"You said you know something about the librarian," Connor interrupted.

"Michael and I were discussing the library one night, and I said I admired Erica for standing up to my husband and his band of loud-mouths."

"Michael told me that Erica fooled a lot of people, that she wasn't a nice person. He said she cost him a lot of money."

"Did he say, how?" Connor asked.

183

"He just said Erica Stark knew how to monetize secrets," Priscilla replied.

"Do you believe he was talking about blackmail?" Rachel asked.

"I wasn't sure what he meant at the time. But after Harold revealed he'd been blackmailed by that librarian, I thought about what Michael said. I believe he was saying that she blackmailed him."

"So, you didn't know until recently that Harold was making blackmail payments to Erica?" Connor asked.

"Of course not. Harold took care of the finances. I didn't know about the monthly payments."

"Could Erica have known something else about the judge besides the gambling problem?" Rachel wondered.

"Maybe. But I don't know what it would be. Michael always had a lot of cash on hand. Of course, he'd lose the money gambling. Max out his credit cards. But then he'd turn around and pay off the balances. I figured he made a lot of money as a judge. He bought me a diamond necklace. I kept it at his place. I didn't want Harold to see it."

"You mentioned all the cash. Do you think the judge could have been taking bribes?" Connor asked.

"I can't imagine that was the case," Priscilla said. "You seem to be grasping at straws."

"Maybe so," Connor remarked.

"Is Michael close to anyone in the legal profession?"

"Well, I know it wasn't uncommon for him to take phone calls from Bob Benson late at night."

"The public defender?"

"I think so. I know Michael said he was some defense lawyer. They were always talking cases. Michael said Benson didn't want to go to trial, loved to make deals for his clients."

"Why did you meet with Olivia Bolton?" Rachel asked, changing the subject.

"How did you know?"

"You met in Smooth Buns. People saw you there," Rachel replied.

"After Olivia revealed publicly that Erica Stark had blackmailed her, I wanted to reach out and let her know what I knew about Michael."

"Or maybe Olivia killed that librarian and you conspired to frame your husband for the murder," Connor said.

"Hold on! I agreed to talk to you about Michael, not to be accused of killing Erica. You print one word of such an accusation and I'll sue you for libel."

"We're just covering all the bases," Rachel said, trying to ease the tension in the room. "There is some thought that Olivia might have murdered the librarian."

"But now you're focused on Michael?"

"Well, yes," Connor said.

"Anything else you can tell us?" Rachel asked.

"No. That's about it."

"You don't sound all that concerned about your husband, yet you are willing to entertain the possibility that the judge killed Erica," Connor said.

"I didn't say that. I said I believe that librarian blackmailed Michael. That doesn't mean Harold didn't stab her. For all I know, he could have done it."

"Then, why stay with him?" Rachel asked.

"I loved Harold once. I'm not going to abandon him now. At the same time, I'm not going to shed tears over his predicament. If a jury convicts him, so be it. I just want this case to be over."

"So, you can go on with your life?" Rachel questioned.

"Yes, that's right. It's my life I'm concerned about, not his or Michael's. Are we done here?"

"Yes," Connor said.

"And you won't quote me on any of this?"

"You've got it."

Brumley ushered the reporters to the door. "You want me to do some digging?" he asked.

"For free?" Connor asked.

"Who are you kidding?"

"That's what I figured. I don't think our editor would approve such an expense."

"Suit yourself," Brumley said as the reporters left the building. He turned toward Priscilla. "That went well," he said, cigar smoke floating in the air like tiny clouds.

Chapter Fifty–Four

A towboat pushed a fleet of grain-filled barges south on the Mississippi, headed for New Orleans. A late afternoon breeze cooled Connor and Adam as they stood on the riverfront steps on the river side of the floodwall. Two hours after hearing from Priscilla, Connor relayed the information to Adam. The veteran reporter didn't reveal his source.

"You're telling me that Erica Stark blackmailed Judge Wachter and now you believe he may be the murderer?"

"That's right."

The police detective laughed. "You've got to be kidding. You've come up with this theory based on the testimony of an unnamed source."

"A reliable source."

"So, you say. But I'm not buying it. Judge Wachter has a sterling reputation in court. Even the defense lawyers say he's a straight shooter. And just what secret would provide blackmail material?"

"Well, our source says the judge has a gambling problem."

"That's old news. Within the police department, it's common knowledge that Wachter likes to gamble. But that's not a crime. It's his business how he spends his money. He's not breaking any law."

"Maybe he has another secret that made him a blackmail victim."

"Oh, I've got to hear this. What would that be?"

"The judge accepted bribes."

"Don't say that too loudly. You might find yourself the subject of a slander suit. If he were taking bribes, I think I would have heard about it. There would be rumors. As a detective, you'd be surprised the rumors that come my way. There's not been any suggestion of impropriety on the part of Judge Wachter. You are so convinced Harold is innocent that you've gone off the deep end, trying to pin this murder on anyone else, anyone including a sitting judge. Ridiculous!"

186

"I admit I have no evidence that he murdered Erica. I just said it's a possibility."

"I hope you're not planning to run this story in the paper."

"Not yet. I don't have concrete evidence."

"No, you don't."

"I just wanted you to know that my source claims the judge implied Erica Stark blackmailed him. I thought you'd want to look into it."

"I'm not questioning the judge based on an unnamed source. I need something more solid. I have to know your source first," the detective insisted.

"I can't do that," Connor said.

"Even you admit that your source has not provided you any information that the judge murdered the librarian. And don't you think that if Erica had blackmailed the judge, he would have revealed that to the police after she was stabbed to death?"

"Not if he was doing something criminal," Connor responded.

"Well, if you find solid evidence, come talk to me. But I don't think there's anything to find. Nice chatting with you," Adam said, gazing at the sunlight dancing on the river. He adjusted his tie and turned westward. Taking long strides, he stepped back through the floodgate and headed for his unmarked car parked on River Street.

Back at the office, Connor updated Rachel on his conversation with Adam. "Too bad," Rachel said. "We could have used Adam's detective skills."

"Yeah, well, we'll just have to go it alone."

"And just how are we going to do that?"

"We need to study the cases the judge has handled. Maybe there's something fishy there."

"That's going to take some time," Rachel observed. "How far back are you going to go?"

"Maybe five years. We'll have to look at both civil and criminal cases."

"I don't think Lansmon will let us do it on work time."

"You're right. We'll have to do it after hours."

"You sure know how to sweep a woman off her feet," Rachel laughed. "Talk about a surefire date night. Court cases and Chardonnay."

Connor smiled. *God, he loved her.*

They spent the next several weeks going through the electronic records of hundreds of court cases in which Judge Wachter presided. And, they began to see a pattern. Something suspicious. The judge suspended imposition of prison sentences in many cases, allowing criminal defendants to have their records wiped clean as long as they paid fines and completed probation without a hitch. The cases varied, most often involving burglaries and even simple assaults where the victims weren't seriously injured. None involved murder or rape suspects. All of them had one thing in common: Bob Benson. The public defender represented all of those defendants.

"Why did the judge suspend imposition of sentence in so many cases?" Rachel asked as she and Connor scrolled through the state's database of court cases one evening at Connor's apartment.

"It makes you wonder," Connor said. "And why do all these cases involve Benson?"

"I know public defenders are often overworked. Too many cases. Too little time to really defend their clients. Getting clients to agree to a deal makes more sense than going to trial and risking a conviction."

"True. But Benson isn't the only public defender."

"Yes, but the records show that Benson primarily handled suspects facing lesser criminal charges. Maybe it's as simple as that."

"Or that Benson and Judge Wachter had some sort of under-the-table agreement."

"You mean that Benson bribed the judge?" Rachel asked.

"Not necessarily. Maybe the defendants bribed the judge," Connor theorized.

"Even if the defendants came up with the money for the judge, it would have had to involve their attorney."

"Yes. I don't think it could have happened without Benson's involvement."

"You realize what you are saying, Connor?"

"Both Wachter and Benson would have motives to kill Erica Stark."

"One or the other could have done it."

"Or both of them," Connor said.

"That's all we need, another suspect," sighed Rachel, reaching for the bottle of Chardonnay on the kitchen table.

Chapter Fifty–Five

Stacks of case files lay atop Bob Benson's gun-metal-gray desk in his cramped office. He and two other public defenders, representing indigent defendants, shared office space in one corner of a former bank turned office building in downtown Elmwood. Connor gazed around the room, noticing everything from the dusty tiled floor to the brown water stains on the suspended ceiling. Dingy green walls shadowed the office with a feeling of despair.

Benson grinned. "Nice place isn't it? State lawmakers seem to always be slashing our budget. Spending tax dollars to defend criminal suspects isn't high on their funding list."

"It seems that way," Connor agreed, taking a seat in a well-worn wooden chair facing Benson, who sat behind his desk.

"The public defender's system statewide needs more lawyers. We're overworked and underpaid," Benson groused. "The system has less than 400 attorneys who handle some 80,000 cases a year. At any one time, I'm juggling 100 to 200 cases. There's no such thing as a speedy trial. Most of my clients spend months stuck in jail waiting for their cases to go to court. It's a damn mess. But you're not here to hear me bitch."

"No."

"You said you wanted to ask me about Judge Wachter's possible ties to the murder of that librarian. I have no idea what you're pursuing, but I agreed to talk to you more out of curiosity."

"Yes, I appreciate you seeing me. The newspaper has been looking into the murder and it's impossible to ignore the fact that the judge found the fraternity paddle that points toward Harold Presson as the murderer. Doesn't it seem just a little too convenient?"

"I don't see how. Judge Wachter chairs the library board," Benson said. News reports indicate the judge had a meeting at the library the day that he found the paddle. Are you suggesting the judge framed that preacher?"

"That thought had occurred to me, although the police discounted that idea."

"You believe the judge framed Harold Presson because he criticized library officials for not banning books?" Benson asked.

"No."

"So, what's the connection? The news reports indicated that police found a bloody shoe in the pastor's office. You aren't suggesting the judge put the shoe there?"

"I'm not suggesting anything," Connor said. "What I do know is that I've spoken to a source who says the judge implied that Erica Stark blackmailed him."

"What?" Benson asked, a surprised look on his face.

"An individual who knows the judge said he told her that Erica knew how to 'monetize secrets.' She interpreted that to mean that the librarian blackmailed him."

"What secret would she have known concerning the judge?"

"I was hoping you could tell me."

"Well, I have no idea. Look, the lawyers I know respect the judge. He's fair and you can't say that about every judge."

"We've learned the judge has a gambling problem."

"So what? Gambling's not a crime. I know he gambles, but it's his money. How he spends it is none of my concern, nor should it be yours."

"Maybe it wasn't about gambling. Maybe it was about bribes."

"Are you suggesting the judge took bribes?"

"Well, here's the thing. I've reviewed numerous court cases going back years. In a lot of cases, Judge Wachter suspended imposition of prison sentences and placed them on probation. And, what's even more surprising, you were the defense attorney on all those cases."

"As a public defender, my job is to get the best deals for my clients. I'm proud of getting suspended sentences for them. If they stayed out of trouble, they wouldn't be saddled with a criminal conviction and could go on and live productive lives. We're not talking about people charged with murder. We're talking about people who faced minor charges, who hung around with the wrong crowd, who didn't have good role models at home; people who just needed a break in life, not thrown in jail."

"They didn't have to bribe the judge to get let off with such a light sentence?" Connor asked.

"Hell no. Do you believe I would counsel my clients to pay bribes?"

"Well, would you?"

"That's nuts. You better not go throwing such an accusation my way. If you do, I'll sue your ass and that damn newspaper too. You better watch your back."

"Are you threatening me?" Connor asked.

"No. But in a war of words, I'd side with the judge. He won't let you smear his good name."

"Thanks for the advice," Connor said, rising to leave.

"As a public defender I hate to say it, but the prosecution is right this time. The evidence points to the preacher as the murderer. Asking all these questions will just muddy the water. Justice won't be served," Benson said. "Not one bit."

Connor didn't reply. He turned and walked outside where a blue sky and soothing early October temperatures embraced him.

Connor returned to the office just in time to field a call from Judge Wachter. "What the hell are you doing?" the judge yelled.

"What are you talking about?"

"You know perfectly well what I'm talking about."

"I assume you are referring to my conversation with Bob Benson."

"Of course. Bob called me and told me about your accusations of bribery."

"It wasn't an accusation. It was a question."

"You asked a dedicated public defender if I was taking bribes from his clients in exchange for favorable sentences. That's slander. I'll throw your ass in jail if you make such an accusation again."

"I haven't broken the law. It just seems convenient that you found a key piece of evidence that points to Harold Presson, who has blasted the library, its staff and the library board regarding the housing of books he views as obscene."

"Are you accusing me of framing him for the murder of Erica Stark?"

"I'm just wondering if there was some secret about you that allowed the librarian to blackmail you."

"You're off your rocker, Connor. I'll sue you and the newspaper if you continue making such scandalous allegations," the judge shouted into the phone. "You're not only attacking me, you're soiling the reputation of Erica Stark, who was my friend. I won't stand for it," he said, slamming down the phone.

Rachel, seated at her desk, overheard the shouting. "The judge sounded pissed," she said.

"Yeah," Connor sighed. "I screwed up. I never imagined Bob Benson would recount our conversation to the judge."

"Do you think Judge Wachter will come after you?"

"I don't know. Maybe he just wanted to scare me, see if we'd drop our investigation."

"I guess we'll find out soon," Rachel said.

A half hour later, Dan Steele barged into Lansmon's office. The publisher's face was red. He slammed the door. The entire newsroom staff could hear Dan yelling. After about five minutes, Lansmon called Connor and Rachel into his office. The publisher glared at the reporters. "What were you thinking, Connor? You accused a respected judge of bribery."

"We were investigating the possibility that the judge might be involved in the murder of Ms. Stark," Rachel said.

"Behind my back," Lansmon groused.

"We were doing it on our own time," Connor said.

"You didn't tell me because you thought I would have told you stop," Lansmon said, raising his voice.

"We needed to see if there was any evidence to suggest that Erica Stark might have blackmailed the judge over a possible bribery scheme."

"And do you have such evidence?" Lansmon asked.

"Nothing concrete," Connor replied.

"Exactly. You pissed off a judge for no reason," the editor said.

"We were just doing our jobs," Rachel insisted. "We have doubts that Harold Presson killed the librarian."

"Your job is to report the facts, not go around slandering people," Dan scolded. "I ought to fire you both. The only reason you're not sacked is because your editor pointed to the good work you've done in the past. But this investigation is over."

"What?" Connor asked.

"You heard Dan," Lansmon said. "Your inquiry is over. If there's any evidence that Harold Presson is innocent, then his attorney, Rush Johnson, should disclose it in court. I want you two to focus on covering your beats. I want stories on city hall and the schools. Now get the hell out of here."

Heads down, Connor and Rachel left the editor's office and returned to their desks, their every step watched by their colleagues in the newsroom. "That's that," Rachel said. "We should have figured Bob Benson would go straight to the judge."

"True. But I'm not about to give up."

"You heard what Lansmon said. He told us we can't investigate."

"Well, we need to talk to Rush," Connor said. "We need to let him know about the suspended imposition of sentences. Maybe he can pursue this."

"Let's hope so."

"If there's one thing I know, Rush isn't one to back down," Connor said.

Chapter Fifty–Six

Darkness had descended on Elmwood by the time Connor and Rachel met with Rush. The attorney unlocked the front door of the downtown building and let them in. They were alone. He led them upstairs to his second-story office with its view of the river, now a ribbon of blackness illuminated by the white lights on the nearby bridge.

Connor and Rachel got to the point, explaining that both their editor and publisher had halted the investigation. Rush, still dressed in suit and tie, listened as they detailed what they had learned; that Judge Wachter had suspended imposition of sentences in numerous cases involving clients of public defender Bob Benson. When they finished, silence took hold for several seconds.

"Wow. That's some story," Rush said, breaking the silence. "You're suggesting that a sitting judge and a defense lawyer are involved in a pay-for-leniency scheme."

"We think it's possible," Connor said. "What do you think?"

"Hmm, I need to check it out. Rumors have circulated in legal circles about the number of suspended imposition of sentences handed down by Judge Wachter. But I don't recall anyone suggesting that there was anything illegal. The assumption made was that Bob Benson did a good job for his clients."

"But what if it was a bribery scheme?" Rachel asked. "What if Erica Stark found out about it and blackmailed the judge?"

"You're suggesting that the judge did a great acting job; that while he praised her, he secretly plotted to kill her."

"Yes," Connor said.

"The trouble is there is no proof," Rush pointed out.

"We need to find former clients of Mr. Benson who would admit they paid a bribe for a suspended sentence," Rachel said.

"That could be a tall order, but it's the only option," Rush said. "I'll make some calls. If I find out anything, I'll let you know. I'm sorry you both are in trouble at the paper. Will you still be able to cover the court case?"

"Our editor said we could," Connor replied. "But we're on thin ice right now. We can't mess up again. We can't ask about anything not in the court files or publicly revealed by the police or stated by the prosecutor or you."

"Well, I guess I'll need to find something quotable to say," Rush laughed.

◆ ◆ ◆

By mid-October, Rush had reviewed numerous electronic court records. He singled out 10 cases involving burglaries, low-level drug possession and assaults. He phoned Brumley, who eagerly agreed to track down the individuals who had served probation and thanks to suspended sentences had no criminal convictions. Rush silently questioned if any of those people would admit to paying bribes. But Brumley seemed confident he'd get at least some of them to talk.

For a private investigator whose business was built on spying on cheating husbands and wives, the chance to do other detective work was downright appealing. Not to mention, the pay was good.

Seated in his downtown office, Brumley clutched a half-smoked cigar as he looked over the list of names provided by Rush. All of them resided in Elmwood. Five had been arrested on home burglary charges, three on charges of possessing small amounts of meth, and two for assaults that occurred outside Jello jazz club.

Brumley read the case files. The 10 people singled out by Rush had one thing in common. They all had cleaned up their act. As a result of the judge's actions, their past misdeeds didn't show up as criminal convictions. Maybe, thought Brumley, justice had been served. One question swirled in his mind. *If they had paid bribes would any of them admit it?*

Over the next week, Brumley tracked down their current addresses. In two cases, he discovered listed addresses were vacant lots. When he did show up at their homes, most of them refused to talk to him, often slamming doors in his face. None of that bothered the stout private investigator. He pushed on, hoping at least one of the individuals would talk to him.

On a windy, rainy Thursday, Brumley, sporting his cowboy hat, walked into Fuel Stop, a Main Street coffee shop in an old brick building that once housed a bakery. The rich aroma of coffee beans greeted him. Brumley spotted owner Johnny Rhodes behind the counter where he was filling a customer's latte order. The private investigator identified Rhodes from an old mug shot. Rhodes had been arrested for burglarizing a convenience store a decade ago when he was 21. Now in his early 30s, he had married his high school sweetheart. Two years ago, he opened the coffee shop. By all accounts, the blond, pony-tailed Rhodes had turned his life around. *But would he open up about his past brush with the law? Brumley wasn't sure.*

The private investigator waited for the female customer to leave. The clock on the wall proclaimed 10 a.m. Brumley had chosen that time to visit the coffee shop, assuming the morning drinkers would be long gone. The woman paid for her latte and exited the shop. Once outside, she opened her red umbrella as it continued to rain. She took a sip of her coffee and proceeded down the street. Brumley was now alone with Rhodes.

"Can I help you?" Rhodes asked.

"My name's John Brumley. I'm a private investigator. I'm looking into some dealings involving Judge Michael Wachter."

"What does that have to do with me?" Rhodes asked, wiping the counter with a towel.

"You were arrested on a burglary charge 10 years ago and given a suspended sentence. After probation, your record was wiped clean."

"Yes. I changed my ways. I'm not the person I was back then," Rhodes said, anger rising in his voice.

"I'm not interested in your past other than your interaction with the judge."

"What interaction?"

"There's been a rumor that Judge Wachter required defendants to pay bribes in exchange for suspended sentences," Brumley said.

"You're asking if I paid a bribe?"

"Exactly."

"Why should I tell you?"

"Because there's a possibility that he was blackmailed by librarian Erica Stark and that he then killed her and framed the preacher."

"You think the judge murdered that woman?"

"Maybe. I've been hired to look into whether the judge took bribes."

197

"Who are you working for?"

"Rush Johnson, the attorney."

"Isn't he defending that pastor?"

"Yes."

"So, you think the pastor might be innocent?"

"I don't know. Again, I'm just looking into the actions of Judge Wachter. What Rush Johnson does with the information is his business."

"I'm not saying anything on the record," Rhodes said.

"Well, tell me this. Off the record, would I be lying if I said that Judge Wachter took a bribe in exchange for a suspended sentence?"

"You said it. No, I won't dispute that statement."

"You must have paid him a bunch of money."

"Several thousand. Again, that's off the record."

"Did the judge personally ask you for a bribe?"

"No way."

"So, I assume your attorney transmitted the demand?"

"Seems logical."

"You're not denying it?"

"No. But again you didn't hear it from me. I don't want to relive my past. I'm a respectable businessman now."

"Still, if it turns out Judge Wachter committed murder, you would want him to be arrested and prosecuted?"

"You bet. I wouldn't want him to get away with killing anyone."

"Glad to hear it. No one should be above the law," Brumley said.

"I totally agree."

"One other thing. Are you aware of others who paid bribes to the judge?"

"Not directly. When I was in jail, some fellow inmates said they planned to pay bribes to Judge Wachter for suspended sentences."

"And you didn't disclose this to the authorities?"

"Hell no. I wanted probation. I wasn't about to say anything to jeopardize my chance to get out of jail."

"Got it."

"Don't you judge me," Rhodes demanded.

"I'm not. Like I said, I'm looking for the truth."

"Well, now you know it."

"Thanks," Brumley said. "By the way, I need a coffee to go."

"It will cost you."

"I didn't expect a free drink."

"Good. This isn't a charity. It's a business," Rhodes said.

"I'm glad you turned your life around."

"Yeah. Me too. I just hope it's not going to be turned upside down."

Chapter Fifty–Seven

The sun appeared over the horizon as Dennis Bertrand brush stroked the canvas set upon a wooden easel perched on a concrete step on the river side of the floodwall. He faced southeast as he painted the rising sun, the light streaming across the river bridge and shimmering along the swift flowing river. Bertrand, dressed in scruffy jeans, long sleeve shirt and sporting a Peaky Blinder cap atop his red curly hair, brushed bright yellow and red acrylic paint across the top of the canvas where it clashed with the emerging blue sky he had just painted.

Embraced by the chill in the air, Brumley sauntered over. He'd phoned Bertrand's downtown art gallery the previous day. Dennis had said he was too busy to talk then, but that the private investigator could visit with him early the next morning on the riverfront.

A prolific artist who had painted numerous murals on the sides of Elmwood's old brick buildings and regularly spruced up concrete pavement with temporary chalk artwork, the now 58-year-old Elmwood man had been arrested on an assault charge 15 years ago. Judge Wachter suspended imposition of sentence and placed him on probation for two years.

Brumley felt sympathy for Bertrand. Police said Bertrand assaulted a man who had threatened to deface his marching band mural on the side of an Elmwood music store. Now, the private investigator hoped Bertrand would disclose if he paid the judge a bribe.

Bertrand heard steps and turned. Brumley introduced himself. Bertrand grunted and turned back to his painting.

"I'm looking into a situation involving Judge Wachter," Brumley began.

"What kind of situation?"

"Bribery."

"What are you talking about?"

"I've tracked down a former criminal defendant who says the judge gave him a suspended sentence in exchange for a bribe,"

Brumley explained.

"What does that have to do with me?" Dennis asked, his back turned to Brumley.

"Well, you received a suspended sentence from the same judge regarding your assault case."

"And you believe I bribed the judge."

"Well, did you pay Judge Wachter?"

"Why should I tell you?"

"I'm not asking you to go on the record. I just need confirmation."

"Why?"

"I'm investigating this matter for Rush Johnson who is defending Harold Presson in that murder case."

"The man charged with killing that librarian?"

"Yes."

"I don't see the connection," Bertrand said, painting thin black lines outlining the riverbanks taking shape on the canvas.

"Well, Rush is exploring the possibility that the judge might have killed the librarian."

"Nonsense."

"Not if the librarian knew about the bribery scheme and black-mailed the judge."

"That's a good story."

"The thing is, you wouldn't want the judge to get away with murder?"

"Of course not. But I don't need the judge and courts to come down on me. A sitting judge has a lot of power."

"Yes, but there's already evidence of his bribery scheme."

"I'm not admitting a thing, but if there were such a scheme you should look at Bob Benson, the public defender."

"I know. He'd have to be involved," Brumley said. "So, do I have confirmation?"

"It depends."

"On what?"

"I'm not stating this publicly."

"Agreed."

"You want confirmation that the judge accepted bribes?" Bertrand asked, turning to face Brumley.

"Yes."

"You got it. But you need to understand, I trusted my attorney. Bob Benson suggested making the payment, said I'd be able to have my record wiped clean after serving probation. Who wouldn't take that deal?"

"I get it. I'm not second guessing your actions. You didn't initiate the bribe."

"That's right, I didn't."

"I appreciate your candor," Brumley said.

"I only opened up about this for one reason."

"Justice?"

"Hell no. I talked to you because Rush Johnson is one of my biggest patrons. He regularly buys my paintings."

"Your large painting of the Mississippi River bridge hangs in Rush's office," Brumley recalled.

"Yes. I've done a lot of paintings of the bridge and the river. There's something magical about that landscape. I never tire of it," Bertrand said, returning his focus to his canvas. Brumley thanked him for his cooperation and headed back through the floodgate as the sun rose higher in the sky.

Big Daddy, an indie rock band, prepared to perform Friday night on the cramped stage at Vinyl Vibes, a Broadway record store and bar. Rachel and Connor showed up just before 9 p.m. The place was packed. The two reporters squeezed their way through the crowd and ordered drinks at the bar: his, an autumn craft beer; hers, a Ginger Collins.

Connor paid for the drinks. At the same time, in a cluttered office at the rear of the building, John Brumley chatted with Parker Davis, the establishment's 42-year-old owner. The balding, thinly built man had been arrested for possession of meth six years earlier. Judge Wachter suspended imposition of sentence. After serving probation, Davis ended up without a conviction. Two years ago, he opened Vinyl Vibes, capitalizing on the renewed popularity of records.

Standing in Parker's office, Brumley suggested Judge Wachter may have secured bribes in exchange for suspended sentences. "You received such a sentence over a drug possession charge," the private investigator said.

"That's ancient history. I served my probation. I have no criminal conviction."

"Because the judge suspended imposition of your sentence."

"Yes, but why are you so interested in the judge's actions?"

Brumley explained that he was investigating the judge on behalf of Rush Johnson and the defense of murder defendant Harold Presson. He detailed the theory that Erica Stark may have discovered the bribery scheme and blackmailed the judge. He added this might have led the judge to murder the librarian. Davis dismissed the idea, questioning why the judge would chair the library board if its director blackmailed him.

"I don't know if all that happened," Brumley said. "But I have confirmed from other former criminal defendants that bribes were paid to the judge in exchange for suspended sentences. I'm asking if you paid a bribe too."

"You think I paid off the judge?" asked Davis, his voice strained with anger.

"Well, did you?"

"Why should I tell you?"

"Because I've done some checking. People tell me you're a stand-up guy, a straight shooter. I believe you overcame your drug habit. And, I suspect you don't want a judge to get away with murder," Brumley said, stopping to catch his breath. "I just want you to be honest."

"And what if I did pay a bribe? Is that Johnson fellow going to come after me in court?"

"No. He is just defending his client on the murder charge. If it turns out the judge committed a crime, I'm confident Rush Johnson will expose it," Brumley told Davis.

"I just don't want my neck on the chopping block," Davis said. "I'm clean. No drugs. I operate a solid business. I don't want any trouble."

"So, you did pay a bribe?"

"Yeah. I mean my attorney talked me into it. I paid the judge $3,000 to get out from under the drug charge. But I won't admit that in court unless compelled to do so."

"Did you also bribe your lawyer?"

"No way. I gave the money to Bob Benson, who told me he gave all the money to the judge. I had no direct dealing with the judge, except in court. The judge never asked for the money himself. Benson handled the matter. But as I told you, I'll deny all of this unless I'm forced to testify in court. I'm not volunteering anything. You got that?"

"Yeah. You're not volunteering anything."

"One other thing."

"What's that?" Brumley asked.

"If this comes out, you tell Rush Johnson I expect him to mount a solid defense for me, and I don't intend to pay for it."

"I'll tell him," Brumley said. The private investigator opened the office door and waded into the crowd at the front of the building as Big Daddy played its first amped-up tune. Seated on chairs wedged against a wall, Connor and Rachel spotted Brumley. Connor waved him over. Brumley sighed. He waddled over, a strained look on his face.

"What are you doing here?" Connor asked.

"Working."

"Are you spying on someone?" Rachel questioned as she spotted the Vinyl Vibes owner glaring in Brumley's direction.

"No. Just asking questions."

"You've been talking to Parker Davis," she said.

"So, what If I have."

"Is he cheating on his wife?"

"No, nothing like that. I'm doing some investigative work for Rush Johnson."

"What work?" Connor asked.

"None of your business."

"It is if you're looking into bribery allegations involving Judge Wachter," Connor said, guessing that Rush might have hired Brumley for just such a job.

"Whoa! What are you talking about?"

"Rachel and I have talked to Rush. We know he's looking into such allegations."

"Why would he do that?"

"To defend that preacher."

"The one charged with murder?"

"Yes."

"How do you know about the bribery allegations?"

"We're the ones that brought the matter to Rush," Rachel said, chiming in.

"Well, I can't go into the details, but I will report soon to Mr. Johnson."

"You can't give us a hint?"

"Not on my life. You're not paying me, Mr. Johnson is. I'm not detailing my findings to you snooping reporters, unless, of course, it's for a fee."

"Sorry. We don't have that kind of money," Rachel said.

"We're not in the business of paying for information," Connor said.

"Yeah. You just want it all free of charge."

"That's right."

"Well, nothing is free," Brumley said. Sweat dripped from his brow as he made his way through the crowd-warmed place and outside into the cool October night. "Damn reporters," he told himself.

Chapter Fifty—Eight

Over the weekend, Brumley listened to the Eagles greatest hits and put together a written report on his investigation. Sunday night, he emailed the report to Rush. Monday morning, Rush called. He told him to stop by his office in an hour.

Brumley showed up 10 minutes early. He didn't want to be late. Besides, he was eager to get paid. A middle-aged, no-nonsense secretary ushered him into Rush's office. He thanked her. Rush, dressed in his favorite high-priced gray suit, greeted him and signaled for Brumley to take a seat. Rush returned to his chair and placed his hands on his imposing desk. "Thanks for coming," Rush said. "I read your report. Wow. I must confess I doubted you'd get anyone to admit to paying the judge."

"Well, they didn't go on the record."

"No matter. Your investigation confirmed that Judge Wachter took bribes."

"What are you going to do now?"

"I'm not entirely sure, but one way or another, I'm going to use this information to help my client. A judge who takes bribes is ripe for blackmail. When Harold's murder case goes to trial, I'll just need to show that the judge had motive to kill Erica Stark."

Brumley spotted the check on the corner of the desk. Rush noticed and grabbed the check. He handed it to the private investigator.

"Nice doing business with you," Brumley said, a wide grin creasing his face. "Oh, by the way, those two snooping reporters saw me the other night at Vinyl Vibes, right after I came out of Parker's office. I didn't tell them anything."

"No worries. I'm planning to talk to those two anyway."

"Why?"

"Because sometimes the best defense starts outside the courtroom."

Connor and Rachel heard the news at lunch. Rush revealed the bribery evidence as they dined at Smooth Buns. "That private investigator came through. We now know that Judge Wachter took bribes in exchange for suspended sentences," Rush said. "Of course, we don't have any of the three former defendants' statements on the record."

"Don't you need them to go public?" Rachel questioned.

"Not just yet. I plan to ask a judge to strike any evidence pertaining to the pledge paddle on the grounds that Judge Wachter is not an unbiased witness. At that point, I can refer to the fact that three former defendants said they bribed him for more lenient sentences."

"But won't the court want to know their names?" Connor asked.

"Yes, but I will simply say that the individuals are afraid to be identified for fear of repercussions from Judge Wachter. Besides, I just need to have the media report on it. That's where you all come in."

"Are you planning to give us Brumley's report?" Rachel asked.

"Yes, I am. But you can't run it until I petition the court for a hearing. Agreed?"

"Agreed," Connor and Rachel said in unison.

"Here's a copy of Brumley's report," Rush said, pulling the lengthy document out of his briefcase. "I marked through the names and any other information that could identify them. I don't want you guys to try to track them down right now."

"What? Don't you trust us?" Rachel asked, pouting for effect.

"I trust you, but you're reporters. You can't help but ask questions. It's in your DNA. I need to control the message if I'm going to properly defend Harold. There's just one thing I have to ask you. Will your boss let you run a story on that report?"

"I think he'll have to let us run it once you file your petition," Connor said.

"I hope so."

"You want the story to run because you believe there could be other former defendants who paid bribes to Judge Wachter," Rachel noted.

"Guilty as charged," Rush said, laughing.

"I love how your mind works," Rachel replied.

"Let's not praise him too much," Connor quipped. "We don't

want it to go to his head."

"Ha, ha," Rush said.

"We're on your side," Connor insisted.

"I never doubted it for a second."

Rush paid for his lunch and left Smooth Buns. Rachel and Connor remained at the table. Ten minutes went by. Connor paid for his and Rachel's meals. But they didn't hurry up and leave. They needed to get their heads around the news: Judge Wachter had accepted bribes. But questions remained. Did public defender Bob Benson take part in the scheme? Connor and Rachel thought it seemed likely.

"We can't say a word to Lansmon," Connor said.

"Yeah. If Lansmon thinks we're still investigating Judge Wachter, he may have our jobs."

"Our asses are on the line here."

"Yours for sure," Rachel laughed. "It's bigger than mine. That puts you more in the line of fire."

"Right," Connor said, shaking his head. "It's so nice to have a girlfriend who has my back."

"More like your ass."

"Well, we better get back to the newsroom. I've got to finish my story on the city's public works cat."

"I'm sure it's purr-fect," Rachel said, grinning. "I can't compete with you today. I'm reporting on a high school robotics club."

"That's interesting."

"Right, if you love a bunch of metal, computer chips and intricate wiring."

"Does the club have a robot reporter?"

"Not yet."

"Good. We still have jobs," Connor said.

"At least for now. I'm worried about what Judge Wachter will do when the bribery allegations come out."

"All hell will break loose."

"Yep. So where will it leave us?"

"In the eye of the storm. The good news is that we're not alone in this. Rush Johnson is taking the lead on this."

"Maybe so, but you can be sure the judge will come after us. Who doesn't want to bark at reporters?"

Chapter Fifty—Nine

Two days before Halloween, Rush Johnson petitioned the circuit court, questioning the validity of the pledge paddle evidence and alleging that Judge Michael Wachter may have planted it to frame Harold Presson.

According to the court document, three former criminal defendants stated they paid bribes to Judge Wachter in exchange for suspended sentences that ultimately left them with no criminal record. The petition suggested that Erica Stark may have blackmailed the judge over the bribery scheme and, as a result, he had a motive to kill her.

Rush called Connor as soon as he filed the petition to suppress the evidence. "You've got your story," he told him. Rush added that he would email a copy of the petition. "I'm giving this to you first, but in a half hour I plan to email copies of the petition to all of the news media."

"That's not a lot of time."

"Don't complain. You have something the others won't have."

"What's that?"

"You have Brumley's full report. The others will only have what I stated in the petition."

"Okay. Thanks," Connor said, ending the call. He turned toward Rachel. "Rush filed the petition. We've got a story to write. But first we need to tell Lansmon."

Rachel and Connor rushed into their editor's office. "We've got some big news," Connor said. He and Rachel explained that Rush had petitioned the court, questioning the validity of the pledge paddle evidence. Connor revealed that he and Rachel had a copy of Brumley's investigative report into the alleged bribery scheme.

"Damn. That's some story. Get it written. We need to get it on our website before our competitors. But you need to call Judge Wachter. We need his comment."

"Right," Rachel said. "We're on it." The two reporters hustled back to their desks. Connor began crafting the story. Rachel phoned Judge Wachter. His administrative assistant answered. The judge was in court. Rachel left an urgent message. Then, she joined Connor at his desk and the two jointly worked on the article.

Ten minutes later, Judge Wachter returned Rachel's call. "What is this nonsense about a petition?"

She explained that Rush Johnson had filed a court document in the Presson murder case, alleging a bribery scheme involving the judge."

"Are you running a story accusing me of a crime?"

"We're running a story based on a court filing," Rachel said.

"A court filing in a completely unrelated murder case that makes the ridiculous accusation that I took bribes from defendants in exchange for lenient sentences. That's poppycock and you know it. You run that story and I'll sue you for libel," the judge shouted.

"We stand by our story," Rachel said.

"See you in court and I'll see that Rush Johnson is disbarred."

"Is that on the record?"

"Hell, yes. You can quote me," Wachter said, slamming down the phone.

"He wasn't happy," Rachel told Connor.

"I could hear every word," Connor said. The two reporters added in the judge's comments. Once finished, they quickly read through it again and then marked it ready to edit. Lansmon spent another 10 minutes reviewing the story. He sent it to the copy desk for a final read. A short time later, the newspaper posted the article under a "breaking news" banner on its website. The headline read: "Defense attorney claims evidence of judicial bribery."

The article began: *The defense attorney for murder suspect Harold Presson has questioned the validity of key evidence in the case and alleged that a judge, who found the evidence, participated in a bribery scheme.*

It went on to name Judge Wachter and recount that he had discovered the pledge paddle that the prosecution contended was used by Presson to strike the librarian on the head before she was stabbed with a knife. The article quoted from Brumley's investigative report. It cited three unnamed defendants who stated they paid bribes to the judge and claimed that public defender Bob Benson facilitated the payments.

Twenty minutes after the *Journal* posted the story online, others in the news media came out with the story. Area TV stations posted the news on their websites and it led the noon news. Mayor Elroy James nearly vomited when he heard the report. Police Chief Blair Bonney's face turned bright red at the news. The news shocked Prosecutor Richard Lamb.

An hour later, the three men gathered in the chief's office. "What are we going to do about this?" the mayor asked, his voice strained with concern.

"I can't believe Rush Johnson would make such an accusation," Blair said.

"Isn't it obvious what that attorney is doing? He's trying the case in the news media. He wants to poison the minds of the future jurors in this case," Lamb said. His thinning hair and rumpled suit made him look less like a prosecutor and more like a cheap salesman, Blair thought as he eyed the prosecutor. The chief wondered, not for the first time, if Lamb was up to the task of prosecuting Harold Presson.

"Does Rush have any real evidence that the judge took bribes?" Elroy asked.

"It doesn't matter. Even if true, which I doubt is the case, the allegations have nothing to do with the murder of Erica Stark," Blair said. "Rush Johnson hasn't offered any evidence proving the librarian blackmailed the judge. He's just trying to muddy the waters."

"But Judge Wachter is a prosecution witness. He found the pledge paddle, which is a key piece of evidence. Rush is trying to discredit the witness. This is a mess," Lamb whined.

"We need to defend the judge," Elroy insisted. "Blair, you need to check out this damn private investigator. You need to discredit him."

"Don't tell me what to do. I'm not looking to discredit anyone. The job of this police department is to protect the community and investigate crimes. Of course, we'll look into these allegations against Judge Wachter. Just leave the policing to us," Blair said, raising his voice a notch.

"Yeah, so far that hasn't gone well. If it hadn't been for the judge, you never would have found any evidence linking Harold Presson to the murder. He did your job," Elroy blared.

"Gentlemen, let's not argue," Lamb interrupted. "What we need to do now is rally around the judge. As prosecutor, I don't want to get on his bad side. You think we have problems now, if Judge Wachter sees the prosecutor's office as his foe, he'll eat my lunch."

"What you need to remember, Richard, is that the police provided you with the evidence that demonstrates Harold Presson committed murder," the chief said. "Focus on that. This allegation of a corrupt judge doesn't change the fact that you have the pledge paddle and the bloody shoe that matches the bloody shoe print from the murder scene. What more do you need?"

"A jury that won't be influenced by all those damn news stories," Lamb replied, frowning.

Shortly after the meeting ended in the police chief's office, Adam Dade called Connor. "Why didn't you tip me off about the allegations against Judge Wachter?" the police detective asked.

"Rush insisted we couldn't talk about Brumley's investigation until after the court papers were filed."

"Yeah, but you could have given me a heads up. Now, we're trying to play catchup," Adam grumbled. "The chief, the mayor and the prosecutor are up in arms. And, now I've been instructed to investigate the claims made by Brumley and Rush. I've read your story. Can you tell me anything else? Do you know who these former defendants are?"

"No, but I'm sure Rush knows."

"Great. We won't get anywhere with him unless a judge orders him to release that information."

"There may be another way."

"I'm listening."

"I think Parker Davis may be one of the unnamed individuals."

"Why do you say that?"

"Rachel and I saw John Brumley come out of Parker's office at Vinyl Vibes one evening. We asked Brumley what he was doing there. He said he was doing investigative work for Rush."

"You sure Brumley wasn't just tracking a cheating spouse? That's his bread and butter."

"We asked him if that's what he was doing at Vinyl Vibes. He insisted that wasn't the case," Connor said. "Although he wouldn't tell us what he had spoken to Parker Davis about, he seemed proud of himself, like he had learned something important."

"Well, maybe you're right. I'll start with him. And, don't you dare quote me. It better not appear in print that I'm going to interview Parker or anyone else in connection with this allegation."

"What about the chief? Will Bare Bones talk about it?"

"You can ask him, but I doubt he'll talk to you. He's pissed."

"He's upset with the media?"

"Of course."

"He's not upset that a sitting judge might have engaged in criminal activity?"

"He's irritated that his department has been thrust into what is now a political firestorm. He's got the mayor, the prosecutor and Judge Wachter all mad as hell. They want the issue to go away, but that won't happen without a police investigation. Blair's getting it from all sides."

"I'm sorry about that, but I'm glad you're looking into these allegations."

"Well, be careful what you wish for. My investigation may show that these allegations are false. If so, it won't look good for you or anyone else in the news media."

"I know you don't think much of Brumley, but I don't think he made up the allegations."

"Let's hope you're right. If Brumley made it up, he's in deep shit."

"Why would those three former defendants make accusations against a sitting judge?"

"For revenge. A chance to get back at the criminal justice system. Afterall, they were branded criminals by the police and prosecution. Suspended sentences didn't wipe away the negative publicity," Adam said.

"I hope that's not the case," Connor said. Adam didn't hear him. He had ended the call.

Chapter Sixty

Dressed to the nines, Rush Johnson spoke to a crowd of reporters at a news conference held outside the Justice Center late that afternoon. He went over the allegations made in his petition and repeatedly cited the report from John Brumley as videographers recorded his remarks and *Journal* photographer Tyler Frazier snapped images of the lawyer facing a forest of reporter-held microphones.

"Are you worried that Judge Wachter will try to get you disbarred?" a female TV reporter in a long-sleeve blue blouse and skirt asked.

"No. I am acting in good faith, based on information obtained by a licensed private investigator."

"But do you have any information indicating that Erica Stark blackmailed Judge Wachter?" a jeans-clad, long-haired radio reporter questioned.

"My client says the librarian blackmailed him. Elmwood College President Olivia Bolton also claimed Erica Stark blackmailed her. It seems logical that she found out about the judge's bribery scheme and blackmailed him too. I anticipate the police will look into the latest allegations against Judge Wachter. I trust they will get to the bottom of it," Rush said, ending the news conference.

Seated at her computer, Julie Halston watched the news conference on a live stream on the local TV station's website. She was relieved the reporters' questions focused on the allegations against Judge Wachter and not Bob Benson. Earlier, she had read the *Journal*'s story. Her boyfriend's name had been mentioned. She called Bob, but he said he was busy with clients. He promised to talk to her soon. An hour after the news conference, Bob Benson showed up. He entered the office and closed the door. She jumped up from her chair, rushed over and hugged him. "I'm so sorry, Bob. How awful.

It can't be true. Who would make such horrible accusations?"

"Sit down. I need to tell you something."

"What is it?"

"Please, sit."

"Okay," Julie said, a worried look on her face. She sat down. Bob pulled up a second chair and sat facing her. She noticed that he seemed tense. But then anyone would be that way if faced with such accusations, Julie reasoned.

"I need to tell you something," Bob began.

"You said that," Julie said.

"Yes, well, here's the thing. Those alleged bribes, they happened. Judge Wachter has taken bribes in exchange for suspended sentences."

"What? You participated in a bribery scheme? You took bribes?"

"No, I never took bribes," Bob insisted.

"But you knew about the judge's actions?"

"Yes. It started years ago. The judge came to me, admitted to a gambling addiction. He said he was deep in debt. He said if my clients, who faced relatively minor criminal charges, paid bribes, he'd give them suspended sentences. At first, I said no. But Michael kept asking me. Eventually, I caved. I agreed to it because I realized it was a way to keep some of my clients out of jail. These weren't hardened criminals. Many of them came from broken homes. They made mistakes but incarcerating them wasn't the answer. They warranted a break. This was their opportunity. And, if they messed up while on probation, they'd end up in jail. Justice, I concluded, would be served."

"Oh, my God! How could you?"

"I know. Later, I wanted out, but the judge warned me not to cross him. He said he still needed the money and if he went down, he'd bring me down also. I couldn't risk it. Don't you see? I had to go along with it."

"You broke the law," Julie cried.

"In a manner of speaking."

"No manner. You participated in a bribery scheme."

"I didn't take a dime. I was just trying to help my clients."

"Tell that to a court. Wow. I never thought of you as a law breaker."

"I know I let you down, but please don't abandon me. I love you."

"I love you too. But you've got to go talk to the police."

"I can't."

"Why not?"

"Because Judge Wachter called me earlier today after the story broke. He threatened me. Actually, he threatened you."

"What?"

"He said he'd get you fired from your job."

"How?"

"I don't know. But he said the library board wouldn't tolerate financial malfeasance on the part of its library director. I took it to mean that he'd find a way to accuse you of stealing from the library funds."

"Oh, my God. What do we do?" Julie asked.

"I don't know. Right now, we can't say anything."

"But how the hell am I going to work with the judge? We have a Halloween morning board meeting. How do I keep my emotions in check?"

"You must. You can't let on that I've told you anything. You can't let him suspect anything." Tears streamed down Julie's cheeks. Bob reached over and hugged her.

Chapter Sixty—One

The day after news broke of the allegations against Judge Wachter, Adam Dade headed downtown. He had an appointment with John Brumley. The private investigator wasn't happy. His office had been flooded with foul messages from the judge's friends, who accused Brumley of unfairly attacking Wachter and expressed hope that the private eye would die a slow, agonizing death. He wanted the police to do something about it. In a phone call setting up the appointment, Adam made it clear his focus fell on the claims made by the former defendants interviewed by Brumley and not on the rants of the judge's friends.

Adam parked his unmarked police car on the street in front of Brumley's office. He climbed out and walked toward the door. A loud boom stunned him. Something had exploded inside the private eye's office. Adam rushed forward, bursting through the door. Inside, the blast had torn through the place. He spotted Brumley, face up, on the floor. Brumley's bloodied, blackened, lifeless face stared back at Adam. Bits of a cigar littered what was left of his mouth.

Adam checked for a pulse even though he knew there wouldn't be one. He called dispatch, his voice cracking with emotion. He relayed the news to the dispatcher. Soon, he heard sirens. More officers were on their way, including those with the bomb squad. Soon, the evidence techs would scour the place for the tiniest thread of evidence. And, the coroner would show up to eye the dead body and offer up, to Adam's mind, some utterly useless comment.

Adam gazed around the blast-damaged office. The force of the explosion had hurled a box of cigars across the room. Cigars lay clumped against the walls. Officers with the bomb squad entered the office. They checked to see if there were other explosives in the place. None were found and evidence techs began processing the scene. Police Chief Blair Bonney arrived. As he exited his vehicle, he noticed onlookers had gathered along the street. He ducked under the yellow crime scene tape that had been placed across the front of the building and entered.

"What a mess," Blair said as he approached Adam. "What happened? Are those bits of a cigar stuck to his face?"

"It appears so."

"Was John Brumley killed by an exploding cigar?"

"That's what I'm thinking. There's a banana-like scent here. Nitroglycerin has that scent."

"So, someone stuck dynamite in Brumley's cigar?" Blair asked.

"I believe that's the case."

"Damn, that's a hellava way to kill someone. Who would do this? You think this is connected to the allegations made against Judge Wachter?"

"I'm afraid that could be the case. I spoke on the phone with Brumley and scheduled a meeting to interview him. He told me that he'd received a lot of online hate messages after Rush Johnson alleged the judge took bribes. At that news conference, Rush spoke of the information Brumley had uncovered."

"Shit. Are you saying Judge Wachter could have done this, could have murdered Brumley?"

"I'm not sure I'd go that far. But we'll have to talk to the judge."

"We need to keep a lid on this."

"What are you going to tell the news media?" Adam asked.

"As little as possible," Blair said.

The police chief and Adam spotted Coroner Joe Sherill entering the building. The rotund man surveyed the scene. He approached the victim. He knelt and eyed Brumley's body. Standing up, he shook his head. "Damn. What a fuckin' mess. Sure doesn't look like an accident. I guess there's no chance it was suicide?"

"Joe, have you ever seen someone kill themselves with an exploding cigar?" Blair asked.

"No."

"Well, there's your answer. We're talking murder."

"I saw the sign on the front of the building. Is this John Brumley, the private investigator?"

"Yep," Adam said.

"From what the media reported, he's the guy claiming former defendants bribed Judge Wachter. I guess that's what got him killed," the coroner observed.

"We don't know that," Adam said. "First things first, we need an autopsy."

"To determine someone blew him up?"

"Don't be stupid. We need official confirmation," Adam said.

"Well, I can't help you there."

"We know. We'll see what the forensic pathologist in Farmington tells us. As soon as officers finish collecting evidence, you need to get the body to the pathologist."

"Yeah. No problem. I might not have any formal forensic training, but I've learned a thing or two on the job. Dead is dead, no matter how you slice it," Joe said.

Adam sighed at the remark. Blair ignored it and headed outside where a scrum of reporters greeted him, shoving microphones in his face almost before he stepped beyond the crime tape.

"I've got a statement," the chief said. "This morning, an explosion occurred at the office of private investigator John Brumley. He is deceased. The Elmwood Police Department is investigating this as a homicide. An autopsy will be conducted. We have no other information to disclose at this time."

"What caused the explosion?" a young, spectacled man who worked for the local TV station questioned.

"We are still investigating the incident."

"Is Mr. Brumley's death connected to the allegations made against Judge Wachter?" a radio reporter asked.

"It's too early in the investigation to know if it's connected," Blair said. The chief retreated into the building as reporters and videographers scurried off to file their stories. Connor stayed behind as did *Journal* photographer Tyler Frazier. The thick-haired Tyler snapped images of officers entering and exiting the building. He ducked under the crime tape and tried to enter, but a large burley sergeant blocked his path and threatened to arrest him. Tyler retreated.

Connor needed to return to the office, but he wanted to speak to Adam. He texted his detective friend. Adam read the text. "Meet me in the alley," Connor had typed. Five minutes later, Connor met Adam by a trash bin behind the downtown building.

"What do you want?" Adam asked.

"Information on what happened here."

"Didn't the chief tell you?"

"He said there was an explosion. I wanted to know if you can tell me anything else. What caused the explosion?"

"I'm not at liberty to say right now. We're still investigating. As soon as we have all the facts, I'll let you know. I've got to go," Adam said. The detective retreated inside the building. Connor headed to his Ford Escape. He needed to get to the newsroom and write up the little information police had disclosed. As he drove several blocks to the Journal building, Connor mulled over the incident. One question kept churning in his mind: *Was John Brumley killed because of the allegations made against Judge Wachter?*

Chapter Sixty – Two

The story of the deadly explosion blanketed the airwaves and topped the *Journal*'s online breaking news. It led the front page of the newspaper's print edition on Halloween morning, although much of the article rehashed the previous allegations of bribery disclosed by Rush Johnson. Tyler's photo of the coroner removing Brumley's body accompanied the story.

That same morning, not far from the crime scene, Adam Dade met Parker Davis at Parker's Broadway record shop and bar. The entrepreneur's hands trembled as he sat in his cluttered office. His face looked pale. He felt nauseated.

"I just need you to tell me the truth," Adam said. "Brumley talked to you. You're one of the three people, cited by Rush, who paid bribes to Judge Wachter."

"I didn't say that," Parker cried. "It wasn't me."

"Do you feel threatened?"

"By you?"

"No, of course not me. I mean it's understandable given the recent deadly incident at Brumley's place. You spoke to that private investigator and now he's dead. That has to have shaken you up," Adam remarked.

"That was horrible," Parker agreed. "I just don't want anything to do with all that."

"With all what?"

"The allegations that the judge accepted bribes."

"In exchange for suspended sentences. You received a suspended sentence on your drug charge."

"Yes, but I'm not saying I bribed the judge," Parker said, wiping sweat from his forehead.

"Look, I'm just interested in finding out if the allegations are true. Did the judge take bribes?"

"I thought you'd be focused on looking into the explosion."

"I am. Don't you see? The two could be related. And, if someone were upset about those allegations coming out, that person would have had a reason to kill John Brumley."

"I didn't kill him."

"I didn't say you did. Maybe the judge killed him," Adam said.

"You think the judge did that?"

"I'm just throwing out a possibility. But it also is true that those individuals who allegedly paid bribes wouldn't want their names publicized. It's one hell of a reason to kill Brumley."

"But doesn't that attorney, Rush Johnson, know the names?"

"I presume so, but the initial report of those allegations came from Brumley's investigation. And, Brumley's disclosures reportedly came from his interviews of three former criminal defendants. Presumably, one of them was you," Adam said.

"Why are you badgering me?" Parker cried.

"I'm not. But here's the thing. Whoever killed Brumley may come after the former defendants just as soon as he finds out who talked to the private eye. Do you feel confident the killer won't figure out who talked to Brumley? Your best bet is to come clean. Tell me what you told Brumley. I know you spoke to him. I have witnesses who chatted with Brumley at your business."

"Damn it. Quit pressing me to talk. You want me to tell you that I bribed a judge, an admission that could land me back in jail?"

"No, I'm not looking to arrest you for anything. I just need to know if I'm on the right track when it comes to investigating Judge Wachter for a possible crime."

"I'll tell you this. You wouldn't be wasting your time to look into it," Parker said.

"Okay. That will do for now. But sooner or later, you're going to tell me everything."

"Don't count on it, detective. Not when Brumley's killer is running free."

Rachel met Dennis Bertrand at his tidy art gallery, located in a Craftsman-style house two blocks from the river. Dennis had phoned Rachel, wanting to talk. Two years earlier, she had written a feature story on the versatile artist who painted everything from downtown murals and chalk drawings to framed paintings in a variety of media from acrylics to watercolors. Dennis liked the story so much that he framed it and hung it on a wall in the gallery aptly name "Picture Perfect." He'd painted the sign himself in a rainbow of colors.

"Thanks for coming," Dennis said, extending a hand awash in dried paint. He directed Rachel into his small office wedged into a corner of the gallery. He moved a stack of canvases off a chair and motioned for her to sit down. He parked himself in a paint-stained wooden chair behind a beat-up wooden desk that looked to Rachel like it would collapse from the pile of finished paintings piled haphazardly.

"You said on the phone you wanted to talk to me about the Brumley case. I assume you mean his murder," Rachel said.

"Well, yes, sort of. It's about the allegations that Judge Wachter engaged in a bribery scheme; and criminal defendants paid bribes for suspended sentences."

"Yes, that's what attorney Rush Johnson has alleged."

"Well, I'm one of the people that Brumley interviewed. But you can't use my name or mention anything that would identify me. I just want you to know the truth."

"Okay. I promise not to identify you. But did you bribe the judge?"

"Well, not exactly. I paid my lawyer, Benson. Actually, Benson said he paid the judge with his own money. I paid Benson back over the course of several months. This was years ago. I had been doing well as an artist until my drinking problem got out of hand. My wife divorced me. I often found myself too drunk to paint. Patrons who used to buy my works avoided me. I was selling my pieces for next to nothing. I barely made rent some months. Why else do you think I ended up with a public defender?"

"Tell me about your run-in with the police. Why did you end up in court?"

"I was charged with assault. I was in a drunken rage."

"Over what?"

"This guy came up to me outside Jello, the night club, and threatened to deface the marching band mural I had painted years earlier on the exterior brick wall of a music store. I tried to ignore him at first, but he kept hassling me. Told me I was a bum, a no-good drunk."

"Did you know this guy?"

"Not really. I mean, he had taken some art classes from me when I used to teach painting in my gallery. But he had no ability. I tend to be blunt. I criticized his painting of a nude model and he just went crazy. Stormed out of class, knocking over an easel on the way out. He hated me and told me so. So, when he bullied me outside the jazz club and I was sauced, I lost it. I turned on him; punched him over and over. The police came and arrested me. He started it, but the cops didn't care."

"I can't see Judge Wachter giving you a prison sentence given the circumstances."

"Maybe so. But Benson told me the judge would go easy on me in exchange for money. When Benson said he'd pay the bribe and I could pay him back, I was thrilled. I thought Benson was being charitable and allowing me to get back on my feet. And, I did get a suspended sentence. I paid Benson back over a period of months and I quit drinking. I got my life back."

"So, why are you telling me this if you won't let me write about it?"

"I've been thinking about what happened all those years ago. I now realize I don't know for sure that Judge Wachter took a dime. I only have Benson's word on that."

"You believe Benson pocketed the money, that he acted alone?"

"Maybe."

"But how do you explain that you and others received suspended sentences if the judge wasn't in on the scheme?"

"I don't know. Maybe the judge had a charitable side when it came to defendants. Benson told me that he and the judge were friends. He said the judge favored suspended sentences for defendants who weren't hardened criminals, individuals who had not been charged with rape or murder. At the same time, Benson told me that the judge felt defendants should pay a price for a second chance."

"I appreciate you telling me this," Rachel said.

"I just wanted you to know the facts. I feel bad about Brumley's murder."

"Do you suspect Benson murdered Brumley?"

"Possibly."

"What about the judge?"

"Don't know. Maybe. Or maybe Benson or Judge Wachter hired someone to kill Brumley. At any rate, I believe Brumley's death is connected to the bribery investigation."

Dennis rose, signaling the interview had ended. Rachel nodded and headed for the front door. She turned to say goodbye, but Dennis didn't look at her. He had turned to straighten a painting hanging on the gallery wall. Rachel exited the place.

Back in the newsroom, Rachel recounted the interview to Connor. "You can't use his name?" Connor asked.

"No. I can't even identify him as an artist."

"Well, you better make sure Lansmon will let you run the story without naming your source."

Rachel agreed. She approached the editor in his office. Lansmon listened as she detailed what Dennis told her while leaving out his name.

"You want to run this story without naming your source?" Lansmon asked.

"Yes. I promised not to identify him."

"Well, then, you better keep your promise. Write it up. Get a comment from Benson. We'll run it inside."

"Why not the front page?"

"This story is controversial enough without pasting it all over the front page. And, I don't need our publisher breathing down my neck. Trust me, this story will get a lot of attention regardless of where it's placed in the paper," Lansmon said.

Rachel returned to her desk and typed up the story. Her first paragraph: *An Elmwood man said he received a suspended sentence in an assault case years ago in exchange for a bribe. At the time, he believed the money went to Judge Michael Wachter, but now he's unsure. According to the man, public defender Bob Benson said he initially paid the money to the judge. The former criminal defendant said he paid back Benson over a period of several months.*

Rachel called Benson for a comment. The call went to voice mail. She left a message. Benson called back 10 minutes later. He denounced the allegation, insisting he never took a bribe or paid the judge to go easy on his clients. Rachel added Benson's comments to the story. She inserted a sentence repeating Judge Wachter's statement that he never took a bribe.

Thirty minutes later, the *Journal* posted the story on its website. Connor called Adam minutes before the story posted. Adam pushed for more information. "Who is the source?" he asked.

"It's Rachel's story. She has an unnamed source."

"What do you expect me to do with it?" Adam asked, his voice revealing his frustration at the news.

"Maybe you could talk to Benson."

"Oh, I plan to do so. But unnamed sources won't cut it in a police investigation. And, none of this changes anything right now regarding the librarian's murder. The evidence points to Harold Presson."

Connor sighed. Adam had agreed to question Benson, but it seemed clear the police detective had little interest in pursuing the latest allegation.

As Rachel put together her unnamed-source story, the Elmwood Public Library board held its monthly meeting in the library's main conference room. Julie tensed up as the meeting began. She refused to make eye contact with Judge Wachter, the board chairman. After what her boyfriend had told her, she felt trapped. The judge could get her fired. Not only that, he could frame her, accuse her of stealing library money.

The meeting lasted about an hour. Afterward, as other board members departed, Wachter approached Julie. "Something bothering you?" he asked.

"No, I just think this business with Harold Presson and Erica's murder have stressed me out," she observed, her voice trembling.

"I just wondered. You seemed preoccupied today."

"It's nothing to worry about," Julie said, forcing a smile.

"Good. Take care," the judge said, his face breaking out in a grin.

Julie watched him leave. Her hands shook as she returned to her office. Her heart pounded. She felt sick to her stomach. She closed her office door and phoned Bob. He tried to reassure her. "Just act like nothing happened," he said. "All of this will blow over once that preacher is convicted of murder."

"But what if he's innocent? What if Judge Wachter killed Erica?"

"The police and the prosecutor insist they have charged the right person. Who are we to say otherwise. Anyway, Harold Presson has been a pain in the butt for the library. If he's convicted, you won't have to worry about him anymore."

"Yes, but I don't want an innocent man to go to prison."

Bob laughed. "One thing's certain, Harold Presson is anything but an innocent man."

Connor hung out at Rachel's house on Halloween. She had purchased several large bags of wrapped candy bars from Walmart. Rachel's street proved a popular location for trick or treaters that night. Rachel had carved a pumpkin. She played spooky music on her I-Phone. She dressed up like a witch, complete with a pointed hat and special makeup. Rachel put rabbit ears on her dog Sammie. Connor felt sorry for the dog. Rachel made Connor dress up too. He had resisted at first, but she insisted. She bought him an inflatable dinosaur costume that made him feel like an old fossil. He was pretty sure most of the trick or treaters came away feeling pity for him. From time to time, Connor eyed Sammie. Connor felt certain that even the dog felt sorry for him.

"Where are all these kids coming from? Do they all live on your street?" Connor asked, grabbing a candy bar to eat.

"No. Parents drive their kids here. We're candy heaven for the trick or treaters. Don't take another candy bar. They are for the kids."

"I'm just trying for a sugar high to get me through the evening."

For nearly two hours, kids came to the door with their plastic pumpkin buckets in search of sweet treats. Every time the doorbell rang, Sammie, tail wagging, rushed to see the costumed kids. Each time, Sammie attempted to stick her nose in the candy bowl, forcing Rachel to rescue the bowl over and over again. The horde of trick or treaters slowed as the night wore on. A boy, who looked to be about 10 years of age, approached. He wore a Harry Potter costume. Rachel smiled and placed a Milky Way bar in his bucket. The boy reached out with his right hand and gave her a scrap of paper. She opened it and gasped. In bold red, typed letters, the message stated: *YOU ARE NEXT!*

"What is this?" she asked as Connor peered over her shoulder.

"I don't know. A man gave me $5 to give you that piece of paper," the boy said, turning to look across the street.

"What man?" Connor asked.

"I don't see him now," the boy said.

"What did he look like?"

"Older dude. Wore glasses. Never seen him before," he stammered. The boy stepped back from the door, fearful he had done something wrong. Harry Potter fled down the driveway. "Happy Halloween," he yelled to no one in particular. Connor and Rachel watched him race to catch up with his costumed friends and their parents. Sounds of laughter floated on the air.

"What was that all about?" Connor asked.

"Someone's trying to scare us," Rachel said.

"The boy said the guy wore glasses. Judge Wachter wears glasses," Connor said.

"You think the judge is threatening us?"

"I don't know."

Rachel closed the door and switched off the outside light. "I think we've had enough of Halloween," she said.

Connor nodded. He didn't say what he was thinking. *If someone killed Brumley for digging into the bribery allegations, what would that person do to two nosy reporters?*

Chapter Sixty—Three

Adam drank a cup of convenience store coffee as he waited to speak to Bob Benson on a chilly first day of November. The public defender was on the phone with a client. Ten minutes later, the call ended. Benson stood and eyed Adam with suspicion as the detective entered the public defender's office.

"What can I do for you?"

"I just have some more questions."

"You always do," Bob said, taking a seat behind his desk.

"I'm sure you saw the *Journal* story."

"You mean that fiction about a bribery scheme?"

"Well, that's the real question. Is it fiction?"

"You think I advised clients to pay bribes to Judge Wachter in exchange for more lenient sentences?"

"I don't know what to think, but the newspaper clearly has a source, someone whom you reportedly represented."

"Who is that?"

"The article didn't say."

"Right. So, someone can smear my good name and get away with it. Damn reporters. They're like vultures, eating away at people's lives."

"Well, I'm not going to defend the news media. But you understand why I need to question you."

"Not really. I told you I didn't participate in any bribery scheme."

"According to the newspaper account, a former client claims you paid a bribe to the judge and then that client paid you back."

"Total lie. You think I would bribe the judge and risk disbarment? No way," Bob said, his voice cracking with anger.

"Do you know if Judge Wachter took bribes?"

"Not that I'm aware of. You'll have to ask him."

"Do you believe the judge killed Erica Stark?" Adam asked.

"Wow. You jump from some insane bribery allegation to murder. I don't follow you."

"Here's the scenario. Ms. Stark learns about the bribery scheme and blackmails the judge."

"No way. My girlfriend, Julie, worked with Erica Stark. Julie will tell you Erica couldn't have blackmailed anyone much less a sitting judge who happens to head up the library board."

"Harold Presson claims Erica blackmailed him. The Elmwood College president says the same thing. Seems possible she also blackmailed the judge regardless of what Julie says."

"Harold hated the library folks; thought they were evil pornographers. That's a solid reason for murder, if you ask me. You should know, you investigated the murder. And, your department arrested him."

"Even so, we have to investigate any and all leads."

"Have you talked to the judge?"

"Not yet."

"Well, maybe you should. I'm sure he'll set you straight. Are we done here?"

"For now. Thanks for your time, Mr. Benson. I feel certain we'll be talking again."

"I hope not. I have a backlog of cases to handle. My clients need me."

"To advise them to pay bribes?"

"Absolutely not."

Adam turned and walked out. Bob kicked the trash can beside his desk. He wanted to scream. *It was all unraveling. How much longer could he lie?*

Connor and Rachel dined on soup and sandwiches at Smooth Buns. The eatery's owners stopped by their table to chat. Truman and Oliver wanted to know about the journalists' investigation. "You all still investigating the librarian's murder? Lately, all I've seen is news about this so-called bribery scheme," Truman said.

"The bribery case has drawn our attention," Rachel agreed.

"But we haven't stopped looking into the murder," Connor added.

"Do you still believe that preacher may have been framed?" Oliver asked.

"Yes," Connor said.

"Do you have any hard evidence that's the case?" Truman questioned.

"No."

"There's one major roadblock to this theory," Rachel said.

"What's that?" Oliver asked.

"If someone framed Harold Presson, how did he or she get into the preacher's office to plant the evidence without anyone noticing?"

"Maybe someone did notice," Oliver suggested.

"How's that?"

"Well, maybe a church staff member saw someone go into the pastor's office when he was away."

"If that's true, why wouldn't that staff member have said something?" Connor wondered.

"Maybe the staff member didn't think anything of it," Truman said.

"Why?" Rachel asked.

"Because the individual who may have gone into the pastor's office may have been someone well known, someone no one would suspect," Truman suggested.

"You're talking about Judge Wachter," Rachel said. "Who would suspect him?"

"I don't know," Connor said, rubbing his right hand on the back of his neck as he considered the idea. "Judge Wachter and Harold Presson are like water and oil. They don't mix. They dislike each other. If the judge visited the church, I'm pretty sure staff would have informed Harold. They wouldn't just let the judge enter the pastor's office."

"Maybe the judge had good reason to visit the preacher," Oliver said.

"The judge might have sought to make peace with Harold, end the conflict between the pastor and library staff."

"I doubt it," Connor said.

"Still," Rachel said, "maybe the judge did visit the pastor's office. Harold Presson has an administrative assistant whose office is located near the front of the church. If the judge or anyone else slipped into Harold's office, she might have seen that person."

"You're right. We need to check it out," Connor said. "We've been so focused on the incriminating evidence collected by the police that we haven't considered exactly how someone could have stolen the pledge paddle and the tennis shoes from Harold's office."

"Glad to offer our advice," Oliver said.

"Enjoy your lunch," Truman said. "We didn't mean to interrupt."

"You're never interrupting," Rachel said. "We enjoy the company as much as the food."

Oliver and Truman moved away, stopping to talk to other customers. Connor eyed Rachel. Her eyes sparkled with excitement. Connor felt it too. They had someone else to interview, someone who might put Judge Wachter in Harold's office before and after the murder.

Connor and Rachel sat in the office of GraceWorks church secretary Gloria Hampton the next morning. Located just off the front lobby, the white-walled office held a desk, copier and several chairs. A countertop, covered in stacks of church bulletins and devotional booklets, stretched along one wall. Crosses adorned every wall of the office.

A no-nonsense woman, Gloria had worked as church secretary for more than 30 years. Her gray hair, piled high in a bun, gave her a stern appearance. She wore little makeup. Only her bright-blue-framed glasses softened her appearance. She wore a silver cross around her wrinkled neck. Her husband had died the previous year. Gloria could retire, but she refused to do so. Harold Presson often told people that the church would fall apart without Gloria's organizational skills.

Connor and Rachel summarized what their investigation had uncovered. They surmised someone framed the pastor, possibly Judge Wachter. "That's why we want to know if the judge ever visited the pastor's office while he was gone, both before and after the murder of the librarian," Connor said.

"We think the judge might have stolen Harold's pledge paddle and his tennis shoes, and killed Erica Stark. He could have smeared blood on one of the shoes and then returned the shoes to the pastor's office," Rachel said. "We believe the judge then may have planted the fraternity paddle in the library so he could pretend to discover it."

"You see the judge as a murderer?"

"Possibly. That's why we wanted to speak with you," Rachel said.

"Did Judge Wachter enter the pastor's office when the pastor was gone?" Connor questioned.

"Not recently. When was the librarian murdered?"

"March," Connor said.

"Hmm. Oh, yes, I do remember seeing the judge. He came by one day, said he wanted to drop something off for the pastor."

"Was the pastor there?" Rachel asked.

"No. I thought it was odd because Judge Wachter called ahead. I told him that the pastor was out, he had a meeting across town with members of his Citizens for Decency group. But Judge Wachter said he'd stop by, said he just wanted to leave something for the pastor."

"Did he drop anything off?" Rachel asked.

"I don't remember anything."

"Did the judge wear a large coat or carry anything with him?" Connor asked.

"Yes. I believe he had a duffel bag. Yes, I remember. He said he had just come from the gym."

"So, he had a gym bag with him?" Rachel questioned.

"No, I wouldn't say that. It looked like more of a large travel bag," Gloria recalled.

"So, he went into the pastor's office?"

"Well, I assume so. He headed down the hall toward the pastor's office."

"How long was he there?" Rachel asked.

"Maybe 10 minutes. It wasn't long."

"Did you see him leave?" she questioned.

"No. I left to go to the post office to pick up the church's mail. I wasn't gone long. The post office is just two blocks away."

"So, did you see him again?"

"Yes. A few days after the murder, I believe. He came back. Again, the pastor was out of the office. I think the judge knew somehow that Pastor Harold wasn't in. I don't know how he knew. He hadn't called ahead. At any rate, he said he needed to drop off something. He said he'd put it on the pastor's desk. I think he said something about some report on the library. He mentioned he chaired the library board. Of course, I already knew that."

"You knew that the pastor and the judge were at odds and yet you let the judge visit the pastor's office anyway?" Connor asked.

"Well, yes, I knew about their conflict over the operation of the library. But the judge said he hoped they'd work out their differences."

"How long did the judge stay this time?" Connor asked.

"About 10 minutes I think."

"Did the judge have a duffel bag with him?"

"Yeah. It looked like the same one he had before."

"You saw him leave?"

"Yes, this time I did."

"Do you remember if the duffel bag looked different when he left? Maybe fuller?"

"No, sorry. I didn't pay a lot of attention to the bag. Like I said, it looked like just an ordinary duffel bag."

"Did you mention the judge's visits to your pastor?" Rachel asked.

"I don't remember. I know that once the police began treating Pastor Harold as a murder suspect, the focus here was on his defense. I know I didn't think much about it."

"You never mentioned the judge's visits to the police?"

"No. They never asked me about it."

"And you didn't volunteer the information?"

"No. I told you, I didn't think much about it."

"Why not?"

"Because I didn't think of the judge as a murderer. Still don't. Of course, I know Pastor Harold didn't kill that librarian. You know those two men used to be friends."

"What? You're kidding," Connor said.

"No, really. They became close when they worked together on a program to assist people after they were paroled from prison."

"When was that?"

"Maybe 15 years ago when Pastor Harold began his ministry here."

"What happened to the program?"

"It depended in large part on state funding. Sure, the church helped some, mostly in providing volunteers to work with the parolees, help them get back on their feet. But over time, Missouri lawmakers cut back funding. Eventually, no more funding. The program went away. It's been gone a long time."

"So, the judge was familiar with the pastor's office. He visited it quite often back then, I presume," Connor said.

"Oh, certainly. He was here a lot. He knew every inch of the office."

"Did the pastor jog a lot?"

"Yes. It's how he dealt with stress. He often jogged to the church."

"Did Judge Wachter know about it?"

"Sure. Pastor Harold used to tell me that he tried and tried to get the judge to take up jogging, but he never did."

"I guess the judge knew about the fraternity paddle too?" Rachel asked.

"He did. He used to say he'd like to borrow the paddle to deal with some of the criminals in the courtroom."

"But even knowing this, you never told the police about it?" Rachel asked.

"No. That was in the past. I haven't thought about that in years. You don't really think the judge murdered the librarian and framed Pastor Harold?"

"We don't know," Connor said.

"We don't have proof either way," Rachel said.

"I just wish the prosecutor would drop the murder charge against the pastor. He's innocent."

"I know his lawyer is doing everything he can to defend him," Connor insisted.

"And what I told you could help Pastor Harold?"

"I think so," Connor replied.

"That's good news, isn't it?" Gloria asked.

"We'll have to see," Connor said.

Chapter Sixty—Four

Judge Michael Wachter greeted the police detective with a forced smile and a deliberate handshake. Adam had reached out to the judge after questioning Bob Benson. Now, two days later, the two men met in one of the places the judge felt most at home besides the courtroom: the local casino.

Standing in the lobby, with its riotous colored walls, the two men chatted briefly about the weather. Adam and the judge knew each other professionally. The courts and police have a common bond: law and order. After a few minutes in the lobby, the judge led the detective onto the casino floor. They headed for a slot machine stationed in a far corner of the casino. The place seemed eerily quiet. Nine in the morning proved early for most gamblers. The judge took a seat in front of a slot machine showcasing a brightly colored treasure-island image complete with an overflowing treasure chest. He turned to face Adam, who remained standing.

"You said you wanted to ask me some questions. I assume it has to with that ridiculous news story," the judge said.

"If you mean the alleged bribery scheme, yes."

"Fire away."

"I've spoken to an Elmwood resident who claims he received a suspended sentence from you in exchange for a bribe," Adam began. "According to the *Journal*, a number of individuals claim to have bribed you in exchange for such sentences."

"That's hogwash. You know me, Adam. Do you think I would risk my reputation by committing such crimes?"

"I didn't say you did take bribes. I said some people have made such claims. I'm just trying to determine the facts here."

"What you have is a bunch of unnamed sources. Those damn reporters at the *Journal* are printing lies, fake news!"

"Well, sometimes where there's smoke, there's fire. The allegations appear to involve Bob Benson. All of the claims seem to come from former clients of his. I checked. You've given many of his clients suspended sentences. I understand Benson is a friend of yours."

"We know each other. Bob's a dedicated public defender. It's not easy defending criminals. He knows they are guilty and I know they're guilty. The question is, should I incarcerate them or give them a second chance. I tend to believe in second chances, but not third chances. I've suspended sentences for those who I believe have a chance to be productive citizens going forward."

"Well, I questioned Benson. I asked him if you took bribes. You know what he told me?"

"No, what?"

"He said I'd have to ask you."

"Did he say I took bribes?"

"No."

"Did he say he advised his clients to bribe me?"

"No."

"Of course, not. That's because this is all a bunch of bullshit. I didn't take bribes and Bob Benson didn't invite his clients to bribe me. Case closed. Why are you bothering with this crap? Does this have anything to do with Erica Stark's murder?"

"Well, there is a theory put forth by some that Ms. Stark knew about the bribe scheme and blackmailed you."

"Are you saying you believe I killed Erica, a woman that I worked closely with as head of the library board?"

"I'm not saying anything of the sort. You asked if my investigation has anything to do with the murder. I'm saying there could be a connection."

"You have your murderer, Harold Presson. You do believe he killed her?"

"We arrested him based on the evidence. But my job is to investigate any and all leads, even after we have made an arrest. That's what I'm doing."

"I trust I've answered your questions?"

"Yes. If I come across any new information on this matter I'll let you know," Adam said. "Have a good day." The detective walked away. Moments later, he turned back to see the judge playing the slots.

Chapter Sixty—Five

Harold Presson waved to his crowd of supporters in front of the Justice Center as he and his attorney prepared to enter the building for a hearing in late November on a motion to suppress evidence in the murder case. Members of his Citizens for Decency group held signs demanding "Justice for Presson" and chanted slogans backing their leader and castigating the police for not finding "the real killer" of librarian Erica Stark.

Attorney Rush Johnson initially filed a petition seeking to suppress the pledge paddle evidence. But in recent days, he'd amended the petition to include the bloody shoe evidence. The hearing drew the attention of everyone from ordinary residents to the news media. People packed the courtroom. Reporters, including Connor and Rachel, crowded together in the front row. Lansmon had instructed Connor to write the main story. The editor gave Rachel the task of writing the secondary article, which would focus on people's reactions to the proceedings. She had spent the past half hour outside talking to Citizens for Decency members who complained of what they viewed as a corrupt system of law and order. Looking around the courtroom, Rachel sensed a restlessness in the audience. People seemed anxious, both those who believed the preacher innocent and those who thought him a murderer. Rush and Harold entered the courtroom. Dressed in one of his expensive suits, Rush swiftly eyed the crowd as he and Harold took their seats at the defense table. The preacher wore a blue suit. A large gold chain and cross hung around his neck. Prosecutor Richard Lamb showed up with his battered leather briefcase. He plopped it atop the prosecution table, opened it and removed a folder filled with court documents and a legal pad. Lamb scowled as he too observed the onlookers. While Rush loved an audience, Lamb wished he could prosecute cases in private. Unlike Rush, Lamb wasn't flamboyant. Normally, pre-trial motions were routine; few people attended. But this wasn't normal. Far from it. Mayor Elroy James sat by the center aisle in the second row of courtroom pews. The police chief sat across the aisle. Julie Halston showed up too. She stared at the back of Harold Presson as she waited for the hearing to begin. Priscilla Presson, wearing a wine-colored, collared dress and pearls, sat in the front row behind her husband. She stared straight ahead, showing little emotion. Elmwood College President Olivia Bolton, clad in a midnight blue business suit, joined her. Henry Carter, who directed Elmwood's regional history museum, took a spot behind the college president. Rachel observed Henry, a history professor emeritus at Elmwood College, gazing around the room. He appeared uneasy with the courtroom's modern style. Rachel knew why. In past interviews, the soft-spoken, bow-tied Henry had confessed his love for historic architecture with its skilled craftsmanship and traditional décor. She knew he hated modern architecture, calling it "ugly as a pig sty." Henry once told her that today's steel and glass buildings "bludgeoned the senses." Angela Pierce, the niece of the murder victim, sat stiffly next to Henry.

"All rise," the white-haired bailiff said as black-robed Judge Stanley Gardner entered the courtroom. The bearded judge took his seat on the bench.

"Please be seated," the judge said. He surveyed the courtroom. "Before we begin, let me be clear. I know emotions run high concerning this case. But I will not tolerate any disruptions. Anyone who disturbs the peace here will be removed from the courtroom." Judge Gardner then silently studied the crowd for several seconds before instructing Rush Johnson to proceed.

"Your Honor, as you know, I've moved on behalf of my client, Harold Presson, to suppress certain evidence in this case. The evidence of a fraternity paddle and a bloody shoe, which have been cited by the prosecution in the charging of my client with murder, involve the actions and testimony of Judge Michael Wachter. Without him, there would be no evidence against my client. And, as news stories have showed, the judge is now alleged to have taken bribes. The murder victim, Erica Stark, almost certainly was killed because she had blackmailed the judge. So, it's a strong possibility the judge murdered the librarian."

"Objection," Lamb said, bolting from his chair. "Judge, these statements are ridiculous, not to mention slanderous. Mr. Johnson hasn't presented a single shred of evidence to back up his imaginative theory."

"Sit down, Mr. Lamb. You'll have your turn. Mr. Johnson, do you plan to present any evidence to support your petition to the court?"

"Yes, sir. I call Detective Adam Dade to the stand." Adam strode to the witness box. Rachel noticed the police detective wore an American flag pin on the lapel of his black suit, which complemented his American flag tie. Under questioning, Adam explained the actions of the police upon discovery of Erica Stark's body.

Rush drilled down on the bloody shoe print and the pledge paddle. "Detective, you mentioned the bloody shoe print. How do you explain a single shoe print? Did the murderer hop about the crime scene?" Rush asked, prompting some in the audience to giggle.

"I doubt it."

"In a subsequent search, did you find a bloody shoe in Harold Presson's office?"

"Yes."

"You found a pair of tennis shoes, correct?"

"Yes."

"Was there any blood on the other tennis shoe?"

"No."

"Doesn't that seem unusual to you? Wouldn't you expect some blood to spatter on the other shoe?"

"Possibly."

"Did the blood found on the one shoe match that of the victim?"

"Yes it did."

"Why would my client leave a bloody shoe in his office?"

"He couldn't explain it."

"Now, tell me, why did you search the pastor's office?"

"Because of the discovery of the fraternity paddle under a bookshelf in the library."

"Did the police discover the paddle?"

"No. Judge Wachter did," Adam said. "He said he was looking to check out a James Patterson mystery after a library board meeting. He said he spotted the handle of the paddle sticking out from under the bottom shelf."

"That was some time after the murder, correct?"

"Several weeks afterward."

"Did you connect the paddle to the defendant?"

"Yes."

"How did you come to suspect the paddle belonged to the defendant?"

"I received a tip from a reporter friend?"

"Who was that?"

"Connor Tate."

"Did you later learn that Judge Wachter suggested the fraternity paddle resembled one belonging to the defendant?"

"Yes, I did."

"Did that concern you?"

"No."

"Why not?"

"I have the utmost confidence in Judge Wachter. And, prints found on the paddle matched those of the defendant," Adam said.

"Yet, I understand recently you investigated allegations the judge accepted bribes in exchange for suspended sentences. How can that be?"

"Just doing my job. There have been allegations made against the judge, but those allegations do not tie the judge to the murder of Erica Stark."

"But you can't rule out that possibility?"

"That's assuming the pastor didn't kill her."

"Can you rule out the judge as a possible suspect in this case?"

"I have no information that connects him to the murder."

"But you do admit that the judge has played an integral part in the murder investigation and led police to suspect my client?"

"I guess so."

"You aren't sure?"

"No, I'm sure."

"Does the library have a security camera system?"

"Yes, it does."

"Did you check the recordings?"

"Yes,"

"Did it show the murder?"

"No. The recording of that time period had been erased, apparently by the murderer."

"After police began focusing on the pastor as a murder suspect, did police check security camera footage for the time period between the discovery of the body and the discovery of the pledge paddle?"

"Yes."

"Did you spot Judge Wachter on the recordings?"

"Of course. He heads up the library board. He regularly visits the library," Adam said.

"In that time, neither the police nor library staff discovered the pledge paddle. Is that correct?"

"Yes."

"So, isn't it likely that the judge planted the pledge paddle?"

"No," Adam insisted, frowning.

"If my client had killed Erica Stark, why would he have left the paddle behind where it could be found?"

"I don't know," Adam whispered.

"What did you say? I couldn't hear you."

"I said, 'I don't know,'" Adam said, his voice louder.

"There appears to be a lot about this case that the police don't know," Rush said, returning to the defense table. He sat down, a slight smile creasing his mouth.

Under cross examination from Lamb, Adam stated that the evidence warranted the arrest of Harold Presson. "We connected the bloody shoe and the pledge paddle to the crime scene and to Mr. Presson."

"No further questions," Lamb said.

Rush then called his second witness, longtime custodian Bill Ramsey, the library's first Black employee. Rush first questioned Bill about his duties at the library before focusing on the pledge paddle. "Did you clean up the library after the police finished with the crime scene?"

"Yes," Bill said.

"As part of your duties, did you clean the area where the judge found the paddle?"

"Yes. Did you ever see the paddle when you cleaned the floor?"

"No."

"Did you clean the library after the discovery of Ms. Stark's body?"

"Yes."

"And you didn't see a paddle?"

"No, I didn't."

"Would you have noticed the paddle sticking out from under the shelving?"

"I believe so."

"No further questions," Rush said.

Lamb approached the witness stand. "Tell me, Mr. Ramsey, have you ever mopped up and found something on the floor later on?"

"You mean like a piece of paper or a pen?"

"Yes."

"Sure, it happens."

"Thank you."

"But not a fraternity paddle," Ramsey added.

Rush, seated at the defense table, grinned at the custodian's final answer. Lamb returned to the prosecution table. His shoulders slumped as he sat down, clearly unhappy with the answer from the witness. Rush wasn't done yet. He called Gloria Hampton to the stand. The church secretary swore "to tell the truth." Gloria eyed the pastor before turning her attention to Rush. After some preliminary questions that drew answers from Gloria as to her duties as church secretary, Rush asked if Judge Wachter visited GraceWorks in the days before and after the murder.

"He did," she said, proceeding to detail the two occasions that she observed the judge. She told the court that the judge carried a duffel bag with him on both occasions.

"Could the bag have been large enough to conceal Harold's pledge paddle and tennis shoes?"

"I think so."

"And on both occasions, did Judge Wachter enter the pastor's office when the pastor was out?"

"Yes."

"Thank you. No further questions," Rush said.

Lamb chose to cross examine. "Ms. Hampton, when the judge came by the church were you suspicious?"

"Suspicious?"

"Yes. Did you suspect Judge Wachter was up to no good, that

244

he intended to frame Pastor Harold Presson for the murder of Erica Stark?"

"Of course not. I knew they had a disagreement over how the library was run, but I had no reason to think the judge might be there to frame my pastor."

"And you don't know that he did? Nor do you know what if anything was in the duffel bag?"

"True. I don't know about any of that," she said as Lamb slowly returned to his chair.

"Mr. Johnson, do you have any more witnesses?" Judge Gardner asked, looking impatient.

"One, Your Honor. I call Judge Michael Wachter to the stand." The judge strolled into the courtroom like he owned it. He smiled at Judge Gardner and nodded toward the prosecutor. He took the stand. He stared coldly at Rush. In answer to preliminary questions, Wachter touched on his legal background and his judicial experience. Rush then dove into issues surrounding the evidence in the murder case. The judge admitted to finding the pledge paddle and suggesting to Connor that it looked like one the pastor had.

"Why did you disclose this information to a reporter?"

"I wanted to help the police."

"Why not just contact the police yourself?"

"I was concerned how it would look."

"In what way?"

"Well, as head of the library board, I had publicly defended the library against the verbal attacks of Pastor Harold Presson and his Citizens for Decency group."

"They wanted the library to ban certain books they felt were pornographic or embraced lifestyles they opposed. Is that right?"

"Yes, that's correct."

"Isn't it true that you thought it would look like you had a vendetta against Pastor Harold?"

"I wouldn't call it a vendetta."

"But you were worried how it might look to the public?"

"Yes."

"So, if you were worried about how it would look, why did you approve a request by the police for a warrant to search Pastor Harold's church office?"

"The police asked for a warrant and I did my job," Judge Wachter said, ignoring Rush and looking at Judge Gardner. "The police connected the fraternity paddle to the pastor. I would have been remiss not to grant the requested search warrant."

"But the police based the request on the fact that you found the pledge paddle that they connected to the defendant. Isn't that correct?"

"Yes."

"Seems like a conflict of interest to me," Rush observed. "And, we now have testimony you visited the pastor's office both before and after the murder. Do you deny visiting the pastor's office when he was absent?"

"No, I did visit the church."

"You carried a duffel bag with you. Why?"

"I had worked out at the gym."

"Why did you want to see the pastor?"

"The first time, I wanted to see if we could settle our differences regarding the operation of the library."

"And the second time?"

"I wanted to ask him if he thought any member of his group could have murdered the library director. I thought he might hold the key to solving her murder."

"The church secretary said you told her the second time that you wanted to leave something for the pastor?"

"Yes."

"Did you leave anything for him?"

"No. I had written him a letter asking for his help in solving Erica Stark's murder but when I entered the pastor's office I decided it would be better to wait until I could speak to him in person."

"Why?"

"I thought he'd ignore my plea; think I was trying to trick him or something."

"So, did you ever get back in touch with him?"

"No. Soon after my second visit, the police arrested the pastor and he was charged with murder."

"But since then, there have been allegations in the press that you accepted bribes from criminal defendants in exchange for suspended sentences."

"Total lies," Wachter growled.

"Both my client and Olivia Bolton, the president of Elmwood College, contend Erica Stark blackmailed them. So, did she also blackmail you?"

"No, of course not. Erica Stark was a wonderful person. It's ridiculous to believe she blackmailed anyone. The worst thing is she's dead and can't defend herself."

"But if she were blackmailing you, that would give you a strong motive to kill her."

"I resent your slanderous suggestion. You are talking to a sitting judge. How dare you attack me!"

"That makes you mad?"

"Darn right."

"Enough to kill?" Rush asked.

"No way. I've spent my life upholding the law, not breaking it."

Lamb jumped up. "Your Honor, Mr. Johnson is badgering the witness."

"I see I've hit a nerve," Rush said. "No further questions."

"Mr. Lamb, do you wish to cross-examine?" Judge Gardner asked.

"No, Your Honor."

"Mr. Lamb, do you plan to call any witnesses?"

"No. Your Honor. I just want to say that Mr. Johnson has presented a tapestry of suppositions that aren't supported by facts. The reality is that the police investigated the murder and secured evidence linking the defendant to the crime. The evidence isn't tainted and there is no reason for you to suppress the evidence in this case."

Judge Gardner cleared his throat. "Mr. Johnson, I appreciate your legal arguments on behalf of your client. However, I agree with the prosecutor. The evidence, while circumstantial, deserves to be considered going forward in this case. Your motion is denied." The judge slammed the gavel and hurriedly left the bench through a side door. Rush patted Harold on the shoulder.

"Don't be discouraged," he told the pastor. "It's what I expected. I just wanted to get the testimony into the record." Then, Rush turned toward the crowd of reporters gathered around and delivered a brief statement. "While we are disappointed in the ruling, we are confident that the facts are on our side. As the testimony today has shown, there is every reason to believe Pastor Harold Presson did not kill Erica Stark. Regardless of what the prosecution may say, the so-called evidence is tainted and we believe won't stand up to the scrutiny of an honest jury."

Connor scribbled Rush's comments into his notebook. At the same time, Rachel pulled out a small digital recorder and sought comments from members of the audience. Some thought the judge's decision was correct. Others, mostly members of the Citizens for Decency who had secured seats in the courtroom, thought the pastor had been framed. No one said their mind had changed because of the court proceeding.

Rachel cornered Chief Bonney before he could leave the courtroom. "Chief, are you concerned that the case against the pastor is built on questionable evidence?"

"No. The evidence is solid or we wouldn't have arrested him," Blair said. He quickened his pace and exited the courtroom.

Rachel spotted the mayor heading for the exit. Rachel moved in front of him. "Mayor, are you concerned about the validity of the evidence in this murder case?"

"Let's not jump to conclusions. Let the legal proceedings play out," Elroy said. "Harold Presson will have his day in court."

Rachel spotted Julie and rushed over to grab a comment. "After listening to the testimony, do you still believe Harold Presson is guilty?"

"I thought so," Julie said, "but today's testimony makes me wonder if he could be innocent. Still, it's hard to believe the prosecutor would have charged Harold Presson if he weren't guilty."

Rachel turned to see Connor and other reporters cornering the prosecutor. Lamb looked as if he were about to be devoured by a bear. In a pinched voice, he complained that the hearing had been a waste of time. He accused Rush of slandering "an honest" judge. "Harold Presson killed Erica Stark and we will prove it when this case goes to trial."

Chapter Sixty–Six

An hour after the hearing ended, Blair and the prosecutor met in the chief's office. Lamb, feeling sick to his stomach, paced as he talked. "That damn Rush. He's assassinating the character of Judge Wachter. He pursued that motion to suppress the evidence to poison the potential jury pool. It's all theatrics."

"What I'm worried about is this. Can you win this case? Can you prove that preacher killed the librarian?"

"What? Your officers arrested him. How can you doubt he's guilty?"

"I didn't say that. I believe he killed her. The question, however, is whether you can prove it in court."

Just then, Mayor Elroy James barged into the office, a look of disgust blanketing his face. "What are you going to do about this, Richard?"

"Calm down," Lamb said even as his eyes betrayed his own fear.

"This case is sinking fast," Elroy said.

"Hold on. We did a thorough investigation. We have enough evidence to convict the preacher," Blair said.

"It appears you didn't do such a good job," the mayor argued.

"Shut up, Elroy. You're clueless. You don't know the first thing about investigating a crime."

"Well, I sat through that motion hearing. Rush poked more holes in your evidence than Swiss cheese."

"Judge Gardner denied the motion," Blair noted.

"That was expected," Elroy said. "What I'm worried about is when this case goes to trial. Will a jury buy the defense arguments?"

"We'll see," Blair said.

"Juries are hard to figure, but I intend to do everything in my power to gain a conviction," Lamb said, his eyes downcast.

"That may not cut it. You need to find more solid evidence," the mayor said.

"Don't tell us what we need to do," the chief said. "If you and the council would give me a bigger budget, we could hire more detectives."

"It's not a lack of manpower that's the problem. It's a lack of proper administration. Your officers should have focused harder on nailing down every detail of this murder, every clue. And that includes investigating the murder victim. The testimony presented at the hearing today will be all over the news. I doubt you'll be able to find an impartial jury here. And a lot of people are going to believe Harold Presson didn't kill Erica Stark."

"Elroy, you're underestimating the intelligence of jurors," Lamb said. "They'll see through Rush Johnson's fiction."

"Don't kid yourself. As I stand here, you're holding a losing hand," Elroy said. He belched and left the office. Blair rose from his chair, strode across the room and slammed his office door. Blair picked up the office phone and dialed Adam's extension. A few minutes later, the detective entered and closed the door. The prosecutor continued to pace.

"Sit down, Richard. You're driving me crazy with all your walking back and forth," Blair said. "Adam, take a seat." After the two men sat down, Blair barked out instructions. "Adam, I need you to take another look at the judge. We need to know everything Rush knows and more. No more surprises." Blair turned his attention to the prosecutor, who looked like a condemned man. "You need to pull yourself together. Your job is to prosecute Harold Presson and make sure you can counter every one of Rush's arguments. Erica Stark may have been a blackmailer. If so, she blackmailed the preacher and he killed her," the police chief said.

"We don't know that she blackmailed Presson," Lamb said.

"It's a pretty good theory. If I were you, I'd go with it. Quit trying to save that librarian's reputation. That's not your job," Blair said.

Lamb sighed and rose to leave. "I'll do my best," he said.

"Good," Blair said. But after Lamb left, the chief told Adam, "That prosecutor needs a huge dose of confidence."

"He promised to do his best," Adam said.

"That's what worries me. His best may not be enough."

Elroy returned to his downtown office on the third floor of Elmwood City Hall. He plodded upstairs, catching his breath when he reached his office. He put his hand on his belly. He needed to exercise, lose some weight, get in shape. He spent too much time sitting in meetings and in his office. Exercise wasn't on his agenda. Not now. Elroy entered his office and plopped down at his desk. He clicked on his computer. He checked the Journal's website. The story on the court hearing had top billing under a headline that read: "Court testimony raises questions about evidence in murder case." Connor's bylined article began: *Courtroom testimony at an evidence suppression hearing showed the evidence depended in large part on the actions of Judge Michael Wachter and suggested the case against pastor Harold Presson might not be as strong as the prosecution claimed.* The second paragraph reported: *Despite the testimony, Judge Stanley Gardner denied the defense's request to suppress the evidence of a fraternity paddle and a bloody shoe that police tied to the defendant. Judge Gardner said the evidence "deserves to be considered" when the case goes to trial.*

"It's a damn mess," Elroy muttered as he finished Connor's story. Next, the mayor read Rachel's story. He studied the comments from those who witnessed the hearing, including himself. The mayor liked his comment. He felt it was a down-the-middle kind of statement designed to avoid criticism from all sides. Still, he wished he could have blasted the police chief. But this wasn't the right time to do so. Elroy planned to run for re-election in another year. He needed the support of civic leaders. Questioning the prosecution's case in public wouldn't help his candidacy, thought Elroy. Judge Wachter had contributed money to his previous campaign. He didn't want to give the judge a reason not to help fund his next mayoral race.

One comment in Rachel's story gave him pause. Julie Halston stated that the testimony made her wonder whether Harold Presson might be innocent. The victim's friend and co-worker, who previously believed the preacher committed the murder, now had some doubts. If she has reservations, the mayor surmised, jurors would too. Elroy sighed. At least, he told himself, as mayor he had one reason to be relieved. *He wasn't the prosecutor.*

Hours after the hearing, an irritated Adam phoned Connor. "It would have been nice to know that Judge Wachter entered Harold Presson's office days before and after the murder. The church secretary never told us about the judge's visits."

"She said you didn't ask."

"Well, why would we? We didn't have any reason to believe the judge had stopped by the church office," Adam grumbled.

"So, what happens now? Are the police going to reopen the murder investigation?"

"We're not reopening anything, but we're continuing to look at all the evidence."

"So, are you beginning to see the likelihood that someone framed the preacher?" Connor asked.

"You mean, do I believe Judge Wachter may have killed the librarian and then framed Harold Presson for the murder?"

"Yes."

"I know Judge Wachter. I don't see him as a murderer."

"Do you believe he took bribes from criminal defendants in exchange for suspended sentences?"

"I've spoken to one of those former defendants, but at this point there's no real evidence to back up such an allegation."

"You don't think Wachter would kill to prevent disclosure of the bribery scheme?"

"You're assuming the judge took payoffs. The former defendant I interviewed believes the judge took bribes. But isn't it possible that the defendant's attorney, Bob Benson, took the bribe? Your girlfriend wrote a story questioning if any of the money went to the judge."

"Benson likely participated in the scheme. But it still depended on the judge suspending sentences. Otherwise, the scheme would have fallen apart if just one defendant paid a kickback to Benson only to be sentenced to prison. The word would have gotten around."

"You don't know that Judge Wachter didn't suspend sentences for first-time offenders on his own."

"Out of the goodness of his heart?"

"Yes, because he believed these offenders could turn their lives around and become productive citizens," Adam said. "I wouldn't discount that Benson cooked up the whole scheme. Public defenders don't make a whole lot of money. It would be tempting to take bribes."

"That would make your job easier," Connor said.

"What do you mean?"

"You wouldn't have to risk angering a powerful sitting judge."

"I resent your suggestion. Off the record, we're investigating the judge."

"Yeah, just not for murder."

"Despite what you think, there's no evidence connecting the judge to Erica's death."

"Well, if I were Benson, I'd be worried," Connor said.

"Why?"

"If Judge Wachter did kill the librarian, what's to stop him from killing Benson to shut him up?"

"You're pitching fiction. Stick to the facts. Besides, I can tell you one thing."

"What's that?"

"Sooner or later, the truth will come out," Adam said. "It almost always does."

Chapter Sixty—Seven

They met at church. The old Catholic church, set on a grassy knoll overlooking Main Street and outward to the floodwall and beyond that the sweeping Mississippi River. Bob Benson arrived first. He positioned himself in a pew along a wall aisle of the aging brick cathedral. Built in the 1850s and restored in the 1980s, the church continued to serve the faithful. But it also drew tourists intent on viewing its artistry and sweeping architecture, with its multiple spires on the outside and its bevy of archways on the inside. Its stained-glass windows offered a kaleidoscope of colors on a sunny day. The white marble altar and large, ornate gold cross drew the attention of even non-believers.

Bob wasn't Catholic. Neither was Michael. It surprised him that the judge wanted to meet there. Bob looked at his watch. The judge was late. He looked around, relieved that he didn't see a priest. The sanctuary seemed empty. Judge Wachter showed up, 15 minutes late. He frowned as he gazed around the church. He spotted Bob and quickly moved to the pew. He sat down. The judge shifted his weight as if he were trying to get comfortable. Bob thought it was a hopeless task. The old pews may have been restored, but they still were uncomfortable. No salvation there.

Michael looked mad, Bob thought. Or was there something else in his dark eyes. Fear raced through his mind as the judge greeted him. The judge had commanded Bob to meet with him. "Damn, Rush Johnson," Wachter said. "He'll never get a break in my courtroom. When I was on the witness stand yesterday for that motion hearing, he treated me like a common criminal. It's all over the news. But he can't prove anything. Neither can the police."

"I haven't told them anything," Bob said, his hands trembling.

"You better not. If they come after me, it will be your neck on the line. Those defendants didn't directly pay me a dime. You handled the money. I'll deny everything. They'll only be able to prove that you took bribes from your clients."

"You can't do that. It was your idea, not mine."

"It's my word against yours. Who will people believe? A judge or a public defender whose clients are criminals. The public will be on my side."

"Don't be so sure. You're not looking too good in the press."

"You just need to keep your mouth shut, for your sake and for your girlfriend."

"Are you threatening me?" Bob asked, his eyes widening.

"I prefer to call it a promise," Michael said. "I'll let you in on a secret." The judge leaned in and whispered. The words stunned Bob, who looked like he wanted to scream. The judge sneered. "You screw me over, you're dead, and so is Julie." Judge Wachter stood up and without another word walked out of the church.

Bob felt sick to his stomach. He sat still, trying to control his emotions. He wasn't sure his legs wouldn't fail him if he stood up. After what seemed to him like an eternity, he stood and slowly headed for the door. He felt numb, like a man heading down the path to his own execution.

Two hours later, Bob met Connor in the bar at The Port restaurant on River Street. Bob ordered a Yuengling lager; Connor, a Coke. Bob, after talking to Julie, had phoned Connor and requested the meeting. Bob hoped the beer would calm his nerves. He felt he might puke any minute. "I need to tell you something, but you can't write about it," Bob said after the waitress brought their drinks to the table.

"So, this is off the record?"

"Sort of."

"What?"

"Let me explain. I want to talk to the police, but only if I'm granted immunity from prosecution."

"You want me to deliver a message to my detective friend?"

"Yeah."

"Well, you better tell me the message."

Bob glanced around the bar. Early afternoon, the place had few customers. None were seated near their table, located at the rear of the bar. "I met Judge Wachter earlier today."

"Is this about the bribery scheme?"

"It's worse than that."

"What is it?"

"Judge Wachter told me he killed Erica Stark and John Brumley. And, he threatened to kill me and Julie if I said anything to the police," Bob said, the words coming out in staccato fashion.

"Wow. That's some confession on the judge's part," Connor said. "Is this all connected to the bribery scheme?"

"Yes. He told me that Erica blackmailed him after learning he had taken bribes."

"Are you still insisting you had nothing to do with the bribery scheme?"

"I did participate, but not like you think. I didn't keep any of the money. I just delivered the money to Michael."

"Why did you do it?"

"It was Michael's idea. I just wanted to help my clients. Later, when I wanted to stop, it was too late. I was in too deep."

"But now you're willing to come forward?"

"Only if I get immunity from prosecution. I don't want to go to jail."

"Why now?"

"Because Michael confessed to murdering those two people."

"That was news to you?"

"Hell, yes. I never suspected he'd murdered anyone."

"But you knew that Brumley was looking into the bribery allegations."

"True. But I didn't think the judge killed him. I figured it more likely that one of the former defendants murdered him to keep the private investigator from revealing that person bribed the judge. And, it's not just that the judge confessed the murders to me. It's that he threatened to kill me and Julie. Don't you see? I'm not safe and neither is Julie. We would constantly wonder if the judge planned to kill us even if we kept silent."

"Damn, that's some story."

"But you promise you won't reveal my identity to your detective friend unless immunity is granted?"

"I promise. But I hope to interview you on the record at some point."

"Not while Michael is free. I can't risk it."

"I'll convey your request for immunity, but you realize I can't promise it will be granted."

"I know. But I can't risk coming forward without such protection. That's why I'm telling you. If you publish anything about what I just told you, I'll deny everything."

"You can trust me."

"I hope so. If not, I'm a dead man for sure."

Chapter Sixty—Eight

Connor sat in a chair beside Adam's desk. He'd rushed to the police station after listening to Bob Benson's revealing news. Connor looked excited, his eyes sparkling. The detective had seen that look before. Such visible excitement meant only one thing: Connor had some amazing information to convey. Adam assumed it had something to do with the bribery allegations, but even he never imagined what his friend told him.

"So, let me get this straight," Adam said after Connor finished talking. "You want me to ask the prosecutor to grant immunity to this unnamed person who is making these serious allegations against Judge Wachter?"

"Yes, I do."

"But you won't tell me this person's identity?"

"I can't. It might put his life in jeopardy," Connor said.

"Spare me the drama. Just tell me why I should have confidence in what you're telling me."

"Because this unnamed individual has access to the judge. He knows about the bribery scheme."

"Are you saying that public defender is accusing the judge of murder?"

"I didn't give a name."

"No, but from what I know, it's the only logical guess. If the bribery scheme involves Bob Benson, he'd want to save himself from legal troubles. He'd want immunity. He'd want to keep his law license."

"Will you talk to the prosecutor?"

"Okay, I'll talk to him. But tell your unnamed source that he's going to have to give me some solid evidence. How do I know he's telling the truth?"

"I believe him," Connor insisted.

"Well, that's great for you. But in my job, people often tell me lies. And, accusing a judge of murder is serious business. It will take a lot to convince me that Judge Wachter murdered one person, much less two."

"But you'll talk to the prosecutor?"

"Yes. I'll let you know where this goes. Just don't get your hopes up."

"Oh, but I am."

"Why is that?"

"Because, Adam, I know you too well. If Judge Wachter is a murderer, you wouldn't want him to go free."

"Yeah, well I also don't want to lose my job," the detective said, looking grim.

***

Adam spent a restless night coping with the thought that Judge Wachter might be a murderer. In the morning, he visited the prosecutor in his office in the Justice Center. Richard Lamb's office looked austere. No paintings or photos adorned the white walls. The prosecutor's desk seemed too organized, no papers piled atop it. The office felt lifeless to Adam.

The detective detailed what Connor had told him. As the detective talked, Lamb's wan face grew even paler. This wasn't what the prosecutor wanted to hear. When Adam finished, Lamb pressed him about the credibility of the reporter's unnamed source.

"Connor Tate believes this person."

"Well, I know he's your friend. But how do we know Connor's source is telling the truth?"

"I need to interview this person," Adam said.

"We could subpoena Connor and ask a judge to order him to give up his source," Lamb suggested.

"I can see a problem with doing that."

"And what's the problem?"

"Such a move would lead to a media circus and, assuming Judge Wachter is a murder suspect, it would alert him to our investigation and could prompt more murders."

"You're right. Okay, tell your friend that immunity is on the table, but first you'll need to interview this individual. If the information proves reliable, we can grant immunity," Lamb said.

"Thanks," Adam said, rising to leave.

"Don't thank me yet. You might lose your job if your investigation goes down the drain."

"Let's hope it doesn't come to that."

Conner set up the meeting at Adam's request. Bob Benson didn't want to visit the detective at the police station for fear that Judge Wachter would hear about it. So, the decision was made to gather at the reporter's loft apartment on a Friday evening. They sat at Connor's kitchen table. The police detective wanted to record the interview, but Bob nixed that idea. Adam relented, but said he'd jot a few notes in his notebook. Bob agreed. The public defender recounted what he had told Connor, that Judge Wachter admitted to killing both the librarian and the private investigator. When he finished, Adam launched into a series of questions.

"Did the judge say why he killed them?"

"He said Erica Stark blackmailed him over the bribery scheme."

"How did she know about the bribery?"

"Michael said she learned about the blackmailing from some-one she knew, who heard it from a fellow inmate."

"Does this person have a name?"

"I don't know the identity of that person. Judge Wachter told me he believes the information came from a petty thief. As the judge tells it, law enforcement subsequently busted the guy on federal drug charges. The Feds placed him in witness protection after he agreed to testify against a cartel hitman. The judge told me he's confident the guy's no longer living in this area."

"And the judge admitted to framing Harold Presson and plant-ing the explosive cigar that killed John Brumley?"

"Yep. He sure did."

"Did he explain why he killed Brumley?"

"He said he'd learned that the private investigator had inter-viewed former defendants. Michael worried that his bribery scheme would be exposed."

"The exploding cigar seems a creative way to kill someone," Adam said.

"At one point during Fidel Castro's rein in Cuba, the CIA con-sidered killing him with an exploding cigar. Maybe that's where the judge got the idea," Benson suggested.

"I wonder where Judge Wachter would acquire such expertise."

"I know that his grandfather did demolition work at an area quarry."

"That might be how he learned about explosives," Adam agreed.

"Are you finished asking me questions?"

"No. I have some concerns about your testimony regarding the bribery scheme. You said criminal defendants paid you in cash and you gave the money to the judge. So, it's your word against the judge's."

"Interview some of my former clients. I will give you names."

"I do want those names. I'll interview them. But from what you tell me, they never handed the money directly to the judge."

"You're not suggesting Bob's lying?" Connor asked.

"No," Adam said. "But it's a question of whether it can be proved that the judge took bribes."

"You told me I'd have immunity," Bob grumbled. "I told you I didn't take a dime. It all went to Michael."

"I'm not looking to arrest you," Adam said. "But it's up to Richard Lamb whether to prosecute anyone for bribery. I'm just trying to uncover as much information as possible so Mr. Lamb may make an informed decision about whether to prosecute Judge Wachter."

"What about the fact he confessed to two murders?"

"We only have your word on that point," Adam said, straightening his tie.

"Do you understand that he threatened me and my girlfriend?"

"So, you told me. But again, it all comes down to proof."

"What proof do you need? My dead body?"

"Calm down! I'm not looking to get you killed. Let me talk to your former clients. Then, I'll take this information to the police chief and the prosecutor. We'll see where it goes," Adam said.

Benson nodded, but his face showed fear and dismay. Connor sympathized. Bob Benson might very well be putting his life on the line, Connor concluded. *If only he could write the story.*

Chapter Sixty-Nine

Adam Dade spent the better part of a week tracking down the list of clients Benson provided. Most still refused to talk, refused to admit they paid bribes. But a handful admitted they paid cash for suspended sentences. The handful included coffee shop owner Johnny Rhodes, record shop owner Parker Davis and artist Dennis Bertrand. None of them shed any light on the two murders.

The Monday after Thanksgiving dawned cold and wet. The forecast called for the rain to turn to snow later that day. Adam joined the prosecutor and the police chief in the chief's office.

Blair Bonney bit his lip. The meeting gave him heartburn. Richard Lamb felt sick to his stomach. Adam detailed his investigation. When he stopped talking, the police chief and the prosecutor sat silent for several minutes.

"What do you think, Adam?" Lamb asked. "Do you believe Benson?"

"I do. My gut tells me he's telling the truth. I've checked his finances. There's no evidence in the bank records to suggest he's taking bribes. Of course, according to Benson, the criminal defendants paid cash."

"Benson could have stashed away the money," Blair said. "But even if he's telling the truth, where's the solid proof that the judge took bribes and killed two people?"

"That's my concern too," Lamb agreed. "If I charge Judge Wachter and it went to trial, I doubt I can get a conviction."

"So, what do we do about Benson? Do we charge him?" Blair questioned.

"No. If he didn't take any money, it would be hard to get a bribery conviction. But my biggest worry is that if this went to trial, Benson's defense attorney would make the case that the judge took the bribes."

"And you don't want to piss off Judge Wachter," Blair said.

"Yeah. I have to prosecute cases in his courtroom. I'm focused on putting away murderers and child molesters."

"According to Benson, Judge Wachter killed two people," Adam noted.

"Find me convincing evidence and I'll charge him," Lamb said, his eyes darting from the detective to the police chief and back again. Gathering his briefcase, Lamb exited the police chief's office.

"Lamb's afraid to say boo to the judge," Adam groused.

"Maybe so, but he's right. There's not enough evidence to charge him."

"But I don't know where else to turn."

"Put it on the backburner for now. Give it a rest. I'm confident something will come up."

Back at his desk, Adam phoned Benson. The news stunned the public defender. "So, if you're a judge, you can get away with murder?"

"That's not what I'm saying," Adam said. "The prosecutor doesn't believe he can secure a conviction."

"Shit, I'm screwed. You realize my life's in danger," Benson said.

"I'm still investigating. This case isn't closed."

"Yeah. Don't bother. You'll just go through the motions. The bottom line is that Judge Wachter will get away with murder," Benson said, ending the conversation.

Adam sighed. He punched in the personal number for Connor, reaching him in the newsroom. Adam informed him about the decision not to arrest or charge Judge Wachter. Connor shook his head as he clicked off the phone. Adam told him the police hadn't closed the case, but it sure seemed like it to Connor.

"What's wrong?" Rachel asked, seated at her desk.

"The police won't arrest Judge Wachter and Lamb won't prosecute him."

"What will Benson do?"

"What can he do? Adam did say that Benson won't be charged with bribery. That's some good news."

"Is there anything we can do?"

"Perhaps we could tell Rush Johnson about the murder allegations against the judge."

"We can't identify Benson. We promised."

"No. We would have to keep his name out of it."

"Make the call," Rachel said. "At this point, it's all up to Rush as to what to do with this information."

Connor phoned Rush. An hour later, Connor met Rush at the law office. He detailed the murder allegations, which he said came from a source. Connor refused to name the source, but assured Rush that this person was very familiar with the judge.

"I believe the accusations," Connor said. "I'm hoping you can pursue this. The authorities certainly won't."

"I'll do my best. My client didn't murder that librarian. I'll pursue any angle that helps prove his innocence."

"Thanks."

"I'm just doing my job," Rush responded.

"Aren't you worried about having to try cases in Judge Wachter's courtroom?"

"Of course, I am. But my job is to defend Harold Presson to the best of my ability. And there's no question that the judge's actions are key to Harold's defense."

Rachel and Connor celebrated Thanksgiving at her place with Chinese take-out. Rachel had worked that morning, reporting on the Salvation Army's Thanksgiving Day meal. Connor was off, but he had few culinary skills. Neither wanted to cook a turkey. Connor and Rachel drank a whole bottle of Merlot and fell asleep on the couch.

Hung over, they showed up in the newsroom the next morning, wondering if they'd ever be able to write about the murder accusations against the judge. Mid-morning, they heard from Rush. The lawyer had scheduled a noon news conference but promised to first email a statement to the Journal. The newspaper would have the story first.

Five minutes later, Connor received the email. The lawyer was asking the prosecutor to drop the murder charge against Harold Presson in light of new information naming Judge Wachter as a suspect.

Connor and Rachel rushed into Lansmon's office to alert him to the breaking news. Lansmon instructed them to write up the story so it could be posted online before the news conference. Connor and Rachel returned to their desks. Connor began typing the story as Rachel pulled up background information from previous stories about the murders of the librarian and the private investigator. She wrote several paragraphs summarizing that information and emailed it to Connor to add to the story.

A half hour later, Connor finished the article. Lansmon reviewed it and then sent it to the copy desk for final edits. At 11:30 a.m., the *Journal* posted the story under a headline that read: "Defense attorney: Police investigate judge as possible murder suspect."

The article, bylined by both Connor and Rachel, began: *Police investigated Judge Michael Wachter after allegations surfaced that he murdered librarian Erica Stark and private investigator John Brumley in connection with a bribery scheme, defense attorney Rush Johnson said today.*

The story quoted Rush, who demanded the prosecutor drop the murder charge against Harold Presson in light of the new evidence. According to the article, the attorney didn't know the identity of the accuser, but believed it was someone close to the judge.

A half hour after the *Journal* broke the story, Rush held his news conference in front of the police station. Despite the cold temperatures, he stood coatless before reporters in one of his immaculate suits. Connor and Rachel stood just outside the scrum of TV and radio reporters who surrounded Rush with hand-held microphones to catch his every word.

"It's time for the prosecution of my client to end. Pastor Presson didn't kill Erica Stark, nor did he murder John Brumley. I don't know if the accusations against Judge Wachter are true, but such allegations only serve to poke holes in the prosecution's case against my client," Rush said.

Blair Bonney and Adam watched the televised news conference from the chief's office. "Damn that Rush," Blair said. "Why does he have to go around interfering in our investigation?"

"It's a mess," Adam said.

"Where did he get his information?"

"I assume he heard it from Connor Tate."

"Yeah, that's what I figure. Can't you reign in your friend?"

"He has a mind of his own. Besides, this could be a good thing."

"How do you figure that to be the case?" Blair asked.

"If Judge Wachter is the murderer, maybe the publicity will lead him to make a mistake."

"Or he just might sue the city for libel," Blair grumbled.

"Let's hope you're wrong," Adam said.

Several blocks away in his office at the Justice Center, Judge Wachter watched the news conference broadcast live on the local TV station. He cursed Rush and Benson. "They're destroying my reputation." He had one overriding thought: *Benson's a dead man. He'd see to it.*

Chapter Seventy

Julie sought to tamper her emotions as she sat in the library's conference room reviewing budget documents with board chairman Michael Wachter. It'd been two weeks since Rush's striking announcement. Now, in early December, most people were focused on the Christmas season. But Julie wasn't in the holiday mood, not when she had to work with a man who had confided to her boyfriend that he was a murderer.

Try as she might, she found it hard to focus on the library's finances. She had made sure to sit across the table from the judge. She watched him like a hawk, unsure if he might attack her at any minute. Judge Wachter seemed oblivious to her thoughts. Either that, or he was a good actor. He showed no sign that the public accusations had hampered his demeanor. By noon, the two had spent several hours going over the finances, crafting a budget for the coming year.

"I picked up some Cobb salads this morning so we can work through lunch," Julie said.

"That sounds great," said Wachter. "I love a good salad."

Julie left the conference room and headed to the employee break room. She retrieved the salads from the refrigerator and two bottles of water. She grabbed some plastic forks from the kitchen drawer. She carried all of the items back to the conference room and placed them on the table. They ate in silence. Wachter greedily consumed his salad. Julie, however, ate little of hers. She felt nauseated just being in the same room with the judge, certain that he had killed her friend Erica.

After finishing his salad, the judge returned to crunching the budget numbers. Thirty minutes passed. Wachter began complaining of muscle pain. "I don't feel well," he said. "I need to go. We'll have to finish the budget work later."

"I hope you feel better," Julie said. She watched him exit. Then, she cleared the table.

The judge drove home, parked his black Mercedes in his garage and entered his three-story downtown condo. He climbed the stairs to his third-floor bedroom. He collapsed in his king bed. The pain only got worse. He screamed, but no one heard him. He reached for his phone but dropped it on the floor. Soon, his sight failed. He found it hard to breathe. Hours later, he was dead.

The police found his body the next day after he failed to show up at the Justice Center for his court docket. Officers moved in and out of the condo, collecting evidence. Adam studied the scene. The judge's face appeared frozen in agony. The police chief arrived. He eyed the victim. "What the hell happened here?" Blair asked.

"We'll have to get an autopsy. We've searched the place. We haven't found any drugs. It doesn't look like a drug overdose," Adam said.

"Could he have been murdered?"

"Possibly. But there's no sign of a break-in. The place has a security system. The crime techs have looked at the security camera recording from last night. It doesn't show anyone in the building other than the victim."

"Let's hope he died of a heart attack or some other natural cause," Blair said. "Otherwise, we're going to be bombarded by a media circus. The press is already crowding around outside. Talk about a bunch of vultures."

"What are you going to tell them?"

"As little as possible," the chief said. Blair headed downstairs. He paused for a second before heading outside to confront the news media. Reporters instantly surrounded him as he stepped on the pavement. Shoving microphones and digital recorders in his face, they peppered him with questions. A videographer from the local TV station stood in the middle of the crowd of reporters, ready to record the chief's every word and action. Farther back, the *Journal*'s chief photographer, Tyler Frazier, snapped images in rapid succession. Connor and Rachel forced their way to the front of the scrum of reporters.

"Today," Blair said, "we are investigating the death of Judge Michael Wachter. An autopsy will be conducted to determine the cause of death."

"Was he murdered?" Connor asked.

"It's unclear if the judge died of foul play or of natural causes."

"Any evidence of a break-in?" Rachel asked.

"None at this time. We will let you know more as our investigation proceeds," Blair said, stepping away from the reporters.

Rachel turned to Connor. "Do you think Bob Benson killed the judge?"

"I can't see him as a murderer," Connor said.

"Well, if it was murder, Bob Benson would be number one on my list."

"Maybe so, but I don't see him as a murderer."

Connor watched as the other reporters scattered. Just then, Adam exited the condo. "Anything you can tell us?" Connor asked as the police detective headed for his car.

"Not right now."

"Was it natural causes?"

"We don't know yet. We'll have to wait for the autopsy, but there was no sign of a struggle," the detective said. "Don't quote me."

"Got it," Connor said before he and Rachel rushed back to the *Journal* newsroom. They briefed Lansmon, who instructed them to write up a short story. Within a half hour, the Journal posted the breaking news on its website under the headline: "Police investigate judge's death."

The story began: *Judge Michael Wachter was found dead today at his downtown condo. Police are uncertain if he died of natural causes. An autopsy will be performed. His death comes only weeks after defense attorney Rush Johnson revealed that police had investigated the judge over allegations that he murdered librarian Erica Stark and private investigator John Brumley to prevent the disclosure of a bribery scheme. No murder or bribery charges were filed against the judge.*

The story popped up on Julie's news feed as she sat at her computer in her library office. Her jaw dropped. She sighed, relieved that the judge no longer was a threat to her and Bob. She read that police weren't sure how he died. Julie grabbed her cell phone and called Bob. "Did you hear the news?"

"That police found Judge Wachter dead in his home? I just heard it on the radio as I was returning to the office from a court appearance for one of my clients. Can you believe it? We're free of that bastard."

269

"Yes, I hate to say it, but it's a relief. We can go on with our lives now. No more looking over our shoulders," Julie said.

Two days after the discovery of the judge's body, Adam received a call from the forensic pathologist in Farmington. Dr. Matthew Burnett conducted all the forensic autopsies in Southeast Missouri. He had completed the judge's autopsy. "I'll email you the whole report, but I can tell you he didn't die of an overdose, and he didn't suffer a heart attack. He died of hemlock poisoning. I discovered remnants of hemlock leaves in his stomach."

"He ingested hemlock?"

"Yes."

"Did someone force feed him the leaves?"

"There's no sign that anyone held him down and crammed them into his mouth. I didn't find any bruising anywhere on the body."

"Are you saying he ate the leaves willingly?"

"I guess it's possible the leaves were mixed into some other food. I did find evidence of lettuce, bacon, chicken, eggs, tomatoes, and other ingredients that one could find in a salad."

"Who would fix such a salad?"

"Someone who wanted him dead. Or maybe it was an accident. The hemlock leaves could have been mixed up with lettuce by mistake."

"Is that likely?"

"No, but it's a possibility. I can't say for sure that someone killed him. But at the very least, Judge Wachter's death is suspicious. It's an agonizing death. The muscles deteriorate and die."

"What about time of death?"

"I'd say he died somewhere around 8 p.m. in the evening."

"So, he'd been dead some 12 hours before his body was found," Adam said.

"Yes."

"Thanks for the heads up. Send me the report. At this point, I'm investigating this as a possible murder," Adam said. He ended the call and hurried into Blair's office. The detective recounted what the pathologist had told him.

"Shit. That's all we need—another murder," Blair moaned.

"We need to retrace the judge's last day; where he went, who he saw, what he did."

"We also need to find out where he dined," the chief said.

"I'll get right on it."

"And, one other thing."

"What's that?"

"Let's hold off telling the press for a day or two. We don't need the press speculating about hemlock poisoning and turning this situation into an Agatha Christie novel," Blair said.

"Fine by me," Adam said. "We certainly don't need the press mucking up our investigation."

At the end of the workday, Adam's voice cracked. He had interviewed the entire courthouse staff. None reported seeing him eating at his desk. Security officers at the Justice Center assured him no one delivered a salad or any other meal to the judge the day before his death. And, there was no evidence anyone had visited the judge at the condo the day or evening of his murder. But Adam discovered the judge had visited the Elmwood Public Library. He called the library. Julie Halston had left for the day. He made a note to call her the next morning. He hoped she could shed some light on the judge's actions.

Adam phoned the library when it opened at 9 a.m. He spoke to Julie, who told him she spent the previous morning with the judge working on the library budget. Adam said he wanted to talk to her in person. They agreed to meet in her office at 10 a.m.

The detective arrived five minutes early. Julie met him at the customer service desk and ushered him into her office. She sat in her desk chair. He took a seat in a chair beside her desk. Adam informed her about the autopsy results. "He consumed hemlock leaves," Adam said.

"Oh, my. How did that happen?" Julie asked.

"We think the leaves might have been in a salad."

"Oh, God, no! The judge ate a salad in our conference room earlier this week."

271

"When was that?"

"The day before the body was discovered. I can't believe it. Judge Wachter consumed the whole thing. It was a Cobb salad. I had one too."

"But you didn't get sick?"

"Well, now that you mention it, I did feel a little under the weather later that day. My muscles ached. At home that night, they hurt. I figured I had pulled something. When I woke up this morning, I felt fine."

"Did you eat the whole salad?"

"No. I only had a couple bites. The judge and I were going over the library finances, putting together next year's budget. All that budgeting makes me nervous. I didn't feel like eating much."

"Did you make the salads?"

"No, I ordered them from Smooth Buns. That place makes great salads. I actually called a day earlier to put in my order. I planned to pick up the salads the next morning, but I ended up dealing with some book shelving issues. That put me behind. I called Bob and he kindly picked them up and brought them to the library."

"What time was this?"

"About 9:30 that morning. The judge arrived around 10 a.m."

"What did you do with the salads?"

"I put them in the breakroom fridge. They were in takeout containers."

"Did you open the containers at that time?"

"No. They weren't opened until I brought them into the conference room for lunch."

"What happened after lunch?"

"About a half hour after he ate the salad, Michael complained of muscle pain. He said he didn't feel well and had to leave."

"Did that worry you?"

"Not really. I figured he probably had stomach flu. I mean, he walked out without any help. I assumed he just needed to lie down."

"What did you do with the salad containers?"

"I threw them in the trash bin in the breakroom."

"Are they still there?"

"I think so," Julie said. "Let's look." She and Adam walked down the hall to the breakroom. She pointed out the trash can standing beside the kitchen sink. Adam put on a pair of crime scene gloves and rummaged through the trash. He pulled out the containers, which held salad remnants and salad dressing. He returned the containers to the trash bag and pulled it out of the bin. Adam tied the end of the bag. "I need to have the trash tested, see if there's evidence of hemlock," he told Julie.

"I can't believe someone at Smooth Buns would use hemlock leaves in a salad."

"Me neither. But we'll check it out."

"Maybe their lettuce supplier screwed up and hemlock leaves accidentally ended up in the produce delivered to Smooth Buns," Julie suggested.

"Maybe. Or someone intentionally placed the hemlock leaves in your salads," Adam said.

"Are you suggesting someone wanted to kill me too?"

"It's a possibility we have to consider. Think about it. If you had consumed more of your salad, it might have killed you," Adam said.

"Oh, no. I could have died too," Julie said, looking frightened.

Chapter Seventy–One

A day after interviewing Julie, Adam received the news. Evidence testing found pieces of hemlock leaves in the confiscated food containers. He informed the police chief. An hour later, the police emailed a news release to the media stating that an autopsy showed Judge Michael Wachter died of hemlock poisoning. The release noted that the poison appeared to have been consumed as part of a salad. Police urged anyone with any information to contact the department.

The news surprised Connor and Rachel. "Hemlock poisoning. What a weird way to die,." Rachel said. "Who would have poisoned the judge?"

"I can think of someone," Connor said.

"Bob Benson."

"Yes. According to Bob, the judge threatened him. Maybe Bob decided to eliminate the threat."

"That's a possibility," Rachel agreed as she and Connor entered Lansmon's office. They showed him the news release.

"Write it up. Let's get it posted online. Then, Connor, call your detective friend. See what he can tell you." Lansmon instructed Rachel to pull up some biographical information about Wachter to add to a longer story for the next edition. Twenty minutes later, the Journal posted a story on the hemlock poisoning. The local TV station broadcast the breaking news. Soon, the story circulated on the websites of other TV stations as far away as St. Louis. The Associated Press also picked up the story.

Connor phoned Adam seeking more details. Off the record, Adam disclosed that Wachter consumed a take-out Cobb salad from Smooth Buns while crunching budget numbers at the library with Julie.

"How did the hemlock end up in the salad?"

"We don't know yet."

"Is that on the record?"

"Yes," Adam said.

"Who delivered the salad?"

"Off the record, Bob Benson did."

"Is he your number one suspect?"

"Connor, you know I can't answer that."

"It was worth a try."

"If and when we know anything definite, I'll tell you," Adam said.

Connor drove to Smooth Buns while Rachel headed to the library. Connor walked into the crowded eatery. He waved to Truman, who was working behind the counter. "Hey, Connor. Hemlock poisoning. I saw it on the news. Crazy way to die."

"It sure is. I understand Bob Benson picked up a Cobb salad the other day."

"Yes, that's right. Wait, does this have something to do with that poisoning?" Truman asked.

"Yes. Police believe the judge ate hemlock leaves contained in a salad from Smooth Buns."

"Shit. We didn't put those leaves in a salad. Oliver, come here," Truman said. Oliver, who had been working in the kitchen, approached the counter.

"Hey, Connor," Oliver said.

"Did you make the Cobb salads for Julie the other day?" Truman asked.

"Sure did. Something wrong?" Oliver asked, noticing the serious looks displayed on the faces of Truman and Connor.

"The police believe Judge Wachter died after eating a salad that contained hemlock leaves," Connor said.

"Holy crap," Oliver said. "No way did the hemlock come from here."

"The order was for two Cobb salads?" Connor questioned.

"Yes. There were two salads."

"One was for Julie?"

"I believe so. She didn't really say."

Connor took out his cell phone and called Rachel. He advised her to ask Julie if she also ate a salad. He then returned to questioning Oliver and Truman, but the two owners of the eatery had no further information on the situation. Connor headed for the exit as Adam entered the building.

"Playing Dick Tracy?" Adam asked.

"No. Just asking questions. Don't worry. They'll tell you the same thing."

"Just keep my name out of it," Adam warned.

"Of course. What are friends for?"

At the library, Rachel questioned Julie, who wondered how hemlock leaves could end up in a salad ordered from Smooth Buns. "You had a salad too?" Rachel asked.

"Yes. Same thing, a Cobb salad," Julie said.

"Did you eat yours?"

"Just a couple small bites."

"Was there hemlock in your salad too?"

"Maybe. I felt bad later. That police detective suggested I could have ingested some hemlock although my symptoms were minor. I felt fine the next morning."

"What about the judge? Did he seem worse after he ate the salad?"

"He complained of muscle pains a short time later and said he had to leave. I assumed he had stomach flu."

"Did you pick up the salads?"

"No. Bob did. Why?"

"Nothing."

"You think my boyfriend poisoned the salads?"

"I didn't say that."

"Bob Benson wouldn't kill anyone," Julie insisted.

"It's just that he delivered the salads."

"Well, the poison had to be in the salads before Bob picked them up. Talk to the folks at Smooth Buns. I bet one of their workers did it, maybe just for fun, not expecting anyone to die."

"I know the owners of Smooth Buns. They run a tight ship. I can't imagine any employee of theirs doing such a thing," Rachel said.

"Well, I'm confident my Bob wouldn't poison anyone, particularly when one of the salads was for me. Do you think he'd try to kill me? That's ridiculous."

"The real question is would he poison the judge?"

"Why would he?"

"What about the bribery scheme?"

"What about it? Bob didn't take any money. The judge did!"

"So, you knew the judge took bribes?"

"Yes, Bob told me."

"If Bob knew about the bribes, it could have posed a risk for the judge."

"Are you suggesting the judge wanted to kill Bob?"

"I'm not suggesting anything. I'm just asking questions."

"Well, I can tell you that I wouldn't have spent hours going over the library budget with the judge if I believed for a single minute that he posed a threat to Bob."

"You didn't ask the judge about the blackmailing allegations?"

"Of course, not. That wasn't any of my business. I'm focused on running the library. I'll let the police handle any suspected crime. Now, I'd like you to go. I've told you everything I know."

Rachel arrived back at the office around the same time as Connor. The two reporters compared notes before crafting their article. Their story began: *Judge Michael Wachter ate a Cobb salad that appears to have contained deadly hemlock leaves shortly before he died. The salad was one of two salads that came from Smooth Buns. The restaurant's owners say there were no hemlock leaves in the salads picked up by Bob Benson, who delivered the meals to his girlfriend, library director Julie Halston.* The article, quoting Julie, said that the judge felt ill shortly after eating one of the salads. The story added that Julie ate a few bites of the other salad and later felt slightly ill. It went on to mention the bribery scheme and included details about Wachter's judicial career.

The front-page story the next morning didn't sit well with Mayor Elroy James who questioned how the newspaper could obtain so much information regarding the judge's murder. The mayor told himself that Blair should have put a lid on that information. The investigation shouldn't be played out in the news media, he thought.

As he sat in his city hall office, Elroy heard shouting sounds. He looked out his third-floor window. Harold Presson and about 50 members of his Citizens for Decency group paraded back and forth in front of the building. They carried signs demanding that authorities drop the murder charge against the preacher. Other signs criticized the city's police department, calling officers "clueless." One homemade sign, showing the faces of Blair and Elroy, read, "Elmwood's idiots." As the protesters marched back and forth, they shouted: "Justice for the Pastor." Harold looked up and spotted Elroy at the window. The preacher smiled and waved. Elroy turned away, disgusted by the spectacle.

Minutes later the media showed up. A little later, a number of patrolmen converged on the scene. Within the hour, Chief Blair Bonney arrived. Still more cops arrived on the scene. They stood outside their patrol cars and watched the proceedings. Blair met with the patrolmen. From his office, Elroy saw the impromptu gathering of lawmen and hurried downstairs. He strode out of city hall and crossed the lawn to confront Blair.

"What the hell are you doing?" Elroy asked.

"What do you mean?"

"Why haven't you arrested these protesters. They're disturbing the peace."

"I don't like it any better than you do, but they haven't broken any law," Blair said. "There is a constitutional right to free speech."

"This is all your fault, Blair. If your officers had done a solid job investigating these murders, there wouldn't be any protesting."

"We made an arrest for Erica's murder. We have yet to solve the murder of John Brumley, but we're doing everything we can to close that case too."

"Maybe you should have taken a harder look at Judge Wachter. There are allegations that he took bribes and that the scheme could have had a bearing on those murders."

"What are you, Columbo?"

"No."

"Then quit sticking your nose into police business. Besides, all these allegations about the judge aren't going anywhere now that he's dead."

"Kind of convenient for you, Chief."

"What do you mean?"

"You don't have to investigate the judge. Still, if that last hearing for Harold Presson was any indication, I'd be worried that Rush Johnson will make your department look like the Keystone Cops."

"Get the hell out of here," Blair barked. Elroy grinned like a cheshire cat and walked back across the lawn, ignoring the protesters. He entered city hall and returned to his office. He collapsed in his desk chair. Opening a drawer, he pulled out a bottle of cheap bourbon and poured himself a glass. He had only one thought. *It's a damn circus out there.*

Chapter Seventy–Two

Adam Dade led a team of officers into Judge Wachter's downtown condo. Police had been there days earlier investigating the judge's death. But at that time, they had been focused on finding evidence of a break-in. This time, they searched for possible evidence that could tie the judge to the bribery scheme and possibly murder.

Built in the 1880s as a warehouse, it sat vacant for more than a decade before a developer renovated it into a luxury condo some 14 years ago. Wachter bought the place as soon as it went on the market. Located on the south end of River Street, the first floor featured an expansive garage and storage space. The living quarters occupied the second and third floors, complete with two fireplaces and wide expanses of windows with views of the Mississippi River. Patio doors on both floors opened onto wide balconies. The second floor featured a kitchen with commercial-grade appliances and marble countertop. The kitchen opened onto a spacious living room whose furnishings screamed of money. The third floor housed the judge's bedroom and adjoining bathroom which had a heated tile floor. The judge also maintained a large office on the third floor, complete with a massive television screen that could be raised or lowered from the ceiling. A series of wooden file drawers lined one wall of the office.

Adam and the officers started in the garage. They searched the judge's car, and the storage area packed full of hunting and fishing gear. They worked their way upstairs, opening every drawer and closet. On the top floor, they worked their way through every inch of the bedroom and the bathroom. Nothing. Lastly, they entered the judge's home office. Officers searched the file drawers. Adam went through the drawers of the judge's polished mahogany desk. Bills and bank statements filled one drawer. Another contained notepads and pens. In a bottom drawer, he found an old law book. He took it out and skimmed through the pages. As he did so, a piece of paper fell out. Adam picked it up. It was a folded note. A red-inked message read, "Pay up or I'll tell the police about your bribery scheme."

It was signed with the initial "E."

"It's clearly a blackmail note," one of the officers observed, looking over the detective's shoulder.

"Seems like it," Adam agreed. The detective turned his attention to the judge's computer. He powered it up. The computer screen wasn't locked. He could see the judge's files. He began checking the documents inside of them, which included photos, newspaper stories about his legal achievements and articles by professional gamblers on how to win at the casinos. Buried among all the icons, he found one linked to the home's state-of-the-art security system. Crime techs checked after the judge's body was found to see if there were any recordings showing an intruder. None were found.

This time, Adam reviewed older security recordings, going back months. He found the right time period, shortly before the judge had reported discovering the fraternity paddle. The detective had a hunch. He hoped he was wrong. Adam scrolled through the digital recordings. He spotted one of the judge entering the condo's living quarters with a duffel bag. The recording later showed the judge in his bedroom. The judge selected a trench coat from his walk-in closet. He put on the coat and pulled something out of the duffel bag. Adam couldn't see it at first because the judge's body blocked the security camera's view. But then the judge turned toward a mirror in the bedroom. He held a fraternity paddle. The camera captured him hiding the possible murder weapon under the coat and then removing it over and over again.

"I can't believe it. The judge did it!" Adam shouted. "He framed that preacher."

On the way back to the station, Adam phoned Connor with the news. "That's off the record," the detective said.

"But you'll have to disclose this evidence to Rush in advance of the trial," Connor said.

"This doesn't prove that Judge Wachter killed Erica Stark, only that he likely framed Harold Presson."

"Keep telling yourself that," Connor said. "But in my mind there's little chance a jury will convict the preacher."

"We'll see," Adam said. "Thankfully, it's not my job to prosecute this case."

Minutes later, the detective sat in Blair's office. He recounted the results of the search and showed the police chief the incriminating note.

"Damn. Who would have thought the judge would do such a thing," Blair said. "Do you think Judge Wachter killed both the librarian and Brumley?"

"I don't know. We can't directly tie Wachter to the murders."

"Well, make sure and tell the other officers to keep a lid on this evidence. There better be no leaks. Do you understand?"

"Yes, but you are going to talk to the prosecutor?"

"Of course. He needs to know that his case might be crap now. But I still don't want this evidence to go public. I mean, I don't see anyone prosecuting a dead man."

"Rush will do it in defense of his client."

"Only if the case goes to trial," Blair said.

They met in Blair's office. The prosecutor listened as Adam went over the new evidence. "It's circumstantial, but it certainly suggests the judge framed Harold Presson," Adam said.

"I agree," Richard Lamb said, wiping his brow.

"If you move ahead with the trial, you'll have to disclose this evidence to Rush at some point," Blair said.

"True. But we can bury this evidence if I drop the murder charge against Harold," Lamb said.

"That makes sense to me," the chief said. "I don't see the need to drag the judge's name through the mud."

"That doesn't concern me," Lamb said. "What concerns me is that disclosing this information could lead defense lawyers to go to court questioning the judge's past sentencings. That would be a disaster."

"Whatever I decide, I won't announce it until after the judge's funeral," Lamb said. "Regardless of what he did or didn't do, Judge Wachter deserves a decent burial."

Chapter Seventy—Three

Judge Wachter's funeral drew a packed house to the Elmwood First Baptist Church, the same church that hosted Erica Stark's funeral. Prosecutor Richard Lamb attended, along with a host of former prosecutors and countless private practice attorneys. Police Chief Blair Bonney showed up in dress uniform. Civic and business leaders crowded into the pews. Some of the judge's former girlfriends sat uncomfortably in a third-row pew, barely glancing at each other. Not surprisingly, Priscilla Presson didn't attend. Neither did Julie Halston nor Angela Pierce, Erica's niece. Bob Benson showed up but sat in the very back row near the aisle.

Some in the news media congregated in one of the pews toward the rear of the church. *Journal* photographer Tyler Frazier seated himself on the floor next to the wall near the front of the sanctuary. TV videographers stood nearby, training their cameras on the raised altar.

Rachel Short sat in the front row of the church balcony. Assigned the task of covering the funeral, she preferred to look down on the scene spread out before her. Pastor Bob Matson, the rotund Baptist minister who also officiated the librarian's funeral, praised the judge as a "font of virtue whose wisdom was ever present in the courtroom." Rachel scribbled notes as the pastor spoke. The sermon, Rachel observed, lasted 20 minutes. By the time it ended, the pastor had practically elevated the judge to sainthood, Rachel thought. But unlike Erica's funeral, Rachel noted those in attendance shed few tears. After the ceremony, she spoke to the mayor and other civic leaders. All of them expressed sorrow for the judge's untimely death. But their mannerisms made it clear, they were glad the service was over, and they couldn't wait to leave the church.

Back in the newsroom, Rachel typed her story. She mentioned the hemlock poisoning as the cause of death and the fact that police had made no arrest but otherwise focused her story on the funeral itself.

In December, Richard Lamb dropped the murder charge against Harold Presson, citing his belief that there was insufficient evidence to secure a conviction. No mention was made of the security recording and the blackmail note.

Harold celebrated, holding a daytime service of "Thanksgiving" on a Friday at his church. Diva Doll, Harold's former girlfriend, attended the service. Seated in a largely empty pew near the back of the church, the stripper wore a tight-fitting red dress, knee-high white boots and a white, faux fur coat. The preacher saw her and cracked a smile.

Priscilla Presson didn't attend. At home, she called her lawyer who assured her he'd file the divorce petition later that day. Outside the church, after the service, Harold and Rush criticized the police investigation. Rush called the murder investigation "flawed from the start." Harold accused police of "a rush to judgment." The *Journal* and broadcast media reported the remarks, which angered Blair.

Hours later, still upset, Blair talked to his top detective. "Where are we with the poisoning investigation?"

"We don't have any solid evidence. In my mind, Bob Benson is the most likely suspect. Still, we can't prove he poisoned the salads."

"Have you ruled out Julie Halston?"

"I don't think she poisoned the salads."

"Why not?"

"Because she ate a portion of hers and said she felt slightly ill."

"She ate a little of one salad, but maybe that was on purpose to convince us she didn't poison the judge."

"I don't think so. Julie doesn't strike me as a murderer."

"What about Bob Benson? He admits he encouraged his clients to pay bribes to the judge. He said the judge threatened him. That's motive enough for me."

"But we haven't found any evidence connecting him to the hemlock poisoning. We know the salads originated at Smooth Buns. There's no indication that the hemlock was placed in the salads there. And there's no evidence that Bob Benson did anything but transport the salads to the library. Both salads were delivered in take-out containers that were carried in a plastic bag provided by the eatery. Benson's fingerprints were on the bag, but not on the containers. Even if we could tie Benson to the murder, we haven't succeeded in connecting him to Brumley's murder or the murder of Erica," Adam said.

"The evidence suggests the judge killed Erica," Blair said.

"Judge Wachter could have killed Brumley too. Benson said the judge confessed to both murders."

"The trouble is that we only have Benson's word. And, Benson had good reason to kill Brumley too."

"To prevent him from exposing the bribery scheme."

"Yep. If we can't tie Benson to the fatal poisoning of the judge, let's see if we can find some evidence linking him to the bombing. At least, we might be able to get him on one murder."

Chapter Seventy–Four

Wet snow blanketed the city in early December, prompting massive coverage from the local TV meteorologists. Connor ended up writing a weather story too, but he wasn't enthused. There were only so many ways you could write a snow story and he'd written plenty over the years. He struggled, attempting not to use the words "white stuff." Still, he'd rather cover a gruesome murder than cold fronts and the pronouncements of the National Weather Service.

At lunch time, Connor and Rachel found the crowd was smaller than usual at Smooth Buns. Not surprising, thought Rachel, considering the weather. The two reporters ordered bowls of chili. As they ate, they mulled over the murders. Technically, police hadn't solved Erica's murder although it appeared they believed the judge killed her. According to Benson, the judge murdered both the librarian and the private detective. But Connor wasn't so sure.

"Something keeps bothering me. I just can't put my finger on it," Connor said.

"Something Adam told you?"

"No. I think it's something that was said in one of our interviews."

"We talked to a lot of people. Maybe one of the people who paid bribes for suspended sentences?"

"No, I don't think so. It wasn't about the bribes."

"Well, it will come to you," Rachel said.

"Wait a minute," Connor said. "I think I have it."

"What is it?"

"Adam said that Bob Benson told him that the judge's grandfather worked at a quarry. Benson suggested that's how the judge could have acquired the dynamite and crafted the exploding cigar."

"So?"

"So, I did a feature story on the judge years ago. He talked about coming from a long line of lawyers, including his grandfather. He didn't mention that his grandfather ever worked in the quarry."

"You think that Benson made up that story?"

"Yes, I do. And there's only one reason he would make up such a story."

"Benson killed Brumley."

"That's right," Connor said. "Now all we have to do is prove it."

"You need to tell Adam," Rachel said.

"Not yet. We need solid evidence."

"There you go wanting to play detective again," Rachel said, a sly look on her face. "I suppose we'll have to go sleuthing."

"We need to find evidence of bomb making."

"How? Do you want to break into Benson's place?"

"That's not a bad idea. We just have to make sure Benson isn't home."

"Leave that to me," Rachel said. "I'm sure I can arrange it."

Two nights later, bundled against the cold, Connor and Rachel visited Benson's home, a 1920s-era two-story, wood-framed structure north of the city's casino. It was an older neighborhood along a street lined with elm trees whose roots had pushed up the sidewalks. An exterior bulb illuminated Benson's front porch. A light shined inside the house, but the reporters knew Benson wasn't home. Rachel had purchased a gift card for use at the Jello night club. She had gifted it to Julie, saying she hoped it would make up for the ordeal that the now library director had endured. Rachel knew Julie loved to visit the night club with Bob. Julie had thanked her. Rachel had asked that she let her know when they were going to the club, suggesting that the two reporters might show up too. Julie did call. They were going to the club that night for music and drinks.

Connor parked his SUV on a darkened street a block away from Benson's place. They wore dark jeans and jackets. Conner and Rachel had driven by the house the previous day. They had spotted an old coal door on the side of the concrete foundation. They hoped it would be their way inside. Connor and Rachel walked by the house once and then turned around at the end of the street and proceeded down an alley, ending up behind the Benson home. Lights shone in nearby houses, but they saw no one looking out at the rear of those homes. Connor and Rachel ran across the back lawn and toward the iron coal door on one side of the house. Connor yanked on the coal door, which refused to budge at first. But with a second yank, the door creaked as Connor opened it. He took out a flashlight, which illuminated the old cellar. Rachel, face down, wedged herself into the opening and pushed hard through the tight space. She dropped, feet first, to the concrete floor, landing between two concrete walls that in earlier times corralled coal that fueled a boiler. Her hands touched the walls, still gritty with coal dust.

"Go upstairs and open the back door," Connor whispered, dropping the flashlight to her. "There's no way I'll fit through this coal door."

"I told you; you needed to work out," Rachel said.

"Very funny."

"How do you know that the inside cellar door isn't locked?"

"I don't. But the *Journal* did a feature story on Benson a few years ago. He talked about having a cat. I assume if he still has one, the litter box would be in the basement. If so, Benson would leave the door ajar so the cat could use it."

Rachel felt something nuzzle up to her leg. She looked down and shone the light on a calico cat. She bent down and petted it. The cat purred. "I found Benson's cat."

"Good. Now let me in," Connor said. Rachel hurried upstairs and minutes later unlocked the back door. Connor entered and closed the door. Rachel and Connor searched throughout the first-floor kitchen, living room, bathroom and den. After 20 minutes, they moved onto the second floor. They searched every closet and even under the bed. Nothing. No explosive. No cigars.

"Let's check the cellar," Connor said.

"Let's hope we find the evidence," Rachel said. "I'd hate to think we did all this for nothing."

Connor and Rachel went downstairs. Rachel led the way, carrying the flashlight that pierced the darkness. They maneuvered around shelves stacked full of plastic containers holding everything from Christmas dishes to discarded laptops and old photos. They spotted a long, homemade work bench along one wall. Cans of paint sat on one end of the bench. Plastic jugs of motor oil dotted the bench, along with an assortment of pliers, hammers, screwdrivers and electric hand tools, including a drill and a sander. Boxes of screws and nails were stacked neatly on the workbench. Rachel noticed a shelf built under the workbench. She shined the light on it. There, on the shelf, sat a box of partially cut open cigars and next to it several sticks of dynamite. Connor snapped photos with his cell phone.

"I can't believe this idea of yours actually worked," Rachel said.

"To tell you the truth, I can't believe it either," Connor laughed as the calico cat jumped up on the workbench.

"Why would he keep such incriminating evidence?" Rachel asked as she stroked the purring cat.

"Because he never figured anyone would connect him to the cigar bomb."

Chapter Seventy—Five

Armed with a search warrant, the police descended on Bob Benson's property the next day, confiscating the cigars and dynamite. Two days later, tests having shown that the evidence matched the cigar and explosive materials found near the private investigator's body, police arrested Bob Benson. The prosecutor charged him with murder. The story topped the local news cycle for days. Connor and Rachel wrote a whole series of stories about Benson, detailing the investigation step by step and disclosing their involvement in securing the key evidence. Weeks after being charged, Benson confessed to killing Brumley. In his confession, he blamed Judge Wachter, saying the judge had threatened to steal money from the library and frame Julie for the theft.

"I couldn't let that happen," a sobbing Benson told Adam. "I love Julie. Don't you see, I didn't have a choice."

News of the confession triggered more media coverage. As usual, Blair took credit for the successful outcome. Lamb, deciding he would run for another term as prosecutor, held a news conference to gain even more favorable publicity.

The whole affair troubled Julie. She felt sorry for Bob. She hated the media for painting her boyfriend as some fiend. Bob Benson had tried to protect her. She loved that about him, regardless of the murder charge. Despite her feeling about the media in general, Julie continued to talk with Rachel from time to time. Julie appreciated the series of *Journal* stories because Rachel had interviewed her and included her comments, which made Bob a tragic figure, but not a monster like some of the TV stories had painted him. Bob had confessed in exchange for a 20-year prison sentence. Julie told Rachel she planned to marry Bob when he was once again a free man. As a former public defender, Bob Benson knew most people sent to prison served far less time than the sentences carried. Crowded prisons meant early releases for most inmates, Bob had informed Julie. He figured he'd be out in seven years.

Two days before Christmas, Rachel stopped by the library. She brought Julie a gift. Seated in her office, Julie opened the present. Inside was a ceramic white angel holding an open book. "I figured this was appropriate for Elmwood's library director," Rachel said.

"I love it. Thank you," Julie said. They chatted for several minutes. "You know I still miss Erica. She may have blackmailed people, but she still was my friend. She didn't deserve to die."

"It must be hard knowing that Judge Wachter never was really brought to justice, at least not in a court of law," Rachel observed.

"It is, but the judge is dead. In a way, justice was served," Julie said. A member of the library staff stopped by, seeking Julie's help in dealing with an unhappy customer at the front desk. Julie sighed. "I'll be right back," she promised Rachel.

After a few minutes, Julie still hadn't returned. Rachel started to leave. She donned her winter coat and pulled out her leather gloves. One of them fell to the floor by Julie's desk. She reached down to retrieve it. Her eyes caught sight of a green pamphlet that stuck out from the partially closed center drawer. She opened the drawer to put the pamphlet back inside. Rachel read the title: "Nature's Poisons."

Intrigued, Rachel grabbed the pamphlet and skimmed through it. On the third page, she spotted a section on "Hemlock." The entire section had been marked with a yellow highlighter. Julie re-entered the office. She spotted Rachel holding the pamphlet.

"I didn't know you were interested in poisons, particularly hemlock," Rachel remarked.

"You know, it's amazing what information you can find in a library."

"And some of it," Rachel observed, "could be deadly."

Made in the USA
Monee, IL
18 August 2025

22485029R00164